BRUSH STROKES

Alvin L.A. Horn
aka
Alvin Lloyd Alexander Horn

*Dear TRACI
Love my Soulful
words & they
will Love you
Alvin L.A Horn*

BRUSH STROKES
FIRST EDTION
FIRST PRINTING
December 2005

RE-RELEASE- SECOND EDTION
SECOND PRINTING
DECEMBER 2016

ISBN-13 978-1541092860

Printed in the
USA

Published by
ROMANTIC BLUES PUBLISHING

Seattle, Washington
www.alvinhorn.com

Cover photo: Alvin Lloyd Alexander Horn
Front and back cover art by Susan McCallum
You can contact Susan McCallum by email:
onepaintbrush@shaw.ca

Acknowledgments

God it has been your will for everything good. When you have stepped aside, it was only for me to know that the stove was hot.

To the woman, my grandmother, who taught me about God, faith, love and patience, Bigmama, I have you in me, and I try to be the man you want me to be. That means you are always talking to me, now and forever more. R.I.P.

To the loves, to the friends, and even the disbelievers, thank you for encouragements in your own way.

Where would I be without, Cousin J, the man -an unmovable rock, R.I.P.

Barbara E. in my dictionary you and friend are one.

The sounding boards I owe you. A short list: TJ, S Mc, DST, VP, and others, I thank you.

The editors: Wow, Ms. Lynn I'm blessed with your true friendship. Your time and comment has been the floor my written words have learned to crawl and now walk. Let's do it again.

Ms. Kendra, I made you work. You did it. You taught me lessons by spilling red blood on every page, and the reasons why. When you were done, my words where running.

Now 2014

Hello,Ms. Nicole, thanks for the up to date editing, your fresh eyes to my writings is more than welcome.

Chapter One

Crawling out of bed at 3 in the morning, I warmed up my motorcycle as I looked at the stars in the sky. I wondered what the impending day had in store for me. Stoplights and a few headlights where my only company as I drove my motorcycle in the dark to a parking garage near the King Street train station. The luggage compartments attached to my BMW motorcycle were packed tight with my travel bags for a three-to-four day stay in Vancouver, British Columbia, Canada. I had a 10 a.m. appointment in Vancouver, so I caught the red-eye from Seattle at 5 a.m. Once I was on the train, I was wide-awake. The two-hour trip gave me opportunity to scan the sports page and stock market section of the paper, and to write some poetry on my laptop.

I arose, I'm alive, Still
My heart pumps
My heart feels you … trembling
My ears hear your cries, no matter the distance
My touch to your skin, I remember when
Made me feel young
Without you
My body is, is, is aging
Tick-tock
My mind is kicking at the damn cuckoo-clock
I refuse to hear an end
Without you
I pray
I hope
As
I arose, I'm alive, Still
Waiting for you

After I arrived in Vancouver, I rode the street trolley down to the wharf. Daybreak, overcast skies, and the fresh sea air pulled me back into a sleepy haze. I started to stroll along the wharf; the sky above me was changing fast. The sun, hazy through the thick clouds, gave off an eerie moonlike appearance. The morning fog would burn off soon. The thought of the sun coming out later and warming my hide gave me a peaceful feeling. After my appointment today, there might be a chance to wander through the park with my camera. Maybe I could find sun-backed silhouettes of beauty to put in my camera's eye that I could use in my art.

Walking along in sync with the moving skies, I stopped and lifted my head to the sky to give thanks for all I've known, all I know, and all that is to be.

Still with some time on my hands, I walked onto a pier with an open-air café at its end. Strong flavors and smells enslaved me. My nose and "*I can taste it*" taste buds told me what to do. Sit. Drink. Eat. I found myself relaxing in a euphoric state of "*Life is good.*" Fresh dark roasted coffee with cream and brown sugar, right-out-of-the-oven homemade bread; that first taste is so good, especially when accompanied by a good book. Sitting here enjoying the view my mind is at ease. I watch tugboats and ships cruising by, and I know it is one of those moments when nothing matters in life. No stress and no problems, just letting what happens happen.

It's been a long time since I last left Seattle's drizzle to let the Vancouver mist kiss my face. I've stayed away from the two-hour trip north into the past. My life has changed directions in many ways from a once-sad experience. The sun shines on me now, and time has dried me out from a downpour on my soul. What happened to me, Tylowe Dandridge, the last time my travels took me north of the border? Twelve years ago, heaven's skies turned to hell and poured on me what felt like hot hail hitting my soul. Twelve years ago, the ocean flooded the desert, chasing my body and soul back over the border.

Chapter Two

The last time I was in Vancouver in 1988, my friend Elliot Piste, a black Frenchman originally from Senegal, came to Vancouver from France for business and pleasure. Our friendship started in 1976 while in college as roommates and teammates on the track team. He had been a foreign exchange student and a middle distance runner, and I had been a sprinter and football player. We had shared many common interests, like riding motorcycles and photography.

Our main shared interest, though, was the scent of a woman, Elliot, more so than I. He had his way with the college girls back then, with his Adonis-like body and a smooth, black-olive, pretty-boy face. But beautiful people can do ugly things, and Elliot used his charm and good looks for bad behavior when it came to being with girls. He sometimes was very controlling, dogmatic, and sinister. He was known to have females do some freaky stuff. Ah, I had fun, too, but I had my limits. Elliot had no limit. He'd pour it on thick with his French accent, deep with rich tones that sounded like a French Barry White, *"Ma chère dame vous allez si bien. Est-ce que je peux renifler vos colottes et observer vous et votre petite amie les chose mè chantes entre eux?"* ("My dear lady, you are so fine. May I watch you and your girlfriend do nasty things to each other?")

Yeah, he'd say shit like that. Girls thought he said something suave and romantic, and he'd play them, deceive them and melt them with his total package of looks and bullshit. The boy was a freak, and he seemed to spot the same. He'd say, "Nice girls bore me. Give me a nasty girl."

He really did not know anything about women; he really didn't care, but he knew nasty girls. It was not unusual for me to come into our dorm room and find different combinations of real sexual fantasies in action. And no, I never joined in. Elliot had the art of spotting girls who played his kind of way, and when they didn't, he wouldn't give them the time of day.

Now, I'm not a brother from another planet. I dated a lot, played a lot and fulfilled a few fantasies. But my roommate was from another world altogether when it came to how many, and how wild a time he could have.

But he was my partner and he never really did anything that offended me back then, or so I thought. A few years later after college I found out that Elliot's freak show had crossed over the line. He had freaked with some of my past ex-girlfriends. He apologized ("thou shall not freak your friend's ex-freak") years later. Hey, girls that I slept with were girlfriends to me most of the time; I stayed faithful for at least a month or at least through finals.

I even walked my lady friends back to their dorm rooms after sex. I was a gentleman! I enjoyed the college life going to class and sharing notes with the ladies. Okay, I used their notes and I let them write my term papers, I mean type my term papers, only! In return for their help I never let them pay for my half of a burger-and-fry date. But Elliot, he thought a "girlfriend" was female body parts sitting on his face or someone else's face with him watching. That was in college, though, and we remained friends. Boys will be boys, and girls were… for boys. Then you grow up, right?

Pro football was my meal ticket after college, but not in the NFL. I played in Canada for the Edmonton Oilers. I had a great season and made the all-rookie team. The next season I decided to go home to the States to try out for my hometown NFL team, the Seattle Seahawks. Well, I didn't make the team and moved on to a new life. I started thinking and acting like a regular guy, looking for a wife and the house with a white picket fence, working regular hours and not using my talents.

I found the average life didn't charge my batteries. I was meant to be a pro. Fortunately I had the chance to make a comeback and become that all-pro. I'm a professional photographer and writer. The photographer thing got off to a great start when Elliot needed my artistic skills with a camera.

Elliot had gone home to France after college and made a name for himself as a motorcycle grand-prix racer. He wanted to model and take advantage of his popularity as a racer. He wanted to market himself to advertisers using his handsome African features and grand-prix racing fame for all types of products. He hit the big time of modeling stardom after the great photo spread I did for him. It worked out for both of our careers.

After Elliot had made it big in Europe, both as a racer and a model, he capitalized on his racer name and body fame to start a chain of European motorcycle dealerships. With his business going well, he wanted to expand to North America. The city he chose for his North American flagship store was Vancouver, B.C., just a ninety-minute drive across the international border from my hometown of Seattle, Washington.

Elliot asked me to meet him in Vancouver to help him set up a photo shoot for a new sales brochure. Added to the mix of working together, we would get a chance to do some riding, like we used to do.

Since he would be staking out real estate and other things that he would need to open his dealership in Vancouver, he knew he would be there for a while, so he shipped in two new, state-of-the-art, not-sold-to-the-public BMW motorcycles. The two bikes were for his lady and him to ride while in Vancouver. Elliot had let me know he had a woman in his life, and she had let him know she would rather shop than slide her hips from side to side on a sexy, macho, motorcycle.

Elliot said, "You can ride my lady's bike and, if you like, you can keep it." Years earlier, he had given me an Italian Ducati 900 as a token of our friendship and for a photo shoot I had done for him early in his modeling career.

My old Ducati 900, a classic motorcycle from back in the day, could not give you that floating-on-a-cloud feeling the new BMW bikes could. I started looking forward to winding and twisting on the grand-prix-like roads of North Vancouver.

I too had a woman in my life. She was much more than just a girlfriend or booty fling; she was my fiancée. Renee Austin, my dream come true, made me hit all the right notes in the shower. She had my heart and the rest of my life. She was my lover and friend, like in a romance novel with the perfect ending.

She had one of those 9 to 5 jobs I had sworn never to have, but it worked for her. We had met in an elevator of the building where she worked. I was there to do a photo shoot for an aerospace work group. Just as soon as our fingers pushed the floor button at the same time, we were one, going the same direction. Renee had a lot going on in the brains and looks department. She had the kind of education that scared weak-minded, *"I-need-a-woman-I-can-get-over-on"* kind of men. Her beauty, it scared me for a while. Halle Berry, Vivica Fox, Sade, and my Renee. Yeah, she was that fine. Most of all, she supported what I wanted in life. This woman had a beautiful soul. She had a free spirit and had her own dreams that were easy to support. She loved me, and with her, I knew what love was.

Renee and I planned a trip to Spain the following month to get married, so I fired off a few pictures of us to Elliot while he was still in France. I hoped he would finish his business in Vancouver and come to Spain to be my best man. He called from France and said yes, he had to be the best man in my wedding. He said I had finally outdone him by getting married. Elliot had been having thoughts of getting married, too, but he wasn't ready to commit. He still liked having his fun and freedom.

So when Elliot invited me to Vancouver for business and pleasure, Renee came along. I let her know the Canadian to American money exchange rate would make everything feel like a deal. Plus she could go riding with me "while on holiday," as the Canadians say.

My woman liked to ride on the back of my motorcycle. She said the vibration and spreading her legs and tightly pushing herself against my ass would give her small personal orgasms. My thoughts on my orgasms: they were always personal, whether by myself or with the help of a woman. Ooh, to hear her say in my ear, "Baby, down shift. Make the motor rev high." Within a quarter mile or so she would be groaning in my ear. Her arms would squeeze me, her hips grinding the seat and my backside.

Next thing you know, we'd find a park or other private place. Couldn't wait to be alone with her, pull her leather riding pants off and taste her, feel her, and have my own personal orgasm. The thought of a little bump and grind on a two-wheeled machine along the rolling and twisting byways and highways of Canada had me singing *"Let's Get It On."*

Chapter Three

I told Elliot the Rivera Hotel in downtown Vancouver was a great place to stay. He was going to be in Vancouver for at least a month, so he wanted a place with a great view, a kitchen and a separate bedroom. He also needed safe underground parking for the motorcycles. Right across the street was the Hilton Hotel with its spinning panoramic view of the city and a great restaurant and jazz lounge. I would have advised him to stay at the Hilton, but there was no parking for the bikes and trailer. Both hotels were close to shopping and close to Stanley Park, one of the world's largest and best city parks.

The park had a lot to enjoy, with a great zoo, an aquarium, a waterfront drive and open-air stages for music and plays. English cricket games went on from time to time, and rugby was a popular pastime. I had played intramural rugby in college, so I enjoyed anytime I got the chance to hang out in Stanley Park and catch a game of pick-up. Having the athletic skills of a professional football player made me something of star while playing rugby. Well, I was a star among the other players at Stanley.

Renee and I both loved the park. During one of our walks, we ended up doing the nasty in the middle of the woods! We didn't start out with that in mind, but we were walking fast for a good workout; nature called, we found we both needed to pee. We walked deep into the brush and found a spot to relieve ourselves. Renee had this thing about taking my penis out and aiming it like a fire hose. Only it started a fire that she had a chance to, ah, help me out.

Her freaky side kicked in and, before you knew it, our sweatpants were around our ankles. Bending over at the waist, Renee gripped a big oak tree and hugged tight with all her might, and not for environmental reasons. She pressed her round booty against my hardness and I pushed my way inside her tight slickness and began pumping away fast, to keep the flies from landing and biting my ass. It felt damn good, enjoying the outdoors and the heat of my woman.

Abruptly, Renee pushed her butt into me as hard as she could and not for her a personal orgasm, but to make me stop. She put her finger to her lips to quiet me.

"What's up?"

I was about to have my own personal orgasm when she moved, or didn't move, breaking the momentum. Damn, I hate that. She pointed forward and gave me a hush sound.

"Look, look," she said.

Twenty yards in front of us was another couple doing what I wanted to finish. A man with his back to us and his pants down to his ankles appeared to be getting some serious head by a woman on her knees with her face buried in his crotch. We watched. My hard-on went south, my personal moment interrupted. But after watching for a while, this woman on her knees, sucking like it was the last food on the earth, got me hard again.

The woman's lips were pressed all the way to the base of his shaft, like she had the entire thing in her mouth, and I thought to myself, "That man must have a small dick." Renee felt me slide back into her with full force. My ego made sure she knew she was not getting a small dick; I stroked her from afar. She spread her legs wide and, leaning forward on her toes, she cocked her ass up at a nasty angle and rode my hardness. She stared forward with intense concentration at the other couple as they dropped to the ground and started humping doggie style.

They were loud, with the man barking and yelping like a dog. He reached a hand around the woman's waist. I assumed he found her clit. His arm began vibrating under the woman like a jackhammer, and I knew he must have found her clit. I reached around Renee and circled my finger on her clit as if I was polishing the tip of her nose. She slid her wet pussy back and forth on my hardness with an increasingly intense rhythm.

Feeling the sparse hair around her sex lips provided a frictional sensation. The heat from her wet crease evoked a mad, nasty hump from me in an effort to cum.

Getting into the freak of it forced me to grab that ass. She got wetter than I'd had ever known her to be before. Her wetness was running down her leg, as I felt her body tremble signaling her orgasm was beginning. The cheeks of her ass clamped me tight. From someplace inside she gave out three deep grunts that exited through her nose. Her body shuddered, and it felt like that 1000-year-old oak tree she was hugging could have fallen down. That caused me to have my own personal moment and spurt a flow of love sap into her.

We pulled our jogging suits back on and kept watching the other couple. I really got off watching my girl watching a live X-rated movie. She was into it. Then my eyes about bugged out of my head when the couple finished doing the nasty. The man lifted off the woman's ass, stood up and pulled his penis off, squatted down like a woman, and peed.

"Shit! You see that, baby? It's a woman."

"Yeah, you didn't know that was two women?" Renee asked calmly.

"Hell, no!"

"Men don't stand like that when getting their dicks sucked. You don't. And a man doesn't hump like that. You just weren't." She smiled a devilish grin and said, "You hump like a dog dancing to James Brown music while riding a female in heat." Renee smirked. "That weak sounding female bark should have tipped you off."

"Well, yeah, but you were getting off so much, and that was getting me off. I was paying more attention to you than them."

"Sure you were, Tylowe."

"So you knew the whole time?" She gave me a sly smile and shook her head as if I should have known.

We loved the park for all it offered.

Chapter Four

We were going to hang out with Elliot and his woman, so our park adventures would have to be relegated to the back burner this trip. The plan was to go to Vancouver by train and meet Elliot and his lady friend. We planned to catch a taxi to the hotel, but when we walked out of the train station, we saw a man in a blue butler-like suit holding a sign that read, "E P European Motorcycles for Tylowe Dandridge." There was a limo waiting for us. Elliot was doing really well in business. I had plenty of reasons to be proud of my old college roommate. The man in the blue suit walked us over to the limo, and Elliot and a woman who could've passed for Serena Williams' body double stepped out.

Elliot's lady's name was Simone, and there could be no doubt that Simone had been in the gym, lifting a lot of weights. She was buffed. Most female body builders lose their sex appeal and almost take on a masculine appearance. But that was not the case with Elliot's girlfriend. She was not over the edge. She had a petite pretty face and soft womanly mannerisms. As they walked toward us, her long legs, one-foot crossing over in front of the other, made her hips yank my attention like a pit bull yanks on his chain. I tried to keep my eyes on my woman and tried not to stare into the face of Simone's extreme beauty, since my woman's beauty was exceptional, too.

As women do, they checked each other out while being slightly hesitant during introductions. After what seemed like an awkward moment the girls hugged and smiled and complimented each other's beauty. It's always so sexy to watch women check each other out. I knew while watching Renee get dressed that morning her choices weren't for me, but were because another woman would be checking her out.

We drove off sipping champagne and laughing as we traveled in the limo, headed down to Old Gastown to get something to eat.

Enjoying good conversation, we ate great crab cakes. The two women had a lot in common: the fashion scene, talking about the upcoming wedding and sports. Simone had been born and raised in England. Her 5-foot-11 frame had been on the Great Britain Olympic volleyball team in 1984. Renee had played volleyball for Bradley University at the same time. What an eyeball delight to see two sexy, athletic sisters sitting next to each other.

After lunch we went to the hotel. Our room was on the tenth floor and had a great view. Elliot and Simone's room was on the eleventh floor. I called Elliot and told him Renee and I were going to take a nap and chill. Maybe we could meet up later at the jazz lounge across the street.

After a brief nap we strolled over to the park for a jog through the woods, peeking around trees as we ran. That night at the club, we all had some belly-splitting laughs as Renee told an abbreviated funny version of what had happened in the park.

"If you guys could have seen Tylowe's face. He about peed down his leg!"

"Hmm, you tease me. But I seem to remember you were hugging that tree like you were going to break it down from the good time you were having." She hit me playfully on the arm. Of course, she left out the part about having the need to hold my fire hose.

Simone poked Elliot. "Maybe we need to go visit the park, baby, and do a little wildlife watching."

"Indeed, ma chère, indeed. It sounds wild, almost like Tarzan and Jane," said Elliot, in his French Barry White accent. We all shared a laugh.

Back in our room later, Renee hugged the bedpost instead of a tree this time. She didn't move at the wrong time, so we both had wonderful personal orgasms.

Chapter Five

We met for breakfast the next morning at 8. Afterward, the girls left for shopping, and Elliot and I made our way to the garage. It was good to be with my old friend. At first, I was uneasy, wondering if my future wife would approve of my best man.

In one of those women's bathroom conferences, Simone, who Renee thought was an absolutely beautiful person, had told her Elliot had other women. Simone was doing what some women do in the same situation: she was doing anything she could do, with no limit, thinking she would be better than the other women who had tried to lock him down. Women usually don't want a playboy friend around their man, but Renee let me know she did not disapprove of Elliot being in our wedding. She said, "I love you, and I know you, and that is all that matters to me."

~~~~~

The bikes were locked in a trailer in the parking garage. We started to unload them.

"Tylowe, these are great motorcycles, ma man. I had one of the best race mechanics in world do some work on 'em right after I got 'em from the BMW factory. Then I had the bikes painted in my corporate colors."

"Corporate colors; aren't you something? Damn, these motorcycles look good."

"Oh, here, my friend, the owner's document, the red one is for you to own. I've put your name down for your legal ownership in the United States. But you have your choice, my man, to which one you want to ride today. They are both fast and sexy looking, much like our two ladies."

"Thanks, Elliot; I'll take good care of it, like the old one. Yeah, my woman is fine. And I love her more than anything. I got no problem telling you or the world what she means to me. Listen, we're so perfect together, we seem to breathe for each other. Can't wait to grow old with her."

Elliot spoke slowly, "I wish to be like you my man. But not yet."

"I understand being single has its advantages, and there will be times I'll feel like you, since I'm only twenty-eight. At times it is scary when I realize I'll be married in one month. But I'm ready for marriage; she's the right woman."

"What will you do with all the pretty girls still wanting you?"

"Please, my brother. I'm ready for the one-on-one thing. I quit being like you, chasing booty, when Renee came into my life."

He nodded with a big smile as he handed me some brand new riding leathers.

Elliot kept preparing his bike and spoke with a somber tone. "For me, I need a woman, but not a woman's love. A woman's love is restricting and controlling. One day I'll be an okay man for the life you are about to be a part of, but not now." He slid into a red, blue-trimmed, one-piece leather jump suit. Mine was red with black trim and fit perfectly.

Elliot's voice and body became animated. "You plan to have big fun before ya marry, hire dancing girls to do ya right one more time, right?"

"No, no. Renee is all I need. She wears my ass out now! She takes care of all my needs, plus some. Two or three other freaks for a night of fun would still come up short next to my girl."

Elliot laughed and handed me new matching riding gloves. "Okay, ma man, a toast to your future wife. This is a super bike, unlike any bike you have ridden before."

We went over all the features of the bikes, then started them. I could tell by how they sounded they were fine machines. We checked our air pressure and gave one more last minute equipment check, and then we were on our way for a day of hard and fast riding.

We crossed over the Lions Gate Bridge heading into North Vancouver to an old closed-down car dealership next to a Jaguar dealership. Elliot liked the location and made notes while we talked about the big glass window where he could have a large display of motorcycles. A circular, lighted sign that said "European Pro Motorcycles" could be on top in his corporate colors. There was a paved side lot, where cars used to be for sale; it would be a perfect test riding area. There were also four oversized doors behind the main building, leading to the bays for the garage repair area. We walked around and brained-stormed some ideas for the site. Elliot wrote down the phone number of the real estate agent. He could have used his cell phone, but walked over to one of the pay phones that are still on most Vancouver corners because of bad cellphone signal caused by so many tall buildings. Cellphone companies were changing from analog to digital.

I laughed to myself because he looked like some secret agent in his riding leathers as he closed the door to the phone booth. He came back and said he got no answer, so he left a message, and his pager numbers. Then we hit the road for two-wheel fun.

We took the back road heading out to White Rock. It was a long, winding and twisting road. The feel of the motorcycle was like no other bike I had ever ridden. Elliot had spent time in the past showing me some pro riding skills, so my skills were better than average, but nowhere near Elliot's, the former European Grand Prix motorcycle champ. He let me lead most of the time, I suppose so he wouldn't leave my ass. As the morning ride went on, we started to pass each other in the corners and on the straightaway over and over. We were having fun.

For the next couple of hours I almost peed on myself from taking corners too fast. I knew this bike had an onboard computer running some of the systems and one of the systems might be keeping my butt from falling off.

We stopped to stretch our legs and relieve ourselves at a marina deli we had stumbled upon. As we walked in, we startled the waitress. Two men in colorful leathers and black helmets we were pulling off which exposed our black faces had her face going pale. Then I got to see Elliot still had a way with women.

"Madame, may we have a coffee and a water and some of that warm bread that smells so good and would be soft on the palate?" he said in his deep voice, as he stared into her eyes and leaned into her space, and in her space were very large, young breasts. The young longhaired bleached-blonde girl started to melt and her round face regained its color.

He cast a spell over the young woman. She stood in front of him like she was waiting for him to do anything he wanted. Meanwhile she never asked me what I wanted. I had to clear my throat twice to get her attention. For the rest of our stay, she was at his beck and call without his ever calling her over.

"Still have the old charm, huh?" I shook my head in amazement.

Elliot laughed slyly and spoke in his know-it-all voice, "But, you see, this is always a good thing for more than one reason." He winked at me and nodded at the young lady.

Without thinking, I said, "Yeah, pain in the ass fatal attractions or maybe an unwed mother demanding child support; a judge handing over half your bank account to a woman you really don't know." My mouth opened a door that let a cold draft blow back into my face.

BRUSH STROKES – ALVIN L.A. HORN

22

"Tylowe, my friend, you are the one getting married, with all those dreamy ideas of the perfect life. You are much too narrow-sighted, Tylowe. Could it be you to handing over your hard-earned money to an ex?"

I went silent, lost in deep thought. The boats in the marina seemed to be getting loud, rubbing against the docks. Forget him! My love is deep, true, and honest, what Renee and I have, it will conquer all. An inner conversation filled the silence between Elliot and myself.

Elliot broke the awkward silence between us by changing the subject. "My dealerships' sales are going very good. I think I've found the right formula. My staff is mostly all female, from sales to repairs, at my dealerships," he said.

"Are you serious?" responding as if I did care; at that moment really I didn't.

"I send women trainees to mechanics school. Then they work in my garage to repair motorcycles, and they wear sexy, tight, work jumpsuits."

"And this is why you sell so many bikes?"

"Yes. Think about it, a macho guy will buy anything from a sexy woman." I had to laugh at his arrogant attitude, even though I knew he was right. Elliot continued to speak. "I train the prettiest women I can find and make sure they lead prospective buyers on in more than one way. Next thing you know, macho guy buys bike." He was so serious in his belief it became funny. "You know sex sells."

The waitress came over again without being asked. Where are they when you need them?

"*Ma chère*, have you ever ridden a motorcycle?" Elliot asked.

She blushed. "I've ridden on the back of my father's motorcycle, but it's been a long time.

"Would you like to learn to ride and learn all about motorcycles?" Elliot interrupted.

She thought she was being asked out on a date. "Yeah, sure."

"Here is my card, and your name is?"

Elliot looked at the nametag that was protruding from the front of her double D breasts. "Lauren it is, right? Why don't you give me your phone number? I bet you like working here, but wouldn't you rather be riding a motorcycle and getting paid for it?" The girl was perplexed by his question and cocked her head to the side.

"Why, of course, I guess."

"Then you call me or I'll call you in a couple of weeks." Elliot handed her an American $20 bill that, with the exchange rate, more than covered our tab and told her to keep the change. She turned away happy, dazed and confused, with her breasts swinging like two tetherballs.

"Your first employee for sales or repairs?" I asked.

"No, she'll be at the customer service desk, laying her best assets on the desk, with a shirt that read, 'European Pro Motorcycles.'

We slammed our fists together in agreement.

Chapter Six

At noon, we hit the road again. We found long stretches of road to really open up and break the speed limit. It was the kind of road where Renee would make me shift down a gear and rev up the motor so she could have a personal moment.

Elliot pulled over an hour later and said he was feeling a bit tired and had business on his mind.

"Would you mind if I head in, Tylowe? You can still ride on."

My eyes about bugged out. I was having a great time male bonding and it was still early.

Elliot put his hands up and stated his case. "My pager beeped from that number I called. Maybe I should try to make contact. Business is business, ma good friend."

I might have acted a bit pissed, because I was pissed off, even though I did my best to let Elliot know riding with him was enjoyable.

"You're going to be here for a while, Elliot. I'm only here for a few days. We talked about at least doing 300 to 400 miles of riding, going six to seven hours on the road. I'm not trying to keep you from your business, but it can wait."

He looked at his watch, his face twisted in thought and cut me off. "Fine, then; we ride on." He rolled his big bottom lip over the top lip and mounted his bike; we rode on. We had only done 150 miles and were having a dream day on the open roads on great motorcycles.

A half-hour later Elliot pulled over again.

"Ma dear friend Tylowe, my bike is not running very good, and I really should tend to business and go try to meet the real estate agent at that lot we looked at. I'm heading back, okay?"

"Okay, cool, but I'm going back to pick up Renee." Might as well let him do what he wanted to do. This was not cool getting on and off the motorcycle. If Elliot didn't feel like riding for whatever reason, he was not going to blow my high. Plus I missed my baby already and she did say she would be back from shopping by three.

"Why don't you keep riding for a couple hours? I'll find my way back to town later after I look into some business. After all, the bike is yours now, ma friend."

"Well, I'll ride back that way with you to make sure you find the place, and then from there I can head back to the hotel and pick up Renee. So I'll ride with you to the lot."

"I'll be fine. I can find the place."

"It's no problem, man. If Renee is back from shopping, I'll take her out riding with me; if she's not, I'll head out by myself."

Heading back into town I really got a chance to see how skilled Elliot was at handling a motorcycle. He swung his hips smoothly and quickly into turns. Every time there was a long straightaway, he would hit the throttle with full force and the front tire would come off the ground for twenty plus yards. He was riding as if he was in a grand prix race, and no way in hell for me to keep up with my lesser skills. It was like two guys out for a jog and one was in better shape than the other one, and for the last mile, the one who's in better shape speeds off. I was not offended; I was sure my riding skills in comparison to his had finally bored him, so maybe that's why he wanted to go talk to the real estate agent rather than ride with me.

After a couple of miles he lost me, so I just took my time and cruised back to the hotel. Crossing back over the Lions Gate

Bridge the view was so romantic. The beauty of the city and the Burrard Inlet made me want to live forever. The tall buildings, rolling hills and greenery were visually arousing, and my breathing raced with big exhales. I wanted to share the visions and feelings with my lover, my soon to be wife. We enjoyed being in each other's presence seeing the world around us. We had completed every lover's dream of finding the *one*. No doubt I was a lucky man! I wanted her near me, her hair blowing in the wind next to me. I started to hurry to be with the one and only woman for me.

I drove down the driveway of the parking garage. The trailer was locked, so I parked the motorcycle next to it. I didn't think I'd be long and figured the parking garage was secure enough, since I was headed right back out with Renee.

I opened the hotel room door anticipating Renee would be there. She wasn't. Damn! I called upstairs to Elliot and Simone's room and got no answer. Maybe she had already come back and gone out again. I pulled my boots off and put my feet up for a while. Sleepiness was slipping over me; a twenty-minute power nap would help.

Wow, it was hour later when my nap ended. Evidently, my woman was still out and about; she must be having a good time. Maybe Elliot was back. I walked down to the garage to check, hoping he locked my bike up. It was too late to go out riding now. Besides my high was blown.

My bike was still parked. I stopped at the front desk for pen and paper and wrote notes to leave in my room and on the door of Elliot and Simone's room.

I knocked on Elliot's door first and then tacked my note on the door; the door cracked open. I walked into the room. Damn, did they leave their door ajar? A voice called out. It was Simone's voice coming from the bedroom. Her voice was breaking into pieces when she called my name. I walked into the bedroom with my eyebrows lifted. My body blocked most of the light coming in from behind me. Then my eyes focused in on shadowy images. I saw Simone and Elliot on the bed. He was lying on his back with his arms folded behind his head. I stepped into the room to clear the light. Elliot just kept staring at the ceiling. Simone was sitting up, her firm, athletic breasts exposed, her eyes staring at me. She shifted her glance down toward the bed, tears running down her face. I was confused. This woman was sitting there naked and crying, and then the bathroom door opened.

Confusion kicked into overdrive as Renee appeared. Dressed in only a sheer robe, she looked at me with no life in her eyes. She crossed her arms and used the robe as a shield from my view. This was the same body I had seen and felt naked so many pleasurable times before; she acted like she was ashamed of her nakedness. I became sick to my stomach.

"What, what is this?" I asked. I trusted my woman and did not want to accuse her of something, and what would I be accusing her of? This had to be legit, I wanted to think, but I have to admit my mind was too far gone. No one answered. Elliot kept counting sparkle specks on the ceiling. Finally, Simone spoke while streaming tears kept pouring onto rumpled sheets. "Tylowe, Renee and I... know each other from some time ago. We... dated the same person."

"The same man? Shit happens. That had to be some time ago, so what the fuck is going on now?" I had never spoken like that around Renee, I didn't speak like that at any time. "I need to know what the hell was going on in here, now!"

"No," Simone said. More silence for a moment before she spoke more words at the bed covers. "We crossed paths for a short time is what happened."

My narrowed eyes looked at Elliot, thinking it might be him they both had dated. The tone of my voice must have hit like a sledgehammer.

"Who was it? Was it him?" I pointed at Elliot and looked at Renee. I kept thinking the world couldn't be that small.

Renee's voice crawled out. "No. Ah... it was another wo... woman, I had a girlfriend, a lover, a teammate back in college on the volleyball team."

"You had what?" My voice had the explosive energy of a four-car pileup at a four-way intersection. "Renee, I thought we had been open about everything in our past. I may not have liked it, but you should have told me. That is not something you should've hidden if you love me like you say you do. But still, what the hell is going on now?"

Simone spoke first. "I knew the girl, too. We kind of all met back then. We played an exhibition match against each other. This girl on Renee's team, well, she and I had a little affair behind Renee's back."

Renee's voice did some more crawling. "Tylowe, I wanted to tell you, about that part of my life. I just thought I had left that part behind me. I've always wanted to tell you about it, but..."

"Yeah, you're telling me you're a lesbian or bisexual or whatever, I still want to know what the hell is going on... now!" The anger in my voice must have hit like another car adding to the pileup. Renee recoiled in shock. She straight-armed her arms downward, her fingers spread wide as if to stop the floor from rising. Her sheer robe fell open; her exposed body at that moment did nothing for me.

"Tylowe, yes, I've had sexual feelings for a woman, but I thought I had put away those feelings or at least stopped acting on them." When she said that, it felt like my eyes opened from a long sleep. I couldn't move, felt myself shaking; my stomach got that motion sickness feeling. What I was hearing and feeling emotionally intimidated me.

More words crawled out of Renee's mouth. "When I saw Simone, things twisted in me, and when we talked about our past we realized we..." Her face, usually light brown had turned painfully red, as she seemed to run out of words to say.

"So you and she are in here? Damn! I let you freak as hard as you want, with me. I've always been more than happy to share any kind of fantasy with you. Dammit! But this? Then to find out like this! You are the woman I'm supposed to marry. You are the woman who would bear me a child."

My head started swimming in the deep-end of a pool of emotional hurt. But I needed more information to know how Elliot fit into all of this "What are *you* doing here?" He didn't answer, just kept staring at the ceiling while lying next to his naked woman, and me standing there looking stupid and mad. Shit, I was confused and sick to my stomach. My naked woman was in this room with him! Am I in the middle of my own pulp fiction? "What are you doing here with your naked black ass?" If I were going to kick his ass I would have to jump over his woman to get to him. He still didn't speak, but Simone did. She let out some monotone sentences.

"Tylowe, it's not Renee's fault. I told Elliot about knowing Renee before. I let him know I wanted to feel her next to me. He has no problem with me being with another woman. He said he just wanted to watch. So I paged him when I knew that Renee would come back with me to be... with me. Renee didn't know I left the door unlocked for Elliot to come in."

I visualized everything and then spoke again. "You just got caught sliding, rubbing and whatever, and you want me to understand? Is that it?! Huh?! It's the least understandable thing in life. Understanding. Exactly what would that be? Renee, I feel better already knowing you would not be with another man, just another woman." My voice trailed off as I was trying to hurt her back with ill-timed sarcasm.

Breathing hard, I wanted to hit something or someone, but what good would that do? Hurt had my stomach in knots. Standing there with my naked future wife and with my old friend directing my nightmare, I aimed my next verbal assault at that arrogant, backstabbing punk who acted like my friend.

"Elliot, this is some sinister shit. Like the shit you always have done. But I know God will make a comeback on your ass. So you're dismissed from my life. *Vous bastard masculin de putain!*" (You male whore bastard!) Thanks for the French you taught me."

"Baby, please," Renee pleaded as she walked over to me with her head down and then looked up into my eyes for a long moment. She put her arms around me, laid her head on my chest, squeezed and trembled. My arms stayed hanging by my sides.

Renee started weeping and sniffling words out of her mouth. "Honey, listen to me, please." She begged like a child wanting relief from pain. "Ooooh, I'm sorry, baby, please but I'm, I'm…"

I cut her off. No way was I going to let her beg me. "You know, this shit is over! You must think I'm stupid!"

"Tylowe, please, you need to listen to me. You are a good if not a great man; the kind of man I dreamed of living my whole life with. What just happened is wrong. I'm wrong, baby, for letting this happen. I'm sorry, but I need…"

"You don't need me, and you don't need to let me know anything anymore!" Now the volume of my voice added a city bus to the pileup in the intersection. "Don't tell me nothing!"

Renee choked my body with her arms. "Tylowe, Tyloooowe… please," she wailed, a wounded siren-like plea. "I'll never let you down again. I'll be a good wife, friend, and the mother of your child."

I started to whisper in her ear but my voice went higher with each of the next three words. "Wife, friend, mother of my child? Renee, maybe I should love you enough to be able to forgive, but I'd be lying on the truth. You can't be any of those things for me. I'm too much in love with you to let what happened just be. I can't trust myself to trust you, and I'm not going to waste our time trying to find out. You have a good life, but not with me." I had to pull hard to back out of her arms.

She lifted her head from my pounding chest. She looked hard into my eyes and said, "Things are not always here today and gone tomorrow."

I turned from her and felt my soul erupting in:
Heartache ... I loved her.
Suffering ... Sometimes you can't be with the one you love.
Anguish ... Because there was no way I could be with her.
Jarring ... It felt like a 100 miles-an-hour motorcycle crash, and I didn't die but felt all the torment of a mutilated, disfigured soul.
Fear ... Will I ever get rid of this ill feeling?
Agony ... The sound of her wail made my skin pull tight at my temples.
Pain ... Instant headache.
Confusion ... My inner vision blurred.
Torture ... I'll live with this day for the rest of my life.

Emotionally I had always been the driest of deserts. Now tears ran down my face, flooding that desert, turning me into an emotional ocean. Requiem for a love not to be; I crossed back over the border, leaving that life behind.

Chapter Seven

(Back to the present)

Twelve years later I'm still single, sitting here in Vancouver, B.C., alone, with no love in my life, but the coffee's good. Life moved on, and I'm just sitting here on the dock of the bay with a good book and time on my hands.

I've seen Renee once since our future jumped off a bridge. Just last year I was late for a flight and walking fast through an airport. Not seeing anyone or anything, until all of a sudden the sight of her walking toward me stopped me in my tracks. I think I felt a hot flash then a cold chill and then another hot flash. As I started a slow stride in her direction, I noticed she was with a man. My eyes flashed to her ring finger. I guess he was her husband, because there was a big ring on her finger. The most telling thing of all, a child walked between them, holding both their hands. The child looked like Renee. I guess she might have been seven or eight, and very pretty.

We said, "Hello, how are you?"

"Fine."

"Good to see you."

A few words covered our past. She stopped; I kept walking past and away. I did not want to meet the husband. We kept going our separate ways through the airport. It's what most people do if they don't want their emotions to get twisted for the other to see: just keep going their separate ways.

Renee was as fine as ever with a glow about her. Sure, I've had second thoughts over the years… Did I do the right thing? Should I have stayed with her and worked it out? When we were together, we had many conversations about having a child. I wanted a girl like her; she wanted a boy like me. I wanted to see Renee's type of beauty grow up in front of me. The thought of one day holding my own daughter's hand and my wife's hand as I walked down the street would have been a dream come true. It's all spilt milk now.

I remember thinking then her man looked and acted pussy-whipped by the way he was smiling. He smiled ear to ear like life was great, but now I realize I didn't know what he was like. It was my jealous heart saying if I don't want her or can't have her, you shouldn't have her either. Remembering how she could turn my ass out in bed, I guess I would have looked the same. Yeah, I was jealous. Jealous for all the things she used to do to me to make me smile ear to ear.

As we walked away from each other, I had to look back at her. Looked at that love swing-set round posterior that from time to time I still have fantasies about. She was staring at me. We locked eyes for what seemed like a long trip to a time that could never be forgotten.

I guess if anyone ever sees an old lover, they might see a memory flash from the past that contains the good and bad of their past affairs. It's got to be natural thing if you were in love, and for a fleeting moment when you encounter that old lover, you might feel a twinge of being in love again. I did. Even before Renee said hello at the airport, I could hear her voice before she spoke. I had not forgotten her scent, even after all those years of being apart. I didn't get close enough that day, but I know her scent even to this day. I know it, as if, I were nestled between her bosoms as I used to do while drifting off to sleep.

Even though it could have been a lifetime since an old lover was in their presence, I imagine, it's the same for most people to turn back the hands of time in their mind. Imagine they still see, feel, and hear the sex they shared, whether or not it was good. I wonder, as I assume most others reflect, do they still lust after the past touch, taste, sounds, and the scent of an old lover. I miss the passion Renee and I shared, and I don't think I'm by myself in having those feelings for someone. I know for a time, I convinced myself Renee couldn't be happy without me. Maybe it was the other way around, and the emotional flame was still smoldering in my soul.

Renee's deep stare held no emotion, but her sad, still-beautiful face did. Her expression said she wanted to talk. Her lips pursed into a circle as if to whistle with no sound, just a release of air. My jaw relaxed, and my lips parted to take in the air she released. I swallowed hard and walked on, lived on.

~~~~~

Elliot had the audacity to ship me the motorcycle shortly after his freak show changed the course of my future. I had the nerve to keep it. He sent an apology along with the motorcycle; I did not respond. He sent letters for a while. Elliot said we needed to make peace about all that had happened, that there were things I needed to know, and to please respond back to him.

To hell with him. Why should I help him feel better about his bullshit? I seem to remember while he was lying on his back staring up at the ceiling, while the bottom was falling out my life. Well, it was a hell of a crash landing, but I lived. My life is not fulfilledby receiving gifts and owning or having possessions or not. The motorcycle and the letter with the apology, I can't believe it came from a good place in his soul, but might of had some guilt attached.

Elliot's corporate office was in Montreal, and I moved around, so I assumed he lost my contact info. When my website went on line seven years ago he evidently found out because I received an email from him through my site. Even though some time had gone by, I still wanted nothing to do with him. He emailed me for a while, letting me know how he was doing. He kept telling me I needed to know some things, and how his business interests were expanding. How his business ventures kept turning to gold and he makes mo-money over mo-money. It makes no difference how much money you make if you don't have friends who trust you. You need friends you can trust and who have your best interests in mind. I was glad when he stopped bothering me with his communications.

On this dock of the bay, the sky cleared above me as I sat. As I watched boats go by, I realized Renee was from another time; yet sitting here, she was on my mind. My entire past was on my mind.

I know there's a time when you have to move on, and I have in many ways. I mean, I've kind of been in love again, but kind of in love is only fun for a while. It's not meant to be forever. So what does it take? A creative soul who will share my world, one who creates passion and is willing to enjoy life's ventures. Passion... I write about it and need it; yet I was alone waiting and wanting to appreciate that woman of my desires. Maybe years ago I missed out on the chance to exhale into that sweet inhale.

Other women who have since come into my life have loved me, but as I said, I've kind of been in love. I've had a hard time giving love back because I haven't felt anyone was the one. So mostly, I have just been by myself. Okay... maybe... I might have issues.

What kind of issues? Trust issues, "being in love" issues, "worrying about being hurt again" issues, and "the woman needs to have a certain kind of beauty" issues, and no one has opened my eyes, mind and soul. My biggest issue is I fear love and because of that, maybe I don't want love. I got issues apparently.

Right now, though, I have no issues to worry about. I'm just chilling by the waterside, here to do some modeling for extra work.

A woman who runs an art school emailed me from Vancouver. She saw my website and asked me to model for her classes. Posting my poetry and short stories on my website, along with pictures of me, kept me involved in a variety of work projects. Between wedding poetry and poetry readings for special engagements, and with one-of-a-kind romantic gift cards, I made a good living. The big picture for me was writing novels and short stories.

Photography was my pure joy, taking sensual silhouette portraits of beautiful women. I would go to the waterfront or parks and other public places to find these women. There are fake wanna-be "I'll make you a famous model" photographers out there. So I made sure they felt safe, and knew that I was not trying to get them to come to my place or invite me to theirs for whatever. To do otherwise is an occupational hazard to jeopardize the cash flow. It would be like a waiter sipping the wine he's pouring - distasteful. I send the women who model free portfolios of their pictures and gift cards. The gift cards have their pictures and a poem I write in exchange for the right to use the pictures. When the cards sell, I send royalty checks to compensate them.

A lot of women buy cards just to have and to give to their women friends, so I used myself as a model in seminude and fully nude silhouettes always with taste and class. No Wild, Wild West macho slinging pictures here. I'm an erotic artist, not a pornographer.

Hard work and staying focused after my heartbreak turned me into the professional photographer and writer I always wanted to be. Working out in the gym over the years kept my body lean with just enough muscle to flex, but not that muscle-bound, caveman look. At forty, I wanted to stay in shape to have a chance to be with that special woman. It would be nice if that woman felt the same: ready to go and do anything, anytime. We could be like black panthers that mate over a 100 times a day during mating season, then hunt together as a couple to survive against all odds. I had been hunting and surviving alone since Renee.

Part of my survival was my ability to be a businessman. But maybe concentrating on my business and art kept me from finding my mate. I stayed busy filling website orders and writing stories for Erotic Digest Magazine and other adult-based publications for open-minded lovers. I have a feature short story coming out in next month's Playboy Magazine. I believe I understand sensual passion, and I love to write about it.

Writing about passion and all that comes with it, and telling stories of romance and emotional love flow out of me like a cascading mountain stream. When I write I feel my tongue sliding along a breast and curving around to the pelvis, while firmly caressing thighs. People who read my erotica should feel mentally wet, moist heat slowly easing up from their toes to meet their own heated, sweet wetness. Imaginations. We all have them, but sometimes we need help seeing the fantasy. Is there anyone who can resist the small of their back being loved like every other part of their body? Is there anyone who can resist every curve of their body being teased with warm breaths of moist kisses that lead to inner thighs? I tried to have my readers appreciate my vision of a man and a woman pleasuring each other. With the turn of each page, it should feel like the reader is breathing the air the people in the story are breathing.

True passion. Sure, any woman or man would love to have it, but many don't know how to give it or create it, visually or mentally. They don't know how to feel physical, seductive play in and out of the bed. The truth is, either you have it or you don't.

Both my agent and lawyer had been on my ass to finish my erotic romance novel. I didn't tell them I was in Vancouver, B.C., posing nude. Hey, you gotta use what you got or someone else will get the money.

Money. Sometimes things fall into place without much effort, and that happened for me in the money department. The early days of doing photo spreads for Elliot snowballed into many photo shoot opportunities. In no time at all it led to my being one of the most in-demand photographers in the world. I made a lot of money for years, but then my joy turned into work. I climbed to the top of the mountain, then I climbed off and invested most of my money. I did well and ran with my money before the markets went south. Now I let the money sit still and safe, and my investments collect small interest dust.

Staying busy with my writing and other web-based projects provided the money I need to live a couple of notches above financial worries.

I lived a good life, but alone.

~~~~~

I was alone in the open café with some time on my hands I started reading an erotic romance novel by this brother, Alexandré Cornet. It had me chuckling. He used lines like, "a woman dropped her panties like rain falling in Seattle." He had written mainly poetry in the past, but his novels and short stories were very good, too.

I wasn't getting as much reading done as I would have liked because the view of the water kept stealing my attention. The sun had already started to burn off the clouds, and I had to turn and face the harbor just to keep the glare off the pages.

Seeing and hearing the sea birds and the waterway traffic kept my eyes busy and my mind lazy.

A little sleepy from the early morning rise, I put on my headphones and sexy notes hit my eardrums. "La La Means I Love You" "The Artist-formerly known as Prince," and now called "Prince" again did his version of an old Delfonics tune. I felt myself get into a tight groove with the atmosphere around me. I started reading again. That led to my laughing at what the author said next: "B.A.D. stands for 'booty after divorce' (sex with the EX)." I was sitting there chuckling, with my back facing anyone who might have entered the café, and that's what happened; a tap on my shoulder. I turned and removed my headphones. My chuckling may have attracted the attention of this woman who had come into the café. She spoke and my eyes rose from her waistline up to very round eyes.

"I take it that's a good book. I mean, excuse me, sorry to bother you. Is that a good book? Who's it by, and what is it about?"

She caught me off guard, not with all the questions, but with her stunning looks and her approaching me with such open confidence. Her skin tone was like a brown fall leaf. She had soft, pronounced cheekbones, and deep-set eyes dancing in sparkling darkness. Her lips were full, like rising bread, and parted like they were going to blow out a row of candles. She had straight, brown hair that flowed an inch past her shoulders and showcased her alluring facial features. A mix of flavors brewed in her. People of color had made love to blend her, sweetly. She had her brew working on me instantly.

At a loss for words, my cool I couldn't find. Entranced by her outward aura, my ego was taking a big hit. "I'm the man in control of this," was gone from my time and space. I tried not to let my body language send the wrong message, that I could overdose on her spices, drown in her liquid hot sauces.

Any other time I could easily come up with sensible, intelligent conversation, but I had to dig deep with this woman.

"Yes, you'll love the author. He puts sensual thoughts into your mind. It's real sexy stuff, mind-tingling romance in a real world setting."

She asked, "The author's name?" Her voice worked on me. Damn. She looked right into my eyes when she spoke.

Deepening my voice I said. "Oh, excuse me, Alexandré Cornet is his name; he has a few works out. He wrote a book of erotic, romantic poetry that was a best seller, and his novel I'm reading just made the top ten of the African American readers' list."

"Oh my goodness," she said and took a deep breath. "I saw him recite at a poetry reading about two months ago."

I tried to come up with something to say to her, but she had me so nervous all I could say was "I heard he was here some time ago. It would have been nice to have heard him speak in person."

"Alexandré Cornet made you believe in his words," she said.

It seemed her body was drifting into a slow dance back to the poetry reading. From my chair, I looked up at her towering over me. I was so mesmerized I had forgotten to ask her to sit down. She kept talking, and I was not going to interrupt her voice working on me as she spoke about Alexandré Cornet's recital. I found myself melting in my seat as her eyes looked skyward and her lips opened and closed.

"His voice, so deep with passion when he recited you, thought he was talking to you personally. Every woman at the poetry reading started giving each other high fives when he said things like:

"Blooming Flower
My love is like a growing flower

That blooms every time you're around
And like that flower
You are so pretty, you are so beautiful
The color of love
A hue of passion
Like the moon, you shine so brightly
The light of the night, my love, is like a blooming flower bringing
desires from the birds and the bees
My love is like a growing flower
That blooms every time you're around
And like that flower
I will care for you and sprinkle your soul with all my love
No harm will come your way
As the birds and the bees arrive, they will help me to my knees and I
will kiss the petals of your blooming flower"

After she recited the poem, she continued to talk. "I remembered those words and how he sounded. His voice is somewhat like yours, if you don't mind my saying."

Damn, now I was stuck not knowing what to say again, so she had to carry the conversation.

"I haven't seen you in here before, have I?"

"No, you have not seen me here before," I said and searched for what to say next. "I'm from Seattle, and ah, Mr. Cornet left quite an impression on you." She was leaving an impression on me.

She smiled for a long moment, pressing her lips together and with the corners curving into a slight half-moon downward; it was so attractive. Then she spoke. "Yes, he did. I've read that one poem over and over; it makes me feel…" Stopping in mid-speech, she went back to that half-moon downward smile, as if she was embarrassed.

"If you don't mind, what did you feel?" I asked.

Her words flirted into a teasing singsong. "Ooooh! A man with passion who lets it show; who will share it, can get into me, like a note from Charlie Parker's horn."

I thought, "Damn, her mind is fine, too!" Her imaginative verbiage began to relax me and I finally had something worthwhile to say, or maybe my ego was coming back on line. "My opinion is, a man like that can be a little eccentric, you know?" Her eyes became deeper with a strange gaze, as if she had received some kind of shock treatment from my statement, but I spoke on. "Sometimes a man who can create and fill you with that kind of passion, may need space, peace and reciprocal passion. You know what I mean?"

Her eyes closed with a doll's gentle closing. Her chin rose, her lips parted slightly. She exhaled a long deep sigh, then said pensively, "I know what you mean. I wish... any, no, every woman could love someone like that. His dreams, his work, his love defined, a man." She spoke with intense yearning, as if she were Dorothy in the Wizard of Oz, wishing to go home. Her eyes opened and either focused on me or in me or from another world. She turned away as though trying to shield her emotions from me. When she did turn, her question-mark-shaped behind was level with my eyes. I kind of got mad at myself to have gotten distracted by her physicality, when her soul was so deep. And I still had not asked her to sit down. What an idiot I am.

"Please. Have a seat, please."
"Thank you." Silence floated after she sat. I thought of a line from a song. I'd rather live in his world, than live without him in mine. My mind had time to drift into "what if" and "what about her."

The shopkeeper brought a cup of tea over to her. I broke the silence with, "You come here often?" I realized just as soon as I said it that I had recited an old pick-up line. My excitement triggered my brain at the moment.

"Well, yes, almost every morning to get my tea." She chuckled as she spoke.

I mentioned the benefits of reading Cornet's novel. "I'm trying to read other authors to improve my own writing."

"You're a writer, an artist... wow. Do you have anything I could read?"

Hmm, she called me an artist. "Yes." Reaching into my laptop bag I handed her a gift card, on the front cover a silhouetted nude image of a man looking out a window with words overlaying, "Waiting For You" She looked at the cover and then at me again with a sheepish grin.

"Ah... let me guess, you're a model, too. Of course, I'm assuming this is you on this card?"

I must have been showing all thirty-two teeth because of her next comment.
"Oh boy, look at that smile!"

My coffee-brown skin might have shone bright red at that moment. Nodding my head yes and saying, "Yes, that is me on the card, even though modeling is not really my thing, I've done some in the past."

"Past and present it looks like to me," she said, as we stared at each other for a long moment.

"You, my dear, look like the model type," I said. She was dressed in gold-toned, beveled-heeled, open-toed sandals, which held perfect root-beer-popsicle toes. Her long, thickly muscled but shapely legs had a form-fitting gold-toned leather skirt spray-painted over her protruding rear. Some might say she had too much of a good thing back there, and she did have plenty, but to me it was good and plenty. She wore no bra under a brown tube top; no bra was needed over what was good and plenty. Her beauty made it hard for me to concentrate on the fact this woman had something to say.

We talked, we laughed, we theorized, we pondered, we debated and came to most of the same conclusions. We had a very engaging talk. A little of this, a little of that, what we understood and what we didn't. The lady was interesting and intelligent. We shared some laughs and I watched her blush at times and show her lovely white teeth. We were enjoying our moment.

Yet, after a while, I felt like something was intruding on our karma. Was there something holding back our vibe? Maybe I wanted more than she was willing to give at the moment?

She opened the card I had handed to her earlier, and she began to read my work aloud with her slow, cello-like voice. Her recital gave my words a life. She turned my words on me and made me feel I had written them for her...

"The seduction of a full moon smiled in her eyes.
A smile returned from her parted lips.
I took the beauty of that smile and the glow of the moon
in her eyes to sleep with me.
I awoke in the morning with a smile on my face.
I waited throughout the day and the night
for the moon to glow, to remind me of the smile
from her parted lips, and the glow of the moon to smile
in her eyes."

She paralyzed me with her delivery of my written words. I felt my body warming up and liquefying my sweat glands. Trying to unlock from her spell, I went to wipe a sweat bead from the back of my neck, but I missed. It ran down the length of my back and crept past the waistband of my jeans. I guess I should have put on some underwear. Damn, I wish it were her hands running down my backside!

A change of subject was the last thing I wanted, but I had to do it.

"Do you have the time?" She placed her hand on the table to expose her wristwatch and no wedding ring on her long sexy manicured fingers. Was there anything about this woman that didn't catch my attention? It seemed everything about her made me want...Damn... going down deeper. Fighting hard to come up I took a deep breath. Leaning over, I looked at her watch. Time, and bad timing. Right now I wanted to be nowhere but with her, but I had to leave. It might have been love at first sight, but for sure I was in love with this time and space. Could she leave with me?

"I have to find this warehouse-looking building that houses an art school. My contact said there would be no way I wouldn't recognize it. Could you help me, point me in the right direction? I think it's close by." She smiled and looked away; her head rose up high and took a long slow nod down, acknowledging yes.

The whole time we had been talking we never exchanged our names. "How about I buy you some more tea and we could walk. You see the name of my production company on my card, but not my name, my name is..."

"Stop please... Don't tell me your name!"

My head turned to the side like a poodle that doesn't understand a command. We had plunged way past names in the conversation we had shared. We had been swimming in a warm ocean of comfort, but now I wanted to know her name. Why didn't she want to know my name?

She spoke. "For mystery's sake I don't want to know your name. Please forgive me. Maybe you thought I was flirting with you...?"

"Oh really, why would I think you were flirting with me?" I smiled and I'm sure my eyebrows rose in question marks, as I stared at her shy look. Those corners of her mouth that always turned downward when she smiled were so sexy. Her voice became playfully assertive. "Okay, don't be too sure of yourself."

Now she was blushing. "I did become interested in that book you were reading because it had you smiling so much. Then you started laughing while you were reading; it was so cute. Then us talking... You're interesting. I'm particularly pleased to have been here with you, only I shouldn't be. The right thing to do is to stop now. I'm sorry; you were just sitting here, and I should have left you alone."

"But you didn't!"

"You're right, I'm sorry. I hope I haven't upset you, but I would not have had a chance to read your poem. For that I'm not sorry."

She stared at my perplexed expression. "Well," I said and then thought for a while. "All right, we'll do it your way, no names."

"I hope you have a good time. Vancouver is a marvelous place. I understand the art school where you're going is an excellent place for whatever you're there for."

"I'm sure I'll have a good time in your fair city. And hey, it's all good — very good, I'm not sorry about meeting you at all. Let's just say in the thirty, forty minutes we have shared I, ah... ah I... well, I guess the cat's got my tongue, can't find the words to say..."

"You don't need words...," she said and laughed. I smiled. "You and that smile! Do you use that on women a lot?" I hunched my shoulders and smiled some more, not knowing my smile had ever made anyone feel that good. "May I keep your card? You have a website here on the back so that I can go visit it. If and when I do, then I'll learn your name. The art school you're seeking is just four blocks northeast of here. You can't miss it."

Wish she'd walk with me, I kept thinking.

"I, I'm..." she faltered, then bowed her head and no words came out of her mouth. I covered her hand with my hand as it lay on the table. She flinched a bit, and I felt her pulse beat hard. I spoke to her bowed head.

"Please take these words with you." I took out a pen and note pad from my inside coat pocket, and wrote some words for her to read and keep. I slid the paper over and under her bowed head. She read my words out loud, as I had hoped she would.

"I'll wait, too... and dream of another time when my eyes will undress your eyes and leave you reaching for my embrace to cover you and comfort you. I'll wait until a time I will be able to ease and erase all, if any, past troubles of your mind. I'll wait until a time you and I cannot avoid our hearts from beating together, dear lady, I'll dream sweet dreams. Until our time, let it be known to you; you're no fantasy to me and I'm not an image from your mind of a dream you want to come true. We are real breaths of air."

Her voice was a symphony being directed by my words. She leaned away and looked into the sky. Her brown tube top moved erratically, erotically, as she exhaled and inhaled. Sliding the palm of my hand under her hand, we rose slowly from our seats. Her fingers were slowly sliding out of mine along my lifeline. Our fingertips stopped, cupped each other's fingertips, held for a long second and released. A slight breeze blew her perfect hair toward me; it was still perfect. An awkward moment, we stared, nothing more to say. With my lips just inches from her lips I lifted her hand and kissed her fingers and released her hand. I might have been a bit forward in my actions, but it happened so naturally.

Her voice touched my eardrums like a feather. "Hmm, you couldn't find any words, huh? Seems to me you have plenty of the right ones." In her slow cello voice, she ended the symphony in our play. Her eyes seemed to transition in color from desert sand to nutmeg and then to the color of sadness. She might have spoken to me for the last time; I hoped not.

She then turned toward the future; I was dejected. Then, with that fine ass, honest heart and long legs, she walked away, down the pier, toward the street.

I watched her turn onto the street and walk to a car, some type of convertible. I could still see her head as she pulled away from the curb, some of her hair flowed through the air and she faded away. Damn, damn… wish that woman was… I don't know. Wondered if I had come on too strong or maybe not strong enough… maybe. Maybe she has a boyfriend or husband, or just my luck, a girlfriend? Maybe she's a nun from the Blow-A-Man's-Mind Convent. I stood there laughing at my thoughts and had one more thought.

Some people we spend a lifetime never really knowing. Some people we forget about just as soon they are out of our sight. Then we can meet people and know them for a few minutes or a little more, and their image, words or deeds can leave a lasting impression on our souls for the rest of our lives.

Chapter Eight

I started walking the four blocks, living in a fantasy of what will be, will be. I looked around, saw a unique billboard on a red brick building while still a block away. Finally, standing in front of the building that looked like a brick warehouse, the artistry above my head stopped me in my tracks. It was way out of bounds for anything I had ever seen before. It looked like an urban-style Sistine Chapel. Pictures mixed with black and white paintings and colorful painted scenes including people from every walk of life were imprinted on the walls of the building. The figures were dressed in three-piece suits and baggy pants and other urban dress; some folks were painted as if they were from ancient Roman times, but all hanging out together.

It didn't stop there. The paintings had photo-like images of sexy women of all walks of life with wings of angels. The women stared at me from the painted walls. Much like the woman from my café and my forty-minute love affair, or whatever you want to call it, the painted women were beautiful.

The billboard was a visual taste of a fantasy world painted on the walls. As I stood across the street, my eyes took in the artwork that spanned a block, the same length as the building. I had reached my destination, and this building was "eye candy." I would love this art for my home. Someone with freaky thoughts and images waved this art like a badge of honor.

Yeah, this was the place for someone to make my image into art. Who would have thought, simply because my nude silhouette had captured an art teacher's eye, I would be here? She thought it would be worth paying me to sit and show off God's work. After seeing the work that had been done on the building, I wanted my body to be painted, for money or no money.

The instructor sent those little smiley faces and funny little sayings in her email. She must have a sense of humor. She stated in her email, "I hope that you are not too shy, because most of the students are women." Returning her email, I jokingly asked if there were going to be any beautiful women I'd enjoy looking at while they were brushing my butt on a canvas.

"Yes," came the response.

I strolled across the street and walked up a marble staircase in the middle of the two-story building. I was in awe of more artwork painted on the walls leading to a long stairway hidden from the street. Rock and brick patterns were painted in all kinds of sizes and designs that blew my mind. The boulders looked real, as if they were not painted. Grains of sand seemed ready to fall on me, but they were only painted, as well. These were fine examples of *trompe l'oeil* — fooling-the-eye painting, giving the illusion of reality.

One scene had what appeared to be a large boulder in the shape of a man's body. Boulder Man seemed to be lying on grains of sand in the shape of a woman. It looked like the rear end of the sand woman was up in the air. She was on her knees with her belly and her very supple nipples barely touching wet sand beneath her as water from the sea washed in. The arms of Sand Woman extended out into the sea. Boulder Man was on his knees with his stone hands spread on the sand woman's back and his hips were pushed against her rear. A rock hard man and the soft curves of a woman in flowing grains of sand, what an imagination! The face of the woman was painted like a light complexioned Egyptian queen from the African side, not the Italian Roman side. The sand woman had me puzzled for some reason, but I thought the artist was a bad mother, for sure. A long chain hung from high above that held a brass-plated sign greeting visitors.

WELCOME
ETERNITY PSEUDONYM ARTISTRY SCHOOL
BE SOMEONE ELSE IN ART
OR BE YOURSELF

I opened a large cherry-wood double door with stained-glass inserts, which had a glossy finish. Everything in the building matched the door. Shining wood floors and more cherry-grained planks spanned left and right and in front of me. The colors in the floor went from apple to dark gold tones to bright orange and brown. The interior design concept was supreme. The walls rose twenty feet high with red lacquered bricks and large paintings in gold-colored frames; it was the same artist's work as the mural outside. There were huge wallboards with scenes painted in every color. God gave someone extra talent and a whole lot more.

Damn. One of the paintings looked like Cleopatra and Caesar in a modern nighttime downtown scene. There were players and pimps, hookers and street people, all adorned in ancient but risqué Roman fashion. This was some very strange vision, unimaginable to most of us common folk. In one scene, Cleopatra and Caesar sat in the back of the rear deck lid of a gold-colored Jaguar XKE. This Cleopatra did not look like Liz Taylor with a bad suntan. She looked like a Black African queen. The faces of the woman and the women in the art had me puzzled. It was not because the faces were of people of color, like I know they should be, but because the faces all looked somewhat the same. Brown and bronze-colored Roman soldiers waving palm leaf fans surrounded Cleopatra and Caesar, while other soldiers sat on half-motorcycle-half-chariot-like vehicles. This painting drew my attention so intently that I didn't notice anything or anyone.

"Hello, can I help you? Are you here for a class? No, you're the new model I heard about."

"Yes, I'm here for a modeling job."

A young girl with coconut-colored skin and a beautiful wide smile stood near me. Her full lips were waiting for the size of her face to catch up. She had high cheekbones of Negroid decent or Native-American, or as the Canadians say, "First Nation." The young girl of maybe 9 or 10 years of age was going to be an extremely pretty woman one day. She was dressed in a soccer outfit and looked like an athlete of the future. She continued to talk enthusiastically.

"Modeling for classes is so much fun. Uh, uh, my ma, uh, uh, is the person who owns the school." The young girl spoke fast, as if she wanted to get the information out as quickly as she could.

While she kept speaking, I focused my attention on one picture of the many mounted on the wall, and I was perplexed. The faces of all the women in the paintings looked like they could be sisters. All were a little different in age, shades of skin, some more voluptuous, some smaller in size, but the faces had me gazing intently. Maybe the faces were of some movie star; it just seemed that I'd seen the faces before.

Then again, all the men in the picture were the same too. All were well-built, black-skinned, Greek mythology godlike bodies. Their faces were all turned in such a way that you could put any face on them, but they seemed to all be the same man in size and skin tone. In my own critique, I did think the artist could have used different male bodies in sizes and shades of brown skin to depict the love of many men for the beauty of one woman. But that was just my opinion.

"The women in the paintings are very beautiful," I said, interrupting the young girl from her rambling. She had been talking the whole time, while my mind was somewhere next to Cleopatra. "Who is the artist, and are the models here at this school?"

She responded, "Yes, sir, she…"

A woman's voice sailed in and cut off our conversation. It came through what must have been a long hallway, because the voice echoed through another set of double doors. She was meant to be heard. "Mr. Dandridge, is that you? Eh? You're on time, eh." It amazes me now how people ask questions and make statements in the same sentence. The voice finished the sentence with the word eh, pronounced like the letter "A." That Canadian-British accent had a certain charm and sex appeal.

The first sight of the woman who belonged to the voice conjured up thoughts of a Smiley Face sticker, not a funny face, but a pretty face with a built-in smile.

Maybe it was shallow on my part but the next thing that got my attention were her breasts. Normally I'm a butt-and-leg man, but her breasts, damn! There was this smooth deep valley in the middle of her blouse and then her breasts reached up and out. Her thin blouse was splattered with paint splotches, and near the nipples dark paint helped showcase the proud and protruding. Her exposed wheat-colored natural-complexioned bosom made me wonder what nationality she was. Medium height, shapely and contoured, she had long legs that flowed down from a rear end that would do in a pinch. Stepping with her short crossing steps in the Arabian style pant that she had on, the lady reminded me of "I Dream of Genie." The pants stopped at her knees, exposing tight calves. On her feet were high-heeled slippers of wood and leather, supporting deep arches. Not a young lady, but a grand woman of beauty and style. She walked into my path. If ever I lived to be a much older man, I hoped my old lady would invigorate my old spirit like the lady that walked my way. I wouldn't mind being Lena Horne's lover right now.

"Hello, Ms. Kraft. Your school building is so unique and you are so beautiful."

"Well, talk like that to me and I'll give you more than a paycheck! Is there anything you would like to have?" she laughed, squinting her eyes while she extended her hand. I guess I must have had an intimidated expression on my face, because I was. "Oh, don't worry, I'm a big tease and please call me Tamara, as in some time tomorrow," she said.

I shook her hand; she caressed it with one hand on top and held firmly on the bottom. "A man with soft warm, large hands can do most anything in life, eh. A man with hot hands, like yours, can heal wounded souls and free the unfree. It feels like your hands have completed most every endeavor you have encountered, eh?" Her voice was less excitable and more prophetic or fortuneteller-like. Listening to her, my inner spirit received a caress. She had power, and I felt even stronger being in her presence.

"Tamara, your accent?"

"I'm from the Jamaica. My mother is of Jamaican and English bloodlines and my father, Western African, Native American, and an Irishman. So, I'm a mixture of some very good ingredients."

I chuckled and said, "Well, I assume you can dance with all those dancing people in you, all except that English part. I can't imagine the Queen getting her groove on." She threw her body forward from the waist up, laughing a hearty laugh and holding her stomach.

"Hmm, never heard that before or thought about it. Yes, the creator gave me some rhythm and a cultured mind, eh. Oh, my English relatives are a bit stuffy and stiff. So as they say, it's all good, eh?"

"You're funny."

"You're funny, Mr. Handsome Man, and charming man, too. Too bad I'm almost old enough to be your mother."

"Can I show him around the school, Ma?" The young girl had been standing with her eyes ping-ponging the dialogue and wanting to break back into the conversation.

"Honey, thank you, but I'll show Mr. Dandridge around." The young girl walked away disappointed. I felt bad; her happy face morphed into such a sad look.

Tamara walked me back though the door from which she had come. "Mr. Dandridge, this way."

"Tylowe, call me Tylowe. Your school, the art, and the layout, it's nice. You got something going on, dear lady." She gave me a tour. Her smiley face was always laughing at whatever I said while I viewed her school.

"Tylowe, a man who makes a woman laugh shows a good sign of being a good man, eh. Yeah? You seem to be a relaxed man, another good sign of a good man, eh."

We walked; we talked the same language. We understood the zeal of the artistic intellect, no limits to hold down the creativity of the soul. We traveled on the main floor from room to room. She showed me great woodwork around doorways and archways, polished to a blinding mirror finish. The hallways had huge stained-glass windows that received light from the outer windows and kept rooms of arts and crafts classes and workshops well lit. In the hallways, there were more paintings. Some of the paintings might have been painted by the same artist whose works I saw outside, including Cleopatra and Caesar.

"Tamara, are you the great painter of the artwork outside and inside? It's outstanding; I envy such…" She cut me off with a hard tone.

"I'm not the artist of this work. They have been painted from drawings of my late husband. Now let me show you your living quarters."

Whoa! I stepped somewhere I was not supposed to. Her whole body language changed. Women just don't understand that when they get an attitude it can be so intimidating. Then again, maybe they do know. We didn't talk for a minute as we walked. We both were deep in thought. I just kept looking at all of the artwork from drawings of her late husband.

Climbing up a flight of stairs with a huge, polished oak handrail, perfect for sliding down, we entered another architectural oasis. Unseen from the street was a loft as long as the building, but not as wide. We entered a long central hallway with large rooms on the sides and enormous stained-glass skylights. This was where Tamara lived. This place was devoid of any artwork except for the painted, leather-like surfaces decorating the walkways and flowers in vases.

At the end of the hallway my eyes danced again. I said, "Tamara you live up here? There is so much space!" I was standing in an elegant parlor at the end of the building. A sunken, rectangular floor of long, cherry-wood planks was highlighted with a huge, black, painted, brick fireplace. The outer walls were lined with six-foot leather *chaise* lounges, something like the ones a stereotypical psychiatrist would have for patients to lie on. Antique end tables were at the head of each one. The middle of the floor was open. It was like having a big dance floor in your living room.

Tamara had not answered my other question, so I tried to get her to speak again. "Would you mind if I come in here to stretch and do my dance workout sometime in the next couple of days? This room is so inspiring."

"This is home; I spread my love among those close to me, or those who get close," she said.

Ah, she's back from her nasty attitude. I won't go near the painting subject again. I like her when she is nice and slightly flirty. Must be my day, I thought, to feel her good and bad attitude. She continued to talk and tell me about her living quarters. "I rent out small studio apartments at the other end. That still leaves me with more space than I can ever use." She spoke a little more as the tour continued.

"Here is the kitchen. Tylowe, you're welcome to come in and cook anytime. I'm much too busy to cook during the week. Plus, I assume with those lover's hands you can do a lot more than one thing right, eh?" As she laughed her large breasts almost popped out of her shirt.

I thought she might have multiple personalities the way she changed up on me.

The kitchen, like everything else inside the building, was spacious. It had many stations, cabinets and counter tops. There was lots of marble on the floor and a huge porcelain stove that had to be from the roaring twenties. If I were the chef in Oprah's house, I'd have a stove just like it.

"You have this big kitchen and you don't cook? I'll bet you make a mean Jamaican jerked chicken."

"Ah, I didn't say I could not cook, Mister." She waved her finger at me in a mocking and laughing way. "I just don't have time, but this kitchen gets used for big dinners. We have art shows with dinner for special occasions."

"Well, I'll probably eat out and enjoy the city as much as I can." My curiosity had me. I wanted to know how she came to have such a place as this. I wanted her history, but knew I'd better tread lightly. I didn't want to step on her toes again. "Could you tell me the history of this place?"

Her breasts rose slightly higher than normal and fell slowly before she responded to me. "Maybe later, Mr. Dandridge. Let me show you your room." She did it again, cut me off, hmm. I had questions; a place like this raises all kinds of questions.

She walked me through a large, tall cherry-wood door into a rather small room. A very tall bed with brass headboard and a tall brass radiator took up most of the space. Everything else was narrow, from the nightstand to the dresser. They had to be, just to walk around the room. The bed was so tall, it squeaked from my climb.

"You ready for a little nap, eh? Good, then you'll be ready for your first session, at one, right after lunch. I'll wake you, eh. The bathroom is the next room over to your left."

Chapter Nine

Sleep. The soft bed held my body like a loving mother holding a baby. I drifted deeply, quickly into the abyss of nothingness. Although my mind was tired from the early start, my body had other plans. You can't hide from your feelings in your sleep.

My testosterone thermometer had been rising, and my sex drive was running a fever. As usual, I'm horny, so I do the usual. Hallucinating intimate feelings, moving slowly from deep sleep to awakened warmth, I kept my eyes closed to keep my lustful dreams alive behind my eyelids.

As my body awoke, I found I was holding myself, thinking about a woman. Just a woman; no name, no face. A woman like the women in the paintings on the wall downstairs. She's urging the blood to fill and harden me.

Deeper into the carnal images from my mind, I'm seeing a woman; her nakedness feeling body warmth real deep, leaving wetness on my lips, my hands, and other parts of my body. Whoever she was, she was beautiful, without a name, but with a curving behind and thighs that motivated the dripping, slipping, sliding fluid of life in me.

Impressed with myself, my size had me smiling in my dream. Told myself to let go of my ego and hardness. It felt good; not as good as the real thing, as usual I did the usual; kept going. The song says, "Until the real thing comes around." So I squeezed my thighs tight, thrust my hips forward, the lines in my palm became the thickness of her insides. Oh, shit, I was so horny. Opened my eyes to see my own hardness. It turned me on more. I rolled over to reach into my travel bag on the floor and pulled out some oil to put me into her imaginary wetness. "Ahhhh, ahhh, huh."

Knock, knock was at my door. "Mr. Dandridge?" It was a young voice, the young soccer girl I met earlier. "Mr. Dandridge, my ma says it's time for you to come down."

The bed squeaked. Ahhh damn… I'll have to finish this later. I hollered back through the door: "I'll be down right after I take a shower." I better take a cold shower and hope my first model sitting isn't totally nude.

~~~~~

"Please sit on this platform." A much older lady with pure white hair that hung down to the hem of her shirt taught the class. She wanted me to sit and curl over as if to tie my shoe. I was told to leave my pants on and shirt off, one shoe on, one off. There were student artists stationed all around me. A bright overhead light highlighted me from the rear; it was as if I was in the middle of a sundial. Everyone had a different view.

For the next two hours, I held private conversations with my inner and outer consciousness to pass the time. Most of the painters were female; I made no eye contact, and just sat still like a statue.

During a ten-minute break, I did look at who was looking at me for art. All the women seemed to be the housewife type, the "not looking for a man" type. I wondered if it was just a man thing or just my thing to check out the opposite sex surrounding me, or do women do the same thing? I often look at people unknown to me and wonder about what it is like for them. I make up stories about their lives, often judging them by the physical cover, body language, speech, and interaction with others. I wonder if others do the same with me, read me like the cover of a book. What story do people read from my physical cover, body language, speech, and interaction with others?

Strolling around the room to look at each easel to see the brush strokes of my image, I saw the many sides of me. Different styles; different strokes. I was a shadow; I was a black and white; I was in living color; I was abstract with some tight lines, some loose, much like all the different sides of my inner personality.

I wondered what these artists would see and paint if a woman was posing with me. Would they see cold or warm images? Would they paint inside or outside the lines of my desire? Could they transmit my views, for which I have no words in a conceptual view of love, into visual images? The last brush stroke, would it tie me to a woman forever? I wondered.

When it was time to sit back into my pose, Tamara came up behind me.

"Tylowe, later this evening the little one and I will treat you to dinner. Do you have a certain preference? Is there something you like to eat?"

"I'm a meat and rice kind of guy, nothing too fancy, please."

Her Jamaican accent shined with laughter and with a rhyme.

"A man loves his meat, like a man loves his woman, to be tasty, tender and juicy. A man loves his meat, like a man loves his woman, to be thick around the bone, well done on the outside and pink in the middle. A man loves his meat like he loves his woman. He just can't stand it when his woman is smarter than the source of the meat." She walked away chuckling.

Assuming my modeling position, I pondered Tamara's rhyme. Maybe she just had a different kind of humor. Maybe she has known people who think like that. Maybe I was thinking too much?

Getting back to my room after my modeling session, and seeing my unmade bed reminded me of my previous horny feelings. I turned and looked at my body in the full-length mirror on the wall; I knew what I had to do with my free time...

Chapter Ten

Hot water poured over my bald head. I was showering from the stress-relieving, forty-minute, hard, sweaty jog. I got to stay in shape. I really needed a good run to help discharge me from my lustful mood. No, I did not do the deed to myself this time. What do you do if there is no one sexually in your life to help you fulfill the need? What do all the lonely people do? All the people you see in life or meet sometimes, what are they doing or what do they do when the body needs touching, kissing, eyeing, warm human feeling? What do people do when it's been a long time since they've heard a groan, and a pleading moan, and a tongue slips and slides and savors a taste? What do people do when they yearn forshared climactic, euphoric feeling?

Sometimes I can wish the feeling away; sometimes! Sometimes I take things into my own hands that others pay for… Some say they do nothing, when they are for sure doing something with themselves or someone else. Then you have those who say they're doing something with someone and the truth is, as the commercial says, "Never have, never will." Plenty of others do it with someone who is just there for one thing only and kick them out the door before the sun comes up. And we all know that a cold shower is just that, cold!

It was time to go to dinner. We walked out into the evening air. I could tell there might have been something going on by observing the moods of Tamara and her little one, whose name was Mia (pronounced MY-ah). Watching two pairs of eyes cutting hard at each other in some type of silent squabble was somewhat amusing.

Mia's rolling eyeballs seemed to be silently screaming, "Why, and how come?" Tamara's crossing eyes seemed to say, "Don't you dare." I did not want to get in the middle of whatever drama they had going. Swimming in a shark tank at feeding time is often the same as getting between two females. If you get asked to pick sides, it can be like being in a blender on high speed.

I stepped into the shark tank anyway. That's what men do; they try to solve the world's problems. Then women come and bail out our macho asses.

"Mia, such a sad look for such a pretty girl, please don't be sad."

"I'm sad just like..." Tamara cut her off like a hot knife cutting butter and breaking the butter dish at the same time.

"Enough." Tamara's voice boomed. Mia's sad expression melted into liquid sad. "We are going to dinner to eat and have a good time. I'm sorry, Tylowe, the little one here is trying to be a little too grown up." Tamara's tone robbed the air we breathed and she addressed both Mia and myself. "The little one here is trying to understand the business of things she is just too young to understand."

"But Ma, I..."

"I said enough!" Tamara's voice drowned out the cars and buses. And made me feel like I was the child fixing to get into trouble. Then her next words gave her baby girl air to breathe again. "Baby, I'm sorry. Please, Mia. It's just this way. Let's not bother Mr. Dandridge with our troubles. He's a nice man who would not like to be involved in such matters." I'm sure she was talking to me as well as little Mia. I crawled back out of the shark tank with my ass still intact; I'll mind my own business for sure. Plunging into the family drama is not what I came up for. If I had kept my mouth closed, little Mia would not have tears running down her face.

When we arrived at the restaurant and were able to sit and order right away and the tension eased. Some small talk followed; the smell of food and hearing others having conversations led to a better atmosphere.

Mia and I talked about sports and photography. I shared my history as a football player in Canada and my travel experiences around the world as a photographer, which brought some interesting questions from Tamara.

"Tylowe, I suppose you have had many different companions or should I say, you have made many friends while traveling?" It wasn't a rude question, yet it was a none-of-her-business-question.

"I'm not quite sure what you mean." I did understand; I just was not going to make it easy for her.

"Ah, come on, my friend. Mr. Tylowe, I can tell by how you carry yourself in such a confident way. You have had many friends from many places. But no judgments. You a man, and a man has but one duty and that is to fill his needs, whatever they shall be." She then repeated part of what she had said to me earlier that day. "A man loves his meat, like a man loves his woman." And the rest of her earlier rhyme she finished with a hearty laugh.

I smiled and ignored her. She was a strange woman. After Tamara, Mia and I had spoken on a number of subjects she asked another slightly odd question.

"Tylowe, you ever had people in your life that you would do almost anything to send them to the moon with a one-way ticket?"

"Oh, yeah, no doubt, but that's life. I try to let bad take its course and pray for a change. What about you?"
"Well, I'm a-praying."

A little silence went by before I spoke to Mia. "Mia, do you have a bike I could ride?" She didn't get a chance to answer because Tamara interrupted.

"You don't want to ride a bike around this town. People will run you over."

Later, when we got back, Mia and I were watching "The Five Heartbeats." I had brought a few of my favorite movies.

"Mr. Tylowe, do you have a girlfriend?" Mia asked.

I laughed; I don't know why. Then I asked. "Mia, how old are you?"

"Oh, do you think, like other old people, I'm too young to know stuff?"

I chuckled, as her eyes, nose, and lips went into a playful pouting expression. I gave her a playful look back and said, "Old? Who you calling old? Oh, so you think I'm as old as your mom?" She didn't answer. She didn't respond in any way. We went back to watching the movie. A little while later, I spoke to her again.

"Mia, like the character in the movie who writes the music for the group, that's me. He thought he had met the only woman for him, but something happened, something he couldn't understand, something he could not overcome." I spoke more to myself than to her. "In the world of love there is no perfect man or woman, and I'm not looking for the perfect woman anymore, just the right woman; just wanting a happy ending. Maybe one day when you're old enough, you'll go through the Humpty Dumpty changes of life. Then you'll understand."

"Mr. Tylowe, I know a lot of stuff, okay? And Humpty Dumpty was stupid for being an egg and sitting on the edge of a wall." She said that like an arrow hitting its target. She meant it. From her viewpoint, she did "know a lot of stuff," as she put it.

"You might be right; my bad. Okay, I don't have a girlfriend, haven't met the right woman."

"If you met her would you make her happy?"

"I like to think so." She smiled, so I guess I redeemed myself. At the end of the movie, we were both smiling with the happy ending.

"Mr. Tylowe, there are bikes you can use in a little room off the main floor hallway. You'll know which room because there are three steps going down to a door. Please don't tell my ma I told you about the bikes. You should ride down through Gastown. There are some art galleries down there." Her steady gaze almost held a plea.

Chapter Eleven

My internal alarm clock went off at the crack of dawn, giving me no hope of going back to sleep. I made my way down to the main floor hallway and the room where the bikes were. They looked new, expensive, and high-tech. I picked a good old-fashioned ten-speed. That is, I picked the one that was the least high-tech. My legs worked hard riding through the streets and right through red traffic lights. I always made sure no cars were coming; I wanted my riding groove to keep flowing with the music in my headphones. Lionel Richie was crooning a train of thought about love will find a way. I peddled into the rising morning sun, enjoying my solitude.

Heading toward Stanley Park, I peddled past espresso stands. I wanted to stop for a shot of caffeine energy, but I kept riding toward the park at a fast pace. I planned to do some photography work while spending some time in the park. My modeling start time back at the school was 1 p.m., which would give me time to shoot some silhouettes of women walking or running with the Lions Gate Bridge as a backdrop.

After finally passing one too many coffee stands, I slowed to take in the scents that came from one storefront. On the outside this place had the red, green and yellow colors representative of African national colors and art. The outside décor, along with strong flavored aromas, enticed me through the screen door.

A Muslim woman stood behind a glass front counter. I guessed she was older than I, but if she was fifty or 100, she showed no negative signs of aging. She didn't smile. She didn't have to; her face was a welcoming live portrait of stately elegance.

She had a polished ebony, smooth-as-silk beauty that could not be imitated by any type of pop culture.
Her African beauty and regal style sent my imagination to the motherland. She was the motherland, a black diamond, the queen of my tribe who would never send her Mandingo warriors out to die, because she valued her men as if they were from her own womb. Her reserved gaze said, "Welcome, my brother." She tilted

her Muslim headdress down toward the glass as if asking me, "What would you like?" I asked for coffee, some rice, hummus, and turkey sausage with pita bread for a breakfast treat.

I sat at a table by the window and stretched out my legs to rest. She first brought my coffee and still no emotion from her, just tranquil presence. Then she brought a tray of food, with some water, and she smiled, bowed her head, and said, "Thank you, my brother." Her English was good with a gentle motherland accent.

The large interior of the place was sparsely furnished with only chairs and tables. There was a raised floor, like a stage, in one corner with some drums on it. Art adorned the walls, watercolor painting in great detail. It looked like one long painting went around the whole interior of a figurative story being told.

Savoring each bite of food gave me time to recover from the first hour of my bike ride. My book relaxed me into feeling at home in this place. In it Cornet asserts,

"A man may admire what a woman does for a living; he may admire her education and social circle. He may be enamored with her physical beauty, but he only truly falls in love with the softest and warmest part of her, her soul."

The five dollars' worth of great food and being in this café with this woman of few words while reading words to believe was worth my ten-dollar tip.

Back on the bike, I peddled back into a groove, listening to "Café Regio's" by Isaac Hayes, before finally arriving at the park. Once there, I cruised around the park and through the marina. As I peddled hard to break a sweat again, soccer and football fields came into view.

Young and older gents were playing rugby. Early in the morning their spirit of competition was loud and aggressive. Walking my bike over to the sideline and watching the men give their physical best reminded me of my past.

Rugby is a rough sport. It's similar to football, but with no pads for protection. I played the sport for recreation in college. Ooh, a hard hit, and a man was down and in pain from full contact. Damn! The smallest player out there tackled one of the biggest, and the big guy was hurt. I think the air was knocked out of him, and his pride.

As he was helped off the field, a voice with a brutish British bellow beckoned from the field of the fallen warrior.

"Eh, mate, you know how to play? Wanna rough house?" He didn't have to ask twice. I was more than ready to use the old skills. As they helped cart off a fallen warrior, I jogged onto the field. I stretched and jogged around a bit. My muscles were warmed up from the bike ride, but running muscles are different.

I had on a brown spandex body suit that was more for track or bike-riding than rugby. The brown shiny material wrapped around my body like the skin of a dolphin. For sure, I looked out of place. Most of the guys were in sweats or gym shorts and had the rugged look. The players looked like members of the United Nations. Some looked to be of East Indian descent, and some had the look of Vikings, and some were other nationalities from tall to short.

I heard a statement from the opposing team as I trotted on to the field. "Eh, do you guys think the pretty boy in the tights can handle a man's game?" Now, I thought to myself, they had already hurt a player with their smallest, so I'm not going to let their slow asses catch me, tackle, and hurt me.

After I had loosened up a bit, I caught some passes from my teammates. Everyone on my team introduced himself to me, and they were all warm and funny. They called their opponents big brutes with no brains. The only one, they said, who had any skill or brains was the one who had hurt their teammate. The person they spoke of wore a hooded sweatshirt hiding his face for the most part. What you could see was painted black under the eyes. "I'll try to avoid that one," I said.

The game started again and it became clear right away I was more athletic than anyone out there. Being a level better than the weekend-warrior type, I was able to avoid being tackled by any of the players on the other team, which allowed me to score at will. My teammates loved me and took advantage of my speed and past football skills and moves. Sooner or later ego is the downfall of all athletes. Running around the corner for another score near the end of the game, I slowed up thinking no one would catch me. Wrong. The hooded sweatshirt hit me hard on my hip and drove me out of bounds and into the ground on my butt. My used-to-be-sexy body suit ripped, exposing my thigh.

"Yer' good, but not that good, mate." The voice was not that of a brute. The hooded sweatshirt, exposed her face as she slowly pulled her hood off, and spoke to me mockingly with a Canadian accent. I'd had the shit knocked out of me by a woman. She smiled a sweet smile, yet she stood over me in an aggressive victory stance.

I'm not sure what hurt more, my hip or my self-esteem. I said, "Well, you and your teammates made me look good until now."

She laughed. "You are good," she said as she reached a hand down to help me up. I thought, this isn't co-ed softball. What the hell is she doing out here?

"Yer stunned there, mate, to see me, eh, a girl knock you down. I love this game because I can rough house it up with the fellows," she said as if she'd heard my unasked question.

"I see." I tried to act like I was okay by moving around a bit.

"You okay, mate?" Her question had a sinister snicker.
I nodded yes. My hip and pride were stung, but I hobbled back to the huddle only to be greeted by quiet laughs.

After the game, the female warrior walked my way looking more like a woman, now. She had stripped off her sweats and was wearing a sports bra and hip-hugging shorts. She was pretty, in a tomboy sort of way, with short straight black hair that must have been dyed. She kind of reminded me of Drew

Barrymore: cute, small puffy lips and appealing facial features. She had the bounce in her walk that also reminded me of how Drew Barrymore danced in Charlie's Angels movie different but spicy. Definitely an acquired taste for some.

"Hey, Mr. Fast Guy, where you from?"

"Hey, Ms. Fast Girl, the name is Tylowe, Tylowe Dandridge, and I'm from Seattle, where women don't play so rough."

She laughed. "Well, you can call me Suzy Q, Q for quick, as your backside might already know!"

We laughed, but I reminded her I slowed up for her to catch up. We got into some small talk for a while. She was cool, but not my type as far as a man-woman thing. Call me sexist, but I don't mind a woman beating me at TV Jeopardy or checkers, but knocking me on my butt is a whole other thing. She soon let me know I was not her cup of tea, either.

"Yer kind of cute there, mate. Nice buns. But don't you worry there none. I like being the like a guy eh, if you know what I mean, you know."

"Well, it's nice to know, but that means we'll be competing for the same thing, and I hate to lose." I laughed. So did she.

Inside my head and heart, I took a hit much harder than the tackle Suzy Q had put on me. Saying we would be competing for women sent back for a moment. I had unknowingly competed for a woman with another before and lost.

She said, "I'm glad we got that out of the way. I'm sure we like totally different types. But I have been known to have some fun. You know, like one plus one plus one." She looked at me like she wanted to eat me. I laughed off her comment. We kept talking and laughing as I walked with my bike. My exposed hip hurt and was starting to stiffen. Riding back to the school on the bike did not appeal to me.

"Suzy Q, I need to get somewhere and I don't think riding my bike would feel good right about now. Do you have a ride?"

"Sure, I'm parked over by the waterfront drive. Just throw your bike in the back of my Jeep." Suzy asked, how and where an African American had learned to play rugby, and why was I in Canada. While she drove me back to the school I told her the short version, the good and the bad. Good was playing pro football in Canada for the CFL and the bad was being in a room with too many of the wrong people being naked.

Strange how we sometimes open up to people with whom we have no history. Something about them feels safe. Maybe they are just like us, and we don't know it as we open up to them. I was not aware I was telling Suzy so much until she said that I told my story with a lot of humor. I guess maybe time may have healed some of the wounds, and I was able to think back in time and not drown in sorrow.

Suzy Q pulled in front of the school, I said thanks and opened the door. "Tylowe." I turned back and she kissed me on the cheek. Caught me off guard, but her pouting lips were soft.

"What's that for?"

"It was for the bad stuff you've gone through."

She was fun to hang out with, and she left me with a number to call if I ever wanted to play rough or have the right people naked in a room. She might be willing to cross over her line and bring a girlfriend along. I gave it a quick thought, then laughed.

"Suzy Q, I'm horny for the crack of dawn. A hole in a tree needs to be careful around me, but the threesome thing? Nah. I'm only for one woman. The kind of woman who only wants one man."

"Okay, Mr. Trying-To-Do-It-Right. Well, I like you for the person you seem to be. Most men jump at a chance to be with two women. Most men jump at anything wet, wild or wounded."

I hobbled up the stairs and looked back as Suzy Q pulled away. I thought about what she said. I'm glad I'm not one of those men.

Chapter Twelve

With a few minutes to spare after my shower, I found Tamara in one of the classrooms. She was sitting on a stool overlooking a charcoal drawing class while reading a book with a Joe Sample CD playing. Her eyes lifted slowly over the book and took in the information that I was walking her way. Her eyes dropped back down to her book as I stood to the side of her.

She spoke to me as if she was reading the words from a children's book. "Mr. Tylowe, you walk with a slight limp. Did you fall off a bike?" She was smiling a bit, so I assumed everything was cool, but she knew I had been on a bike.

"Yeah, ah, I… did. I found a bike around here this morning and I went for a ride to the park. Damn squirrel couldn't make up his mind which way to go. Anyway, do you have any aspirin?"

"Uh huh, look in the pantry in the kitchen on the middle shelf. You'll see a bottle that says 222. Take two; you'll feel better. Don't be late for your class."

Sitting still for hours was tough with the pain in my hip. It didn't hurt so bad walking around, but sitting made it hurt. The aspirin kicked in after my first break. During my second break that afternoon, Mia found me stretching my sore stiff body in the hall.

Mr. Tylowe, did you go down to see the art galleries in Gastown?" Her smile made me smile.

"Hey, Mia. Nah, I didn't get a chance to, and just call me Tylowe." She cut me off with a frown. She rolled her eyes. Ouch! She walked away with some serious attitude. I spoke to her disappearing act, "I caught a rugby game in the park." I'm not sure she heard or cared to hear me.

After finishing my modeling session, I sought Tamara out for info on where to find a YMCA. I found Tamara and Mia in the kitchen smiling and laughing.

"Help! I need a whirlpool or hot tub. I've overdone it for one day. This playing and posing has hurt my body. I'm a writer and photographer, and I'm too old for this. I need to find a spa or a YMCA to go soak my body."

Mia took a verbal shot at me. "Not old, huh?" She giggled and sneered.

Tamara turned her head in thought, then she spoke in her singsong Jamaican accent, "Well, you be hurting, huh? We do have a pool that Mia goes to. She likes to swim like a fish, and I do believe dat they have a small hot pool next to the swimming pool."

Mia shouted with a lot of air. "Ma, Ma, they do! Can I go? Tylowe can take me," Mia shouted.

"I suppose so, but you need food, my dear."

"Oh, I'll feed her."

"Ma, Tylowe and I can stop at Mickey Dees."

"Oh, no, we won't, we'll find something I can eat, too, and Mickey Dees is not on my list." I tried to roll my eyes like Mia had earlier. She did it back at me, better.

Tamara took in a deep breath. Then she spoke with an almost resigned sigh. "Would you mind having Mia with you? Normally I call a cab to pick her and to bring her back. The place is a long walk away, so I'll call a cab for you."

"No, don't do that. We'll walk; it might also help loosen up my hip. I think the sitting didn't help."

"Okay, but after you come back from the pool could you stop and get her something to eat?"

"Hm, I guess I can put up with her." I laughed and stuck my tongue out at Mia.

"Whatever, I'll be ready in a minute." Mia left the room, and I turned to go get ready to leave, but Tamara spoke in a soft voice, like a reggae blues ballad.

"Tylowe, me tired from doing all I know to do." I looked at her like I did not understand, because I didn't. She continued to talk. "You a man, but you don't have to act like any kind of man. Give a woman an honest heart, don't break a woman's heart."

She turned and walked out of the room ahead of me. I stood standing, staring and wondering. "What the hell is she talking about?" Maybe she thought I would befriend Mia as a male figure while I'm here and not keep up the friendship. I'll make sure I don't do that. I knew sometimes children enter into your life, and they make you feel love that feels like it will never end.

Gathering my things for a soak in the hot tub and maybe a swim, I waited for Mia quite some time. Finally, I knocked on her door. "Hey, slow poke, what's taking you so long?"

"I'm coming," she responded. I heard her in there singing or talking to someone. Tamara, I guessed.

I walked down the hall and hollered, "I'm leaving." A moment later as I got to the door, Tamara was there and Mia came running down the hall with her gym bag in hand.

"What took you so long, kid?" I said to her happy face. She didn't answer; she just smiled as we walked down the stairs. The paintings on the stairwell walls still amazed me.

"Mia, who painted these walls?" She smiled some more and changed the subject.

"So you want to lose in a race, huh? Bet you can't beat me in swimming." I just wanted to get to that hot tub.

I teased her. "Yeah, well, I'll be sure to give you a big lead and when I beat you, don't be whining like a big baby." Mia and I laughed and teased while we walked to the pool. It was still daylight, but the sun was slowly fading.

Walking with Mia, sharing the moment, made me think about what I might have missed out on by not having a child of my own. As we walked by a building, our thin shadowy images made window art. It was another life walking by, a life I knew nothing about: the love of a growing child. Maybe I missed out, but it's not something I thought about a lot. A child's love and trust might have been something I could have used in my life. Every so often Mia would skip and swing her arms, then swing her whole body around and around as we walked and talked. I thought about how she had told me before she was not so young in the head. But she was a child and a beautiful thing to see.

"Mia, stop right here for a second."
"No, we need to keep going, please?"

"What's the hurry? I just want to take a few pictures of you and me."

"Okay."

"Stay right here." I pulled out my portable tripod and mounted my camera. I walked back twenty yards and set up the camera for photo shots. The sun channeled down the street between the buildings. We walked into the last of the sun that would be perfect for a silhouette shot. I set the timer on the camera to give me enough time to jog back to Mia. We walked away from the camera holding hands. She liked it that I held her hand. Her smile said so. She skipped as we walked. There was no way of knowing what the pictures might look like. I just wanted to have that picture with her. There was no one else on the sidewalk, just the two of us, and that was perfect.

After jogging back on the sore hip and gathering my equipment, we made our way to the pool. The thought of relaxing in a hot tub made me walk fast, but Mia walked just as fast for the last few blocks. We went through the door of the public pool and paid our entrance fee, then Mia went to the women's locker room and I went the other way. My sore hip was in that spa relaxing for a long time before Mia made it into the swimming pool. When she did hit the water, she swam like a fish; maybe racing her wouldn't be a good idea. I'm a bit nearsighted and I had taken my contacts out before getting into the hot tub, but I could see well enough. Shit! I kind of freaked out when at the last second I saw Mia complete a beautiful swan dive off the high dive. People around the pool clapped their hands and shouted their approval.

There was nothing so wrong with my sight that I couldn't tell the difference between the women and the girls. One of the women with long body lines stood on her toes with her back to the pool. She jumped high, folded her body and recoiled into a straight arrow to enter the water with hardly any splash. It was James Brown super-bad!

Seeing what I could see let me know I'd have to find a high dive in hopes of maybe taking pictures of women diving outdoors for a sun-backed silhouette shot.

The hot water made me relax; it made my hip feel better. I also had taken some more of those 222 aspirins. They were strong and had some codeine in them to help you relax. I was feeling a bit better. I put on my headphones with Regina Carter bowing her sexy violin soul.

Cornet's next sexy passage made my hot tub experience even better.

"She awoke early in the morning and with her fingers on auto-control, she started touching herself. She lay next to her lover while he slept. Lying on her back, she propped her legs up and pressed her feet flat on the mattress. This allowed her to lift her hips up and out wider. One hand slid underneath her to where two fingers slid into throbbing,

lusting wetness. Her fingers did not fill her up with the physical girth like her lover could, but she did not want to wake him.

This moment was for her, she enjoyed her lover immensely, but she enjoyed her self-pleasuring moments, too. Her other hand's middle finger vibrated on her clitoris. Her whole body jerked and vibrated, deeply involved in her masturbation and near the point of her orgasm she pulled her hand from underneath her and reached over to her man's limp penis. She held a handful of him, and he pleasurably moaned out of his sleep. A loud breath came from a big intake of air; she let out small erratic verbal squeaks. Her legs tensed, toes grabbed the sheets until they cramped, then her body relaxed. She still held on to him and felt him lengthening and widening. She sat up and slid under the covers."

I let out a big breath, hot from the passage and hot from the heat of the water. I took a deep breath, preparing for what might be on the next page. I reached for my towel to wipe the sweat from my face, but my towel wasn't there. Looking around, Mia was standing behind me using my towel. Damn, how long had she been standing there? This was the second time she had disconnected my personal moment.

"Hey, get your own towel." I wanted her to leave me alone so I could keep reading. She pointed to the other end of the pool.

"Why don't you take a swim, Tylowe?"

"In a while."
"No, come on, get in, please."

"In a minute, okay?" She gave me that pouting look again and rolled her eyes. "All right, I'm coming." She got the response she wanted and she smiled. I pulled myself out of my hot wet session. I'm not much of a swimmer; my lack of body fat makes me sink like a rock. My 6-foot-1 body and 190 pounds was strong enough to move through the water, so I dived in from the edge of the pool. Mia had jumped in next to me and we did the kid thing, splashing each other a while. Then she wanted to race to the other end. I agreed, but I was going to swim under the water. It was less work and I can my hold breath a long time.

She said, "Go," and off we went. My vision in the water made the other end seem so far away. It was an Olympic-size pool and the people in the pool looked so distorted. A moment later I was at the other end and came up for air. I looked around for Mia, but she was not there or behind me. Maybe she swam under the water too and was just slower than me. I peeked under the water, I didn't see Mia. Where did she go?

"You're so slow." I turned and looked up. Mia was out of the pool and standing over me. I guess racing her was not good for my ego.

I felt a touch on my shoulder and I turned in the direction of the touch. The person in front of me made me feel like I was drowning, I couldn't get any air all of a sudden. It was the woman from the open-air café on the pier; she was just inches from my face. Her closed-lip smile and deep-set eyes once again had me at a loss for words. Finally, I took one deep breath, and a bunch of short, shallow breaths followed as I stared.

She noticed my confused feeling and teased. "Cat got your tongue again? Would you like an underwater pen to write with?" Her pearl white teeth flashed in my eyes as she laughed.

"Uh, I guess I thought I'd never... see you again." She slowly bobbed up and down in the water, her long reddish-brown hair floating. I'm confused, is fate really like this, an irresistible power to control time, place, and space?

"Tylowe. So your name is Tylowe. Nice name."

"How do you know my name?" She nodded at Mia, who was standing over both of us, grinning from ear to ear. I was confused, but my eyes started to clear up some of the issues. "You two must be sisters. Tamara is your mother, too. I can see it. You look like twins." My eyes bounced back and forth. I was pleased with myself for my newfound awareness. Their smiles became giggles.

"Tylowe, Mia is my daughter!"

"Huh?" I looked at her with a question mark on my face. Then I looked back to Mia and spoke to her. "You call Tamara Ma?"

"I call her Ma, short for Grandma." Her face was not as happy as it had been a few seconds before.

Mia's real mother spoke. "Tylowe, I'm going to take a few more dives, and we'll all go get something to eat, and talk."

"That's cool, but there's one thing, one thing I need to know now!"

"What is it?" Her voice had that same slow cello tone I had remembered.

"What is your name?"

"My mother's name is Meeah," Mia said proudly.

Meeah started to float away on her back. Damn! Even the bottoms of her feet were pretty. As she backstroked away, her eyes still felt two inches from mine. Mia dove in and swam toward Meeah. I swam back to the other end under the water for as long as I could with my eyes closed.

I went back to the locker room to put my contacts back in. I needed to see more clearly. Returning to the side of the hot tub, I watched Meeah and Mia dive from the high dive. Such beauty flowed through the air and parted the water. Meeah had been the woman I noticed earlier diving with such grace. I thought about our first meeting. Her beauty had overwhelmed me then; her spirit and passion had been with me ever since.

That feeling she had left me with when she read my poetry at the café had floated in my daydreams while I was posing during the art classes; yet she had left me with no name. I thought for sure I would never see her again. But here she was. What is their story, Meeah and Mia?

Chapter Thirteen

Dinner with a beautiful girl and a more beautiful woman made me feel like a king. I kept looking at them and wondering why I had not picked up on their familial resemblance. From their rounded cheeks to their perfectly painted-looking dark eyebrows, they were the dual result of inherited bloodlines. Those sensually perfect pillow lips that graced Meeah's beautiful face were just developing on Mia. She had yet to grow into all her pretty features. Their deep-set eyes shone brightly. Their smiles were the only thing that set them apart. Meeah had that downward curving smile and Mia had her own smile.

Meeah and I shared some small talk and flirted with our eyes while we walked, looking for a place to eat. Mia was all smiles, looking back and forth from her mother to me. We skipped over the Mickey Dees treat and found a pizza parlor instead.

Mia showed her age and started coloring on the children's place mat, falling into a coloring frenzy. After we ordered our pizzas, Meeah and I headed over to the salad bar. Face to face again, we stared, and lettuce was not on my mind. I'm sure I was not hard to read.

We both held salad plates in front of us, the only things keeping me from getting closer.

"Tylowe, life is strange. I thought about you and wondered about you, knowing you were at the school with my mother and my daughter."

We stared at each other not saying a word. I didn't know what to say, until I said something that didn't quite fit. "Well, ah, tell me, what do you want on your salad?" I asked as I tossed the greens in the bowl.

She gave me a coy look that I didn't understand, and then she shaped her lips into a sly smile and said, "Do you always play in the salad?" We did some more staring, then burst out laughing. Our laughter became silly as we walked around the bar and she braced herself, pressing her hand slowly against my shoulder.

I placed the palm of my hand over the back of her hand. My fingers filled the spaces between her fingers for one nervous moment. Then she said something I had heard before: "A man with soft, warm, large hands can do most anything in life. The warmth of a hand will heal wounded souls!"

"I heard something like that from your mother."

"I'm sure you have heard a lot from my mother!"

"Well, I had not heard of you; I had not heard she had another daughter, or should I say, I did not know who was the mother and who was whose daughter? Tell me what's going on."

"I'll tell you, but there's a lot to all this and it would take some time. But if you need to know any one thing you'll have to ask."

"Okay, if it will take some time that's all right, because that means we'll have to spend some time," I stopped in mid-sentence and thought before I said, "together."

Mia's voice carried over to us, "Mom, Tylowe, come on, the pizza is here." Her voice teased as did the expression in her eyes. I noticed Mia no longer said "Mr. Tylowe."

I spoke to Meeah as we went back to sit with Mia. "Let's get together tomorrow and talk. I should get Mia back pretty soon." I turned to Mia after we sat down. "Were you on the phone talking to your mother in your room before we left?"

"Yeah."

I said to Meeah, "I take it that Tamara does not know you were to be at the pool," Meeah laughed, but it was a sad laugh, and she shook her head.

After we ate, we walked out of the pizza parlor. It was really evident that Meeah was going in a different direction from Mia and me. The two of them hugged and held each other as if they held all the earth's air between them. When they separated, Mia's round brown eyes became a deep dark lagoon of sadness. She walked ahead and away from her mother; I reached for Meeah's hand, but she took both her hands and covered her mouth. Standing between the two of them, I could feel pain erupting; a city block was shaking its bricks loose.

She spoke through her hands, "Tylowe, please could you give my little one a hug before she goes to bed? She can give you directions to my place. I'll be there all day." She tried to turn her head to hide her tears, but sorrow sung the blues in her slow cello voice.

"I don't have to model tomorrow since it's Sunday. So could I come by in the morning and spend the day with you?"

"Yes."

She walked away with me not knowing much more about Meeah and Mia other than they were mother and daughter, and they loved each other. We walked home under the light of night, car headlights, taillights, neon lights and streetlights. I asked Mia if I could take a few pictures of her and of the two of us. She never said anything, but just stopped and waited for instructions.

At an intersection, Mia stood at the crosswalk. I stood back about thirty feet with my camera. She stood facing me with the streetlight highlighting her image. When I looked through my viewfinder I saw two more things that stood out. She had no emotion on her face, and the traffic light across the street put a glow on her to make a silhouette. Along our way there was a homeless man; I gave Mia a pocket full of change to give the man, who was sitting in a doorway. I took a picture as she handed him the change; the dim overhead light added an eerie feel to the image. By the time we had to go back, I had shot two complete rolls of film.

When we walked back through the door at Mia's home, I went to the kitchen first and found Tamara sitting in the breakfast nook with a book I doubt she was reading. The light in the room was too dimly lit. Before she got a chance to ask any questions about why we were gone for so long, I spoke.

"Sorry we took so long, but Mia made a good model for a photo project I started. She's very photogenic."

"Nighttime pictures, eh? Are you that good, Tylowe?" I sensed she doubted my reason for us getting back so late, but I was telling the truth, mostly.

I gave her a playful response with a mocking Jamaican accent. "I am art-teest!"

I was so worried about Tamara I did not notice Mia went the other direction when we came in. Tamara called her name in a motherly fashion, and Mia entered the room a minute later. Mia spoke to Tamara before the woman I had thought was her mother got a chance.

"Ma, we had a good time, even though Tylowe can't swim."

"He can't swim?"

"Yeah, he thought he could beat me, but I was in and out of the pool before he was half wet." Mia laughed and made Tamara laugh at me. I was amazed at the turnaround in Mia's attitude, but I knew the little girl was not as happy as she seemed to be.

"Did you get something to eat, dear?"

Mia stood there in silence. I knew her happy spirit went back to the pizza parlor, so I answered quickly to cover up for her daydream about another place of only a short time ago.

"Yeah, she ate," I said in a sarcastic tone. "We stopped for pizza and she ate all the pizza in the place!" I forced a laugh.

In the morning I was going to meet with Meeah. I needed all this to make sense. I should not dive into this shark tank of mysterious misinformation, but I knew I would anyway. Meeah had been on my mind since our meeting at the café, before I knew her name or thought I would see her again. I guess Mia, having taken a liking to me, wanted and planned on me meeting her real mother.

I went by Mia's room; she had the door still open and I could hear some Shaba Ranks Jamaican hip-hop playing. I knocked on her wall to get her attention. She was lying on her bed gazing at what, I don't know. Without me saying anything, she got up and walked over to me and handed me a business card. I looked at the card as she stood there. It had a phone number and a name on it.

ECCENTRIC PLACE ART GALLERY

Remembering how Meeah seemed to be shocked a bit when I said a man could be a little eccentric made me smile inside. I turned over the card; a map was on it that led down to the gallery in Gastown, near downtown Vancouver. I put the card in my pocket and looked at Mia. She reached out and hugged me like I was supposed to have hugged her, as I was asked to do by her mother. I went to bed mentally tired, but unable to sleep, feeling like a little boy on Christmas Eve, hopeful of things to come. I just did not know what I was hoping for.

Chapter Fourteen

Half the night I spent tossing and turning, staring at the dark ceiling, and sleep came late. But I woke up early, really early, just as the dark was ebbing from the sky. I sat up in bed and just read page after page of my book. As I read another sexy passage this time, I enjoyed what Alexandré Cornet wrote, but I was not in the mood to read about what I wanted to do.

"She slid her thick shapely thighs forward, squatting and on her toes. Placing one hand under his head and reaching back with her other hand, she held the base of his blood hardened outer vein. Lowering, spreading herself nastily over his mouth, she felt his tongue part her, lick her; probe her from end to end."

No physical or mental rise from me this time. My sensuality preferred the real thing, like the feel of a woman's soft baby hair near her… I needed to see and touch ladylike curves, the kind that bend and twist like a country back road.
I checked the light level coming through the window. My hip felt better and I thought about getting back on the bike and riding down to Gastown, but changed my mind when I thought about having body odor when I met up with Meeah.
I went down to the kitchen and dialed the phone. "Hey, I know it's early, but how about some coffee and warm bread down on the waterfront?"

She sounded so sleepy when she said, "I had hoped you would call." We talked awhile.

I jumped into the shower and shaved my face and head and dressed in my tan jeans. A burnt-orange knit shirt and tan suede shoes matched my jeans perfectly. Not knowing what the day might hold for me, I packed my small leather one-arm backpack with a variety of things and hit fresh air and a slightly overcast sky. I started to walk, but within a few steps I turned around and went back to get my camera bag. Stepping back through the door and walking down the hall, I walked right into Tamara.

"Mr. Tylowe, you up so early, you going somewhere?"

"I'm going out to take pictures for the day and just hang out. Maybe I might catch the ferry over to Victoria and stay overnight."

"Oh, do you know you are to model on Monday? It is your last day to model."

"Yeah, I know; I'll be back in time to model. Ah, would you mind if I stayed a few more days? I found some things to do."

Tamara stared, then responded. "You are welcome to stay as long as you like. Would you like some coffee before you leave?"

"Nah, I'll get some while I'm out. Thanks, though."

After heading back out, I walked until I got down to the wharf. My new friend, Suzy Q, was waiting for me in a colorful horse jockey outfit. "You're looking good, real good." She licked her lips like I was a juicy barbecue rib.

"Thanks, Suzy, you're such a flirt. Thanks for meeting me. I like your outfit with all these colors. Let me order you something."

"Nice place you picked." She scanned around to see the same thing I saw when I first sat there. "I'll have Earl Grey tea and warm bread; while you're at it turn around and let me see that butt in them jeans. Damn!"

"Stop flirting with me when you know you don't play with real boys. Plus, you're not my type. I don't like it when a woman can tackle like you." I laughed hard and so did she. I ordered some food and struck up a short conversation with the Arabic man who owned the café. "When I was here a few days ago there was this very beautiful light brown-skinned lady who came in while I was hanging out and..."

"Oh yesss! I know her. She come in for chai spice tea and cinnamon bread often. Maybe she come later, huh? She is pretty girl. I saw her talking to you. She never speaks to a man, but men always talk to her. You find another woman, I see?" The man raised his eyebrow and looked over at Suzy.

"No, no sir, she is just my friend." I returned to my table with coffee and food. "So what's with the jockey outfit?" I asked. "It looks like the real thing."

"It's a long story, but if you've got time I'll tell you." I looked out over the water. Listening to someone else instead of the rattle of my own mind talking to me about what my day might hold was just what I needed.

When I called Suzy Q and woke her up, I shared a little of my story about meeting Meeah later. "I got time. It's way too early for me to call Meeah."

Suzy told me of her early years as a pre-teen horse jockey, and since she always loved the clothes from the sport, she wore them around most of the time. She even had a seamstress custom-make the horse-jockey-fashioned clothes. Being a jockey was something her English father wanted her to do. He treated her more like a son than as a daughter growing up. She played rough and tough and always with boys in traditional boy games, and her father encouraged it.
Then she went away to college in the States to play soccer, and she became one of the best in her conference. After college she tried her hand at a lot of things, but at the moment she was still bouncing around looking for her niche in life. Sue thought her life was good, but what she always knew and felt was she didn't want

a relationship with a man. Sex with a man was okay, but was never her cup of tea; she was much more into being with a woman emotionally and physically.

Suzy never let dear old dad or mum, as she called her mother, know about her preference in mates. She kind of thought they always knew until she did her version of Guess Who's Coming to Dinner, and the shit hit the fan. Dad's reaction was "How in the hell are you going to give me a grandson?"

"To make it even worse my dear old dad is R.C.M.P,"

"What in the hell is that?" I asked.

"Oh, you Americans don't know much about us, do you? And you even spent a lot of time in Canada. We Canadians know everything about you Americans!"

"And your point is? What is an R.M.M.P?"

"No, silly! I said R.C.M.P and it stands for Royal Canadian Mounted Police."

"Oh, I knew that. I just forgot what the acronym meant. I know about Dudley Do-Right and Bullwinkle and Rocket J. Squirrel; Snidely Whiplash and Boris and what was the woman's name?" I was laughing so hard watching her trying to keep a straight face, and she couldn't.

"Okay, funny guy, you know your old school cartoons, and it's Natasha, my dahling dear," she said in a mockingly deep cartoon voice. "Although, you know, only Dudley is from the Great White North.

"Anyway, my dad is really high up in command with the drug trafficking department. With my dad, homosexuality and drugs are almost the same."

"I'm sorry to hear that."

"It's okay. Dad and I get along better nowadays, but I'm not Daddy's Little Girl or Boy. So, Tylowe, that's my story. So tell me more about this woman you're going to meet."

"Sure, but first tell me if Natasha was bisexual, I had this thing for her when the cartoon was on. She dressed so sexy, but she seemed to have that dominatrix thing going on with the little man Boris."

Suzy almost threw her back out, laughing so hard.

"Tylowe," her voice went real high, "you have to be a freak to have freaky thoughts like that. But when you think about it, she might have been. Now tell me about this girl you're up so early for."

"Well, she's kind of a mystery to me. It's strange the things I don't know about her. I know some of the people who are in her life."

"Well, is she pretty, my kind of pretty?"

"She is everyone's kind of pretty!"

Sue gave me a smirk I understood.

"Don't get no ideas." I shook my head and smiled for her to understand. "Don't even think about it. You know I've been down that road before."

Suzy said, "I know, big boy, you told me before what happened to you and your wife-to-be. I must say I'm proud of you for even considering me your friend after what you've been through."

"What do you mean by that?" I asked with a puzzled look.

"Tylowe, most men only talk to me because they think they'll get a chance to watch me and another woman do the nasty, and maybe they'll get a chance to join in on the party. Here you've been hurt by that kind of thing and you still sit down and talk to me, a woman who has been and will be with another woman."

"You're a person, Sue. It's not up to me to prejudge you for something that has not happened between us. You're not one of the people who broke my heart. Anyway, all that happened way back when, and I'm nowhere near any of that now."

"Where are you now?"

When I first met Sue, I had told her some of my past and I told her more now. I also told her what had happened so far with Tamara, Meeah and Mia. I guess it helped me review all that was going on. It really wasn't a big deal, when I thought about it. I just happened to meet a different kind of family and I had met them in a strange way. Strange the way we meet all kinds of people. I was sitting down having coffee with a woman who had knocked me on my butt playing rugby, then introduced herself, and to top it off, she was cute and a lesbian. But she was good people.

Sue was the kind of real person you knew you could trust right away. She had this funny outgoing way about her that made people trust her.

"Suzy Q, You might know there are times we trust others, and we get burned, burned by letting our guard down. Why, it's human nature to reach out for companionship on all levels."

"I hear ya. And the thing that kills you is that everyone says 'just trust me.' So don't worry, I won't say that to you, but if you like you can trust me." We laughed while we watched a barge of garbage being pulled out to sea by a tugboat. "Tylowe, I have felt what I thought was real friendship before, and it just seems like…" She stopped talking and I didn't press her.

Listening to Sue since the first time she had knocked me on my butt, to her taking me home from the park, and now sitting here watching the world go by, I felt she was a friend I could count on. Maybe somewhere along the line I think the things she wanted the most in life, like me, she had partially found, then lost what she had found. So I asked her, "Where is the love you get to keep?" Maybe she had an answer from her past experiences.

"Hell if I know about how to keep it, but I do think love has no winning formula. Shit! Tylowe, you just never quit throwing your heart out there and hoping someone wants it and most of all needs it in a healthy way. Me mum tells me love is like school. You take class after class and you pass or fail, you move on or retake the class. You use what you learn, you love what you learn; you gain by what you learn. You have good instructors and bad instructors, and if you're lucky, you get to teach the class. Some classes you like; some you don't, but one thing's for sure: you never graduate. There's always new stuff to learn."

I laughed and felt sad inside. "You know, those are some wise words; are you trying to live off dear old mum's advice?"

"I'm just living it out, what will be, will be." After she said that, I thought maybe I had dropped out of school, the school of love. Had I given up on the learning and living for love? Maybe school was out on me? I just couldn't see ever giving myself to another woman to learn more bad shit! I gave every drop of love in me to Renee many years ago. The too few women I had crossed paths with since Renee had not put any life-love juices back into me.

I was in my own little world for a while; I just stared out over the water. I watched a tug go by towing an empty barge. My life was empty like that barge, but that barge had a destination. Where was I going? The only time I ever cared to hear Diana Ross's voice was when she sang the words, "My world is empty without you, babe."

"So, Sue, if your mom said you don't graduate, what's the point?"

Sue asked me, "Why you asking me about love? You're the love and romance writer." She laughed.

"Well, I never know the ending of the stories. I just write until the end comes."

"Don't your stories have happy endings?"

"Some."

"Then you shouldn't be having any problems finding and making love work. It sounds like you loved someone before, and there is no reason you can't have it again. If you can write from your heart the things you know, want and feel, that puts you ahead of most of us. You have to be willing to let someone in, too." She stopped short of finishing what she had to say, shook her head and took a deep breath. I took that to mean "stop feeling sorry for myself," or maybe an indication of what had been happening in her own life.

"Suzy Q, it's strange; I can talk the talk, or should I say, write the talk, about my feelings. I am emotionally and sensually in touch with myself. But I'm not in touch with someone else to share my flowing juices. It has been months; okay, it has been a year, and then it was only physical. I just don't want anyone else's drama. Maybe I'm being selfish for not wanting to give up the kind of time a woman would want of me. I need another creative mind to understand me. It just seems I'm alone, wanting to feel passion with only a woman who has no fear of letting go all inhibitions. I'm looking for passion, and wanting to give it. I'm looking for the woman who will make me feel her love is not measuring me for a tux first. I mean, she really has to like who I am and not what she thinks I should be. Her mind and body need to be like an umbrella to cover us. She has to be my friend and my lover."

"Well, Tylowe, there is one thing very clear. You are not afraid of being who you are. Even if it means you'll have to suffer the pain and frustration it might bring you."

"I'm not sure what you mean by that."

"You've just met this woman and her daughter, and they both have your attention. If by chance she might be this woman who fills all your needs, would you let her into your life from head to toe? Would you do whatever it takes to have her forever? So being you, will you suffer the consequences of that?" Again, Sue shook her head and took a deep breath in.

I let a deep breath out. Her words flew at me like a Matrix kick in the head. My mind went back to what I was going to do today. Spending some time with Meeah. The first time we met she said she had a situation. Well, don't we all? What is Meeah's?

"Sue, you ever heard how the mechanic's car doesn't run that well, but everyone's car he works on runs great?" She nodded, "Well, maybe that's me. I haven't fixed my own love life, but I know how to." She stood up and stretched in the early morning breeze and then leaned over and kissed me on the cheek.

We didn't talk for some time. I'm sure her mind was going in circles like mine about my own life. I motioned for her to follow me out to the pier. I took out my camera and used the rising sun to highlight my friend and the colors of her outfit. She was a good model and a better friend.

~~~~~

9 a.m.

"Suzy Q, could I have a ride down to Gastown?"

"A ride, sure, but will you do me a favor? Will you give your heart a fair chance? Just give it a real chance, don't run if it doesn't seem perfect. Because it hurts all the same whether you give a little or a lot." I nodded. "If you lay all your heart out there, no matter what, you can't question yourself if you did all you could. Besides, it all hurts the same when you find yourself alone. Let go of the past!"

Chapter Fifteen

It was a quiet ride to Gastown. Everything had been said. The truth and nothing but the truth. Before getting out of her truck, I put my finger to my lips, kissed it and placed it across her Drew Barrymore lips. She gave my finger a short, teasing, trying-to-be-funny bite. Since I didn't want to be dropped off in front of Meeah's gallery, Suzy Q pulled up to a corner, next to a big old London-type steam clock down in old Gastown.

As I walked down the block, I did not notice Suzy Q had backed up her jeep. I heard her say through the window as she slowly pulled next to me, "Tylowe, any woman who wants a man would want you." I stood there appreciating her for a while as she drove away.

Strolling onto the next block in a fit of nerves, I stopped in front of a window. The art in the window brought me to a halt. Murals on the outside walls of the Eccentric Place Art Gallery would stop anyone.

It was the same type of art that highlighted the art school.

Black and brown Cleopatra and Caesar with pimps, hookers and street people in arousing Egyptian fashion. Many shades of black and brown African queens adorned the brick walls. This time I was not puzzled as to where I had seen the female faces before. It was Meeah's face, all in different expressions of her beauty. While Caesar, and the soldiers, pimps and all male figures were dark in color, all were still faceless Mandingos.

In the window was a full-length picture of a river. It portrayed women standing and sitting in the water. They were washing their God-given natural beauty. On the edge of the river, a black man stood in a leopard print loincloth, a bowtie and no shirt with Stacy Adams two-tone shoes and no socks. He stood there with a book and pen in his hand as if he was overseeing his flock. A black panther lay beside his feet as his loyal friend. Beside the picture in the window where I stared, Meeah looked back at me, and she was smiling.

She passed a cup of coffee to me as I came through the door, and we hugged a friendly hello.

"Good morning, pretty lady."

"Hey, you found me okay?"

"Yes, how could anyone miss this eccentric art?" We smiled at each other, remembering what I had said about the eccentric mind when we first met. "When I first saw the school it blew my mind; I'm in complete awe of the skill involved in its creation and beauty. Kept thinking I'd seen the face of the women in the art. I had. It was you."

"Yes, it's me. Come over by my desk for a minute. I need to make a few calls and then we can talk. If I can get someone to come in early, you and I can take off for the day." I followed her like a pet on a leash.

"For the day, that sounds good. How about I look around?" She nodded as she dialed the phone. The first thing that caught my eye was the way she sat on her desktop. She moved with a rhythm that needed no music, but there was some. George Benson's guitar played a popish groove in the background. She spun her rear around and adjusted her cut-off jeans by rocking and rolling her posterior, almost in rhythm to the music. She crossed her long bare legs; her thighs were enticingly perfect. She leaned her head in a rolling fashion rotating it to the back and her hand removed her hair that had been draped over her heart. She was art!

Tall gallery walls were covered in fabric panels of black and gold streams. Hanging from the walls were large paintings. Many different artist signatures contributed their talents in assorted styles. Shorter wall dividers in black and silver silk-like fabric made small, three-walled rooms, and smaller art hung on those walls with large chandeliers centered over each cubicle. Looking up, you could see the whole gallery. Overhead, the ceiling was lighted and mirrored in graduated layers on some type of suspended ceiling. I could see Meeah on the other side of the gallery, still on the phone, making animated movements. My maze-like tour led to a back area that had a spiral staircase, which led to a loft.

"Tylowe, we are free." Meeah walked up behind me and pressed her hand against the center of my back. "Go up these stairs." She followed behind me up the spiral staircase and said something with a giggle I did not fully hear.

"You say something?" I stopped and turned and looked down to her.

"Noooo," she smiled, I could tell she was watching me from the waist down, but then she said, "I have someone coming in to watch the gallery. She'll be here at eleven and then we can take off."

Why is it I have a hard time initiating a conversation with her, I thought to myself. Every time I've been in her presence it's taken me a while to warm up and open up. Her presence might have had me nervous before, but now, not knowing her story might be the subject of my inner conversations. Maybe I don't want to know her story.

At the top of the stairs, another world away from the gallery existed; a spacious loft-living area with modern furniture.

The floor had deep plush carpet all around, but a section I walked by had a slightly raised floor of beautifully polished wood. It might have been cut out of wood from a big ballroom dance floor; it glistened deeply. The area was approximately twelve feet by twelve feet. Even more of a highlight: there was a large classic brick fireplace against the far wall, with a wood mantle that matched the wood of the floor.

A long piano bench sat in front of the fireplace. A wine goblet marked with a lip print sat on the bench. The lipstick color, deep reddish-brown, was the color Meeah had on every time I had seen her. Next to the wine goblet was a book. I acted like I was checking out the floor and the mantelpiece, but I really wanted to see the name of the book. It was Alexandré Cornet's book of poetry:

THE WORLD THAT FELL INTO MY DRESSER DRAWER
A Romantic Man's Passion, Love and Blues

A bookmark was in the book; it was the piece of paper I had written the note on at the café when I first saw her. Under the piano stool a pair of tan high-heel slippers, one was standing up and one lying on its side. In my mind's eye, I could still see her feet in them. I could see Meeah sitting there warming her skin by the fire, and seeing all that put me in an oasis daydream.

"Meeah, do you fire up the fireplace often?"

"Last night, as you can see, and most every night I read by the fire. It relaxes me before I go to sleep."

"It would relax me to see you relax," I wanted to say but I did not.

Just past the wood floor in the center of the room there was a sunken bed with two steps going down into the floor. The mindset is always step up to a bed; sit on or lay down on a bed is all I'd ever known. The headboard extended up out of the floor about four feet and on the side facing the fireplace, the headboard was the padded back of a couch where the two of us sat down. A triangular shaped coffee table with African-like warriors with spears and shields adorned the table, along with foreign periodicals. Japanese, British, French and Italian publications were fanned out next to a glass vase with glass flowers.

As we sat down on the couch I picked up a magazine. The music floated up from below and filled in where there were no words passing between us. I flipped pages. Neither she nor I had said anything in a while.

"Meeah, when we first met, you said you didn't want to know my name, and you couldn't or wouldn't see me because of something going on in your life. You must know I am tripping over so much that I've heard and seen so far. I don't understand. Help me, please?" Not looking up I kept looking at pictures of the Rhine River.

She took a deep breath in. Words escaped back out. "I'm married!" She said it once, but it reverberated in my ears like a jungle drum. Laying the magazine down, the only thing I could see was the little African warrior figurines, pointing spears at me.

"Married." I grunted from low in my throat and focused on her face. She slowly batted her eyes once then gave a short nod.

"Well, nothing ventured, nothing gained." She did not respond to my comment. She was not my woman, she was just someone I met under slightly strange circumstances. She had not lied to me or deceived me. She had not done anything wrong to me, yet I felt cheated. Sitting up straight I craned my head from left to right in hope of relieving the stress tightening my neck. She must have felt the same stress, because her head did the same thing.

Chapter Sixteen

Blues. I never thought of George Benson as a blues singer. The music had turned sad. The music floated down, not up anymore. Not bad sounding, but an emotional "Masquerade." I closed my eyes and tried to listen objectively as Meeah, her voice almost a whisper, droned on, like she was collapsing from the inside out.

She told me about her love story gone wrong. To call it a love story would be a lie. How she gave a man her love and she was treated like a toy. He lived a lie that punched her soft, naive heart over and over. Blues from a pool of spilled mental blood poured forth from her lips. Meeah drained her soul through her voice for the next hour and a half. Her strong drive for life was the only reason I had a chance to sit next to her.

She lived apart from a man who owned her misery. She stayed married to him for the right to keep what she had left, some contact with her daughter, the gallery and the school.

"Runway" is what she called her husband, which is now her married name, Meeah Runway. They had met at an art gallery eleven years ago in Quebec. Meeah's father, somewhat of a prestigious Jamaican artist, had been showcased for an art show. Runway was at the art show procuring art for his own personal collection. After buying a lot of her dad's art and commissioning him to do some other works of art, the two men became good friends.

Runway, at first, did not show any interest in her; he was more interested in her father's art. Meeah said she had had a crush on him, but she was ten years younger than he was and gullible when it came to men. She was twenty-one, beautiful, and emotionally wide open for anything that came her way. She spent a lot of her life up until then being a model for her dad and other artists. She had art skills, too; her mom and dad had blessed her with their talents. Dad was more of a pencil-and-charcoal artist and mom was a painter. Meeah combined her God-given talents and would take dad's drawings and paint them in color.

Runway and Meeah's dad struck a business deal to open an art school. It was something that dad and mom always wanted. Runway fronted all the money they needed.

Dad and Runway commissioned Meeah to paint elaborate artwork on the school building. Because her dad always used her as a model, her face was used on all the women in the paintings.

Runway kept his distance from Meeah at the start of his relationship with her dad. He just never had a lot to do with her. She didn't see him around all that much except for business dealings. Tamara was usually in control, but she had no way of controlling her own husband's marital treason. His lifestyle included being with a lot of women.

Meeah said, "I loved my dad more than anything in the world; he treated me like a queen, but Dad had women stored away like spare pencils in his coat pocket. It was just an accepted thing that went on as I was growing up. I thought it was something special the way I would see women always looking and talking to Daddy."

Her father had passed away nine years earlier from cancer, but Meeah still meets her father's other women and grown kids or almost grown half brothers and sisters. They appeared out of nowhere at times to contact her or her mom.

"I'm sorry to hear about your dad. Meeah, where is this husband of yours now? Do you and he share this place? As much as I want to be here, should I be, uh, worried? Should I go?"

She took in a deep breath and shook her head no. "He doesn't come around here often. He lives in a city on the East Coast, but he still controls much of what I do or don't do."

"So how did you hook up?"

She told me about her relationship with her husband. They became lovers when she flew out to his places of business to begin taking over her father's art projects and business. When she stepped into her dad's shoes, Runway welcomed her as a partner and as a friend. She admired him for that and she let him know it.

That started a lover's train with no brakes. On one of those nights of failed contraceptives, Mia started her nine-month pilgrimage into this world.

Tamara pushed for Meeah and Runway to be married. So they did. Runway was basically a good guy until right after her father died. Mia was barely a year old when Meeah opened her eyes to what had been going on with her husband. Besides having stray children around the world, he also had stray women all over, just like her father. She decided she was not going to go through her life being a fool like her mom. This is when she and Tamara started having more problems.

Tamara said, "Just stay home and be a mother. Let him do what he wants to do. He takes good care of you. He bought us this art school, he bought you an art gallery; he has bought you a car. He gives you credit cards and you never see a bill or pay a bill. Just let him do what men do."

Meeah said no. "I wanted my husband to be with me and no one else." Meeah started traveling with her husband all she could; leaving baby Mia with mom. In her eyes, she was trying to tell him she loved him and would do anything to make him happy, to no avail. She instead spent many lonely nights in grand hotels with no husband and without baby Mia nearby.

He became abusive as time went on. Verbally he hurt her to the core. When she told me about how his evil tongue had spilt her soul like a cleaver, I could see her body language change. Meeah looked just like her daughter right then. Like a little girl who was teased about budding breasts, she was ashamed of how Runway had made her feel about her femininity.

An old pop-rock song from the band Journey played while Meeah's verbally expressed grief went on. The singer sang, "Who's sorry now?"

At that moment, I was the one who was sorry, sorry for coming into her life on any level and letting her voice tell a sad tale of how love can torment.

"He said I was not good enough in bed." With her wet eyes, reddened cheeks, trembling lips and tentative voice, I could feel her pain. It was like I witnessed her falling off the high dive and hitting the water in a belly flop.

"Meeah, you don't have to say anymore, it's okay." I wasn't sure I could take much more, but she chose to tell me, so I listened.

"I bored him." Her voice shrilled and then trailed off into silence. Her breathing became deep and irregular. I asked her if I could get her some water.

"No, no, I'm fine. This is a great place to live, except that all the running water and the bathroom are downstairs."
I needed to let my blood circulate, I could have used new air in my brain, I had to move, so I told her,

"It's cool, I'll go down and get something to drink."

"I'm supposed to be the host here." It was the first smile I'd seen from her in a while. That smile disappeared like hot breath in the cold rain when she went back to talking about her husband Darth Vader, or Runway, or whatever his name was. She continued to tell her story.

"I tried everything I knew to please him. I read books on how to please a man, I asked other women and I watched movies." She laughed without smiling. "I let him do anything he wanted to do to me, he just said I bored him and that's why he had other women. So maybe you don't want to be here, if you're thinking about being with me."

Thinking to myself what an ass this man was, to tell her some bullshit to justify his self-absorbed crap.

"Meeah..." Her eyes lifted up from some place too far away to ever go alone. I wasn't sure she really saw me, but she was looking in my direction. "Meeah, once is all most people ever get to love and be loved. Most just have some good times and settle for the best of what is left. We find ourselves with someone who loves us kind of okay, but our heart still dreams and craves to be in love with someone who has passion for us. I would think he just didn't have enough passion in him."

Brushing the back of her hand with the back of mine, I said, "I can tell you have a creative heart and mind, so you not being able to satisfy a man sounds like a false accusation to me. You sure as hell look like and sound like a good woman; a good woman would want to please a man." I stopped myself from saying anymore, or maybe it was her smile that came back in full force that cut me off from saying anymore. Plus, I didn't know what else I was going to say anyway.

She appeared to be looking around the room, but she was scanning me out of the corners of her eyes. Angie Stone was singing an old Curtis Mayfield song, "The Makings of You."

A gentle female voice called out from the gallery floor, "Meeahaaaa."

Meeah called back, "Ms. Lydia, I'll be right down." She lifted my hand and began kneading it like it was bread dough. She spoke in a fractured voice, "Would you still like to spend the day with me?"

"Let's go."
We prepared to leave, and I was introduced to Ms. Lydia, who was an elf of a gypsy woman. She let Meeah know it would be okay to be gone for as long as she wanted. She would close the gallery when it was time.

"Feel the breeze in your heart, you two. Let your souls be like sails and guide you where you are lost in each other," Ms. Lydia said as we exited. I wasn't sure I wanted to be lost with Meeah, but I wanted to sail with her to find out.

Chapter Seventeen

We went out the back door and in the single parking space there was a classic gold-toned Jaguar XKE convertible, just like the one Meeah had painted in the artwork. Sometimes you don't know how to play things out. I didn't know if it was cool to be riding around in this car. She did say he gave her cars, and this was the kind of sexy car you give a woman. She may have purchased this car, but this kind of classic sports car I would have assumed her husband had given to her. I just didn't know if it was cool or not to be riding in the car her husband had bought.

"Would you like to drive?" Meeah held out the keys, and I reached for them. Forget him! I opened the passenger door for her. I don't know him, and he don't know me, I'm driving this car! I thought with an inner laugh.

"Where are we going?" I asked.

"You heard Ms. Lydia, let the wind get us lost." She laid her head back and closed her eyes; maybe she just needed to rest her mind.

The turn of the key and the car rumbled to a macho roar. The sleek sports car made me think of a long drive along a winding road. Twists and turns in this car might straighten out any path I was on for the moment. I shifted gears to get out of the city, and we made our way to the highway. I asked Meeah to reach in my bag and take out the CD that was in my portable player. She slipped it in the car CD player. Marvin Gaye began to sing: "If this world were mine, I would give you everything."

The highway followed along the Fraser River. It was another one of those moments when nothing matters, no stress and no problems, just letting what happens happen.

Then Meeah asked, "Tylowe, you know most of my story, what's yours? Everybody has one."

Damn. Just when I thought the stress was going away. I started out by first telling her how it was I came to be in Vancouver and then about meeting my friend Suzy. I told her I had recited my life story to Suzy over the last couple of days and the last parts of it just that morning.

"It's nice to have friends, Tylowe. Please believe me, I know. I have a few, like Ms. Lydia. Something I like about you, you seem to accept everyone for who they are. People say they do, but they lie. Action always speaks louder than words."

"True, I guess. We all know most people think about themselves and what others can do for them. Which can keep us from seeing people as real friends. I've let a few people get too close and they used me. But I'm still trying to let people get close enough and judge them as they come."

"Well, what about any love interests? Do you let women get close?"

"Meeah, I know about the pain of love, having loved someone so much I almost wanted to kill for her. Yes, the pain of love makes it hard to love again. I was going to marry this woman, but she and a friend crossed the line. Now my career as a photographer and writer are the most important things I have going on. I'm just staying true to what I like to do."

I told Meeah a little of this and a little of that about my life. It was a bit too much for me to rehash my complete story that day. I talked about where I was from and how I grew up, but I didn't go too deep. Hearing her sad story was enough for the both of us for the moment.

"Meeah, could we just ride and maybe I'll feel like telling you more of my life as it's been and how it's felt?" She nodded her head, and smiled an "it's okay" smile.

With the sun almost directly overhead, its warmth heated my bald head. The sun soon received some help, as a tender hand stroked me over and over from my forehead to the back of my neck. I moved my head around to feel her touch caress my every nerve ending. I started to hum to the music, like a cat purring from being loved by his mistress.

Donny Hathaway's daughter Lalah's voice sang through the speakers, For All We Know, then Donny's voice articulated the same song.

Stress gone! Something good was entering me. For long stretches of road I drove on, unaware of the speed or distance we traveled. There were things I still did not know about my co-pilot for the journey we were on. Where was this journey headed? Didn't matter. I just wanted her there next to me. What do I do if I want more? For now I'll drive on. . .

The great northwest scenery framed Meeah's now peaceful expression. It brought thoughts of words I wanted to put down on paper. I turned down the music and said, "Meeah, will you reach into my bag and pull out that spiral-bound book, please? There should be a pencil in it. I need you to write something down for me." My glance altered between watching the road and her every move.

She said, "I'm ready. What is it you want me to write?"

Sitting next to you
Smiling wide thinking about you and you only
My inner vision sees deep in you
A window to your beauty only my eyes can see
The sun and you fight for which one shines the brightest
over me
Highlighting amazing expressions of beauty
Your aura
> *Wanting God to let me sleep... I want to be alone with*
> *dreams of your passionate expression*
> *Wanting God to wake me... to see you in my eyes for an eternal*
> *dawn seeing your beauty forever*

Meeah paused, frozen for the next mile, her eyes cast down, yet with another pensive expression on her beautiful face. I turned the music back up and another mile marker passed. She removed her sandals, and put her heels up on the edge of the seat. Wrapping her arms around her knees, she held on to herself like she was either protecting herself or holding on to a feeling she did not want to let go of. Laying her head on her knees, she stared at me. Somehow I was able to watch her root-beer brown toenails wiggling and the oncoming traffic at the same time. Some of her hair blew back with the wind. I felt all possible logic flying out with the wind and love blowing back in.

"Tylowe, I like your music."

"I like you hearing it."

Meeah reached for the volume and turned it up some more. I wondered if she heard that one violin, or did she hear the piano player tinkling the keys in the background; did she notice that one pause of silence? Did she hear and love it like I do? We let the road and music calm any rough seas in our mental journey for the next couple of hours.

Meeah rubbed her tummy at mid-day to let me know she wanted to eat. I was hungry, too, but my mind had tricked my stomach into living off Meeah's dopamine. As I pulled off the road, Corey Glover was singing Only Time Will Tell.

I stopped at some kind of sports lounge restaurant over-hanging the riverbank. The restaurant advertised "all you can eat hot wings." I locked our personal belongings in the trunk, and when I turned around I received another friendly hug from Meeah. But friendlier than before. She pushed her forehead into my chest and took two deep breaths before she turned her head to the side. Her eyes closed and she held onto me with her hands rubbing the center of my back.

A noisy crowd greeted us at the door. Big screen TV's were on the walls everywhere showing Canadian football games. Meeah and I moved outside to the balcony where there was less noise and long benches for viewing the river.

"You two are an attractive couple." The waitress kind of embarrassed us, but Meeah's face glowed at the praise. We ordered hot wings with all the different dippin' sauces, a dark beer for me and a strawberry margarita for her. Our shoulders nudged while we viewed our surroundings.

"Meeah, if you could, please tell me about this arrangement between your mother, Mia, and you. Give me the short version; you don't have to go into it too deep. It doesn't matter what it is, because I'm here, my dear; I will not walk away from you."

"You sure?" she asked.

Her expression said she seemed to be all right, so I joked, "Well, I don't want to walk back to the city."

"Oh, so you're a comic?"

"No."

"I know you're not, Mr. Smart Ass. Since you have such a beautiful butt, I'll let you be my funnyman."

"What you doing watching my butt?"

"How can I not? I caught you looking at me."

"How can I not?" She rose up from her seat, leaned over me and kissed the top of my head with a long, lips-parted kiss. Then her lips moved to my forehead as her fingers rubbed in the moisture she had left on top of my head. I had to move around in my seat, and spread my legs; my blood was flowing from my speeding heart.

"I'll be back. I'm going to the restroom. Will you be all right if I leave you here by yourself?" Before I could answer, she turned her rear toward me, hesitated, and then she walked away.

I spoke to her disappearing rear. "Well, ah… I'll be right behind you in a sec. I'll check on the food before I head to the restroom myself." The truth is I had a semi-growing sensation to deal with, so I had to give her a head start.

"Tylowe, when I get back, I'll tell you the rest."

When I came back from the restroom, hot wings and Meeah were there. Another couple had come out to the deck, so Meeah moved into my inhaled and exhaled space as she talked more about her life.

"I became depressed over how things were going between Runway and me. This is so hard because of what you might think."

"Try me."

"I let wanting to make everything right become bigger than God. During all his ill ways, I left Mia stay with my mother, while I got ill chasing him all around the world. It almost became natural for her to be with my mother.

"Then I let it go too far. I couldn't sleep, I just couldn't sleep." Meeah stopped talking for a minute, and I didn't press her. When she did talk again, she went someplace I knew nothing about from anyone I'd ever known before.

"I lost it, and maybe it was to get his attention, but I lost it. I took… too many… pills… one night seven years ago. I know now I did not want to die because of some man, but the whole thing took its toll on me. I became so weak in my soul. I just wanted to sleep and not wake up and know what I had been going through would still be there."

Meeah had my attention in so many ways, but what was I supposed to feel? Sometimes when you care too much, you become an enabler. Would saying "it's all right" be all right to say? I just kept listening.

"And once again he took advantage of me. He and my mother had me committed for many months to a mental hospital. My dreams became nightmares. You know that movie Girl on the Outside?Well, my ass was on the inside, and like her, I knew I did not belong there."

Meeah went on to tell of how the real-life bad dream caused her to legally lose custody of the only true love she had, Mia. Tamara demanded, and Meeah was too weak to fight back against Runway and his expensive lawyers. Since Runway would stand to lose half of his money kingdom, he and Tamara worked together to keep her in a bad way.

The school was legally controlled by Tamara, but still owned by Meeah. Tamara could and did limit how much Meeah and Mia interacted, but Mia had complete love for her mother and made their relationship special.

The only thing Meeah had total control of was the gallery. She had, on a whim, put the gallery in the gypsy-like lady Lydia's name, right after her dad died. The lady was like another mother to her and had worked with Meeah from the first day the gallery opened. Runway tried hard to get control of the gallery, but Meeah won that battle.

I listened to Meeah without interrupting her. Trying to let her know what she was telling me was okay. I fed her hot wings while she talked, but I had a question.

"What was this promise you mentioned when we first met?"

"My mother holds Mia's custody over my head and just out of my reach. She always says if I don't cause waves, I can see my daughter more often, and maybe have her to hold as my own again one day."

"So you and Runway don't have anything to do with each other?"

"He, ah… he comes to town every once in a while. He calls Mia to let everybody know he's coming, but she is basically irritated with him, because she can see the truth about him. He comes to the gallery, acts like it's his home, and acts like we are happily married. Even has the nerve to think I'll have sex with him. I'd touch myself with a splintered broom handle before I'd let him get anywhere near me again!"

"I say that's a bit definitive."

"Damn right it is!" She was angry but it wasn't directed at me. It was directed at a haunting past.

"Okay, let's change the subject."

"Not much more to say, anyway. Do you still want to be here with me?"

"Like I said before, too far to walk home." She picked up a hot wing.

"What kind of sauce do you like?" she asked.

"Honey mustard." Meeah dipped the hot wing in the sauce and acted like she was going to put it in my mouth, instead she rubbed it on my cheek. I gave her a puzzled look.
"You're kind of sweet, Mister. Used to be So Shy Guy."

"What are you talking about? I'm letting you do all the talking! I'm just listening to you."

"You listen well, too. Plus that poem you wrote in the car, the music you played and that butter-melting smile. What's a girl to do?" She leaned over and removed the sauce from my cheek with her lips and tongue. She took away more than just some sauce.

"Don't start something you can't finish." And I wasn't joking with her when I said that.

"You started this!" Her tongue rested near the corner of her partly open mouth.

"Huh? What are you saying?" My eyebrows were raised.

"From the time you decided to walk into the café and laughed out loud while you read your book, you started this."
"If you say so..."

"I say so." Her tongue shifted to the other side of her circled open lips.

I changed the subject. "Oh, hey, I had a chance to sit and eat at another café while I was out bike riding. It was over by Stanley Park. The most beautiful mature African woman served me the best hummus, lamb and rice I ever had. The place is so inviting, the art and décor. I just sat back and relaxed. It was really nice." I put another hot wing to Meeah's mouth; she nibbled the meat off the bone and licked the juice off my finger. If my fingers could have an orgasm, I'd have been screaming. As it was I was groaning.

After Meeah released my fingers from her mouth she responded, "The place is called The Blue, The Black and Tan Nile Café."

"Yeah, that was it. Did you have anything to do with the art that's in there?"

"No, but I know the people who own the place. The lady you're talking about is the artist. She used to teach different forms of Ethiopian art, from clay, to watercolor, to tribal face painting at the school. Speaking of that place, that is where Alexandré Cornet gave his poetry reading I told you about."

"I did see the stage in there." Meeah put her finger in the honey mustard and slid it between my lips. I watched her eyes roll back in her head, and she held her breath for as long as I held onto her finger. And that was a long time. When I did let go she spoke faintly.

"You know if we leave now we could go to the café. It's Sunday night and people do their thing, from solo instruments to vocal performances, spoken word artists, or just whatever. It's an open microphone thing for whatever someone wants to do."

"Let me go to the boy's room and change my shirt. I brought an extra one that's in your trunk since you spilled food all down the front of me."

"You complaining about me, putting food on you?" I got up from my seat and rolled my eyes at her and that downward smile of hers turned into an all-teeth smile.

"You're a big flirt, you know that?"

"You complaining?" She licked her fingers, and her glance was intensely flirtatious. "Tylowe, while you're out there would you bring me my bag please? I'll change, too." The way she said please, and everything else she did, turned me on, let me know her husband was full of shit, saying negative things about her sexual ability. He must be one of those guys who puts his weak ass out there as some kind of stud. Then when they find a woman who wants some serious passion with the sex, they can't handle it.

I finished cleaning up and changed and was standing out by the car waiting for Meeah. When she walked out of the restaurant she had changed into an outfit that made me laugh. She didn't look funny, she looked good, damn good!

"What so amusing?"

"It's just I've seen that I Dream of Genie type pants before on your mother." Meeah wore almost sheer burgundy wine-colored Queen of Sheba clothes. A tight bodysuit was wrapped around her breasts. The pants came up to her navel, which accented her hips to perfection. Tan, open-toed, leather stiletto heels adorned her feet. She had many layers of tan, burgundy and pearl-colored bracelets on one arm. A tan scarf and tan hair wrap that let her hair flow back topped her off in grand style. Her appearance said a lot about this woman. Class is not always conservative; her style was classy.

"Yeah, I know. My mother does have some good points, and I inherited her sense of fashion. She is an artist." I know I brought it up but I really did not want to think about Tamara. She had given her daughter a sense of original style. But the mothership connection reminded me of the fact that she was a married woman. Maybe not in spirit, but married nevertheless.

"Well, you look good, my dear."

She moved her hand and placed it over my heart and asked, "Tylowe, please don't say the words… 'my dear.' Your voice sounds like a baritone angel. It makes me feel weak, but tended to, when you talk. But please don't say 'my dear.' I know that might sound weird, but I need you to do that for me. I do love to hear you talk. When you asked me to write down the poem for you, to hear your voice say those words… I felt like clay in your hands. I felt you were molding me into something more beautiful than anything ever to have been on the earth. I don't know you, but it feels like we have known each other for a lifetime already. Does it sound crazy that I feel something for you? I have no fear of you, and all I've known for years is fear."

"So you like me, is that what you're saying?" Her downward smile caught a tear from her wet but clear eyes. I lifted her hand off my chest and placed her fingers to my lips and held them there. She removed them and replaced them with her lips. Soft, inebriating moisture, hot, like a new terry-cloth towel steaming and being laid over your face. The warmth entered me, putting me into a daze. That was her kiss.
We pulled away from each other with the speed of two turtles. On the highway heading back to the city, she leaned her head on my

shoulder. If she wasn't sleeping, she was dreaming. I was dreaming of more kisses and much more of her.

I desired her to distraction: I had been driving for hours and it felt as if only one minute had passed!

Sometimes someone can exude so much passion, you know they will make you babble like an idiot from the pleasure they can make you feel. My body was feeling non-stop visual physical echoes thinking about the love I had not yet made.

My thoughts raced. Forget about her husband; he didn't love her. Forget she tried not to wake up one day; being with her now has let me know I have been asleep. I also thought about my friend's words, "If by chance she might be this woman who fills all your needs, would you let her into your life from head to toe? Would you do whatever it takes to have her forever?"

The answer was yes, though that didn't seem to be a strong enough word. Suzy Q's other words, "If you lay all your heart out there, no matter what, you can't question yourself whether you did all you could to make it work."

I shifted gears, as we headed back to the city. I slipped in a CD of John Coltrane's ballads, and his emotional sax flowed out with his rendition of My Favorite Things. Meeah leaned in and held onto my arm. Maybe she fell asleep, but for sure, she was in a calm place. I flowed with the road, and the music got cool, but I was as warm as can be as the sun lowered. In my mind, I wrote words into my memory bank, words to say about love being my co-pilot.

Chapter Eighteen

Conga sounds greeted us before we came through the door of The Blue, The Black and Tan Nile Café. This time, unlike my last visit, it was full of people of the world. A sharing of cultures looked to be almost a mandate inside the café. The heads and bodies of intellectual minds tuned in by appreciative ears, were nodding, rocking, and patting.

A stand-up bass thumped out notes, going up a scale in between conga beats, boom bop, boom boom bop, boom bop, boom bop. An electric piano played over and under and through with chords, runs and tinkles of mini solos.

A wooden flute peeped from an enormous beard on the stage. A bearded, blond, dreadlocked man stood in front of the other musicians, chirping out notes in any empty space the bass and conga left him, while the electric piano made a bed for all of them to lay on. All four musicians used their instruments as body shields and let the music show its own beauty.

The beautiful African woman walked through the crowd toward us. I had my hand in the small of Meeah's back, moving her forward.

The African woman brought her eyes within a nose length of Meeah's eyes and said. "Sister Meeah, you come. It's so good to see you." The lady placed a slender hand on my forearm. "Ah, look here, I see you in here just a day ago, you with the good manners and big tip. You know my spiritual sister? Sister Meeah very good, very good indeed." I was all smiles with her acknowledgment.

Meeah leaned me forward into a tight circle with the African woman and said, "This here is my friend Tylowe, Ms. Julia. He did not know I knew you, but because you are so beautiful, he in passing told me of eating here and how you touched him so."

"Then he sounds like a good friend to have. You be ever wonderful my new friend. Let me find you a table." Ms. Julia had wonderful, contrasting demeanors from yesterday to today. She led us through the gathering of artistic minds. The bearded flute player on stage made the microphone disappear like a cat hides a parakeet in his mouth, and words flowed out of the speaker system. It sounded like Joe Crocker reciting poetry to a groove.

"Playing my jazz
> *My jazz holds all the notes in time from my past, present, and future*

I'll sing to you lyrics from stories untold
> *My jazz can be deep blue with lost loves, emptiness, sadness and contempt*
> *My jazz can be sky blue with the pleasure of love, knowledge, and places*

I've seen and dreams come true
Everyday a new note I find to scale a new or old challenge
> *My jazz is pure, simple and naked for all to see and hear all the notes of my jazz"*

The bearded performer let the microphone escape his mouth and he recaptured his flute and made it chirp in rippling arpeggios like a bird. We sat at a table and Ms. Julia said she would send someone over to bring us water or anything else we wanted. I pulled Meeah's chair into my space. Our conversation level had trickled to a drop; maybe having so much to say all through our day had worn out our mental and verbal motors. I had let go of any apprehension of being with her. I stopped thinking about the what-if and the what-now. I had to let whatever control my thoughts and feelings.

Meeah held my hand in her lap, touching, stroking each finger, each cuticle. We listened to several artists perform their verbal or instrumental art. Meeah's attention to my finger became more intense, to the point where she almost bent the ends of my short nail back. It hurt. I looked at her feeling my physical pain, but her face showed she was the one in pain.

"What?" I asked. Her eyes showed her emotional distress.

"I told you about how my mother has this don't-make-waves-control over me. Well, there are people here who might mention I was here with a man."

"You don't want me here with you?" Though my mind was content being with her, she had other thoughts.

"Tylowe, please, there is more than you involved here. Yes, I want to be right next to you."

I wasn't trying to be selfish in my thoughts, but I guess I was. "Okay, you're right." I pulled my hand from her lap. She reached back for my hand and stared at me hard.

The electric piano player was floating chords in a melodious flow, as a woman's voice recited a poem from the stage. I leaned over to speak into Meeah's ear, but hesitated so that I could listen to the passionate words.

"What is the whole of this man?
What features am I drawn to?
Is it all of him or is it some?
Can his mind lift me and hold me?
Will he keep me safe and warm?
Will his eyes put me in a trance?
Is that safe?
Will I be safe?
  Can his lips flow words into me like a warm breeze and make me
  follow him?
Can his lips make me melt in his arms?"

I cut into and off the woman's words and whispered in Meeah's ear. "Meeah, I'm here with you. And if you let me, I'll be here with you. I know you have Mia to think about, I know you have a lot to think about. But we are here in this place and at this time. I want to be here with you. Let's not allow what's right between us be outdone by what is wrong."
I was holding her hand as I whispered in her ear. Her tears were wet kisses on the backside of my hand. Meeah shook her head to

let me know she heard me. "How can a man be as kind as you? Tylowe, you make me feel safe. I feel better. Thank you. I know I said it before but, I don't know a lot about you, but what I do know, I love. You smile and I get warm and happy. You make me laugh without trying to make me laugh. You're as sexy as they get, and those lips… And these hands, oh Lord."

Like a little boy blushing I looked around to deflect the attention Meeah was paying me. I saw Ms. Julia standing behind the counter, so I patted Meeah on the leg and said, "I'll be back." I walked toward Ms. Julia.

A deep-and-rich voice was coming from a small woman singing onstage. She was just finishing a jazzy version of James Brown's, It's a Man's, Man's, Man's World. Ms. Julia walked up on the stage, and in her clear English African accent, she spoke. "To all my people here at The Blue, The Black and Tan Nile Café let us welcome our brother who calls himself Romantic Blues." The audience clapped and welcomed me to the stage. Not knowing if my name would get back to Tamara and cause any trouble that may already be brewing for Meeah, I used my gift card pen name as a stage name. I asked the piano man if he could imitate a type of Donny Hathaway electric piano tremolo loop. He was good; he gave a smooth, unhurried, thick groove that made what I wanted to do so much easier. I walked up to the microphone and let the piano mix with the words in my head, and then I let the words come out of my mouth. The words were directed toward only one, but were for all to hear.

"If the sun was hot enough
Or we were hot enough being next to each other
Enough to dwindle the amount of our clothing
> *Our barely covered tops and bottoms longing for the touch of each other*
Exposed my chocolate flexing limbs and your ample curves
> *Sitting, lying on a rock overlooking a cove, relaxing to the sound of soulful heartbeats and the slow incoming tide rocks us*
> *Alone with you, you with me, feeling like this is the only place for us to be*

So you please me and tease me, excite me by wiggling your
    pretty painted toes in front of me
Kneeling down
You lean over looking into my eyes
Your lips caress my lips
    I reach to stroke the curve of your arches and slide my hands up
    your calves to your thighs"

    I heard the people in the audience, "ooh-weeing' humming ah-weeing, yeah baby, talk that talk," I kept my words slow-dancing, tight as I could get to what I was feeling.

"I squeeze
Our noses nudge softly
Eyes lock
We...
Dive
Deep
Come up for air
Float on the surface
Play in the water
Dance on the waves
Create a riptide that takes us
Under
As we meet, we dance in the night
Time was changed
From flight to float
As our souls look beyond the blue sky
    Leaving land to see from the sea the world that couldn't hold us
From a world rarely touched, only dreamed of
As we float and drift
We cruise with a freedom few ever find
    We listen to the melody of our inner spirits in pure rapture and
    delight
And we dive deep
We find
We need no air
We breathe into each other
Our spirits are floating free
Our desires swim and soar like a dolphin

Our souls are at peace
We are safe with each other
As we gaze upon each other as the tide slackens
Passion grows
As we draw each other closer
Much closer than water washing ashore
We twirl so slowly as we float up from the deep
　　Sharing this beauty that comes from the mating of our bodies
There is no time in eternity
And eternity is where we are
To taste the glories of life beyond
We have been given the freedom to explore
The freedom of the purest of wanting
So hold in the night as great depths we reach
Dive with me my lover
Search out the pearl beds for the greatest pearl
Love and Passion
In the mists of
Warm blue water, and hot blue skies
Compassion, Ecstasy, Truth
Everlasting
The feeling for which we have been waiting for
Diving deeper and it gets warmer the deeper we go"

Looking up I saw and heard the look of love from the people, but didn't see Meeah. Before I walked off the stage, I shook the piano player's hand and gave an approving nod to the other musician. I walked through the people; I felt appreciation pats on the back, eye contact and high fives. I heard, "Right on, my man. You were good. Really felt that. Thank you for sharing. That was deep." I still saw no Meeah.

I may not have acted as if I was nervous during my performance, but my bladder let me know. I walked toward the bathroom and ran into Meeah in the hallway.

I said, "There you are."

"I needed someone to hold me while you were up there on the stage making me float. Ms. Julia and I held each other while you were the best we have ever seen up there."

"You saw Alexandré Cornet up on that stage and he left an impression on you."

"Ice cream by itself is good, but ice cream and cake and pie is the best it gets." Her eyes smiled, her lips smiled, a halo lay upon her head and I was high from inhaling her golden verbal dust.

"If I was good it was because every word was for you… and… me." I received another hard stare.

"What am I to do, Tylowe? This is not easy. It's a stage of my life I'm not prepared for, yet I know I need."

"Do as I say, let's not let what's right between us be outdone by what is wrong."

"I want to do as a man tells me to do. I want to trust like that, I do, but the last time I did what a man told me to do, my life went into a storm, and won't end, it seems."

"Wrong!"

"What do you mean?"

"Wrong; you did what a male told you to do, you did not do as a man would have you do." Her hand spread over my chest, and she was either testing for my heartbeat or reaching for what she needed. I pulled her body into me and the whole world disappeared.

Chapter Nineteen

We both kissed Ms. Julia on each cheek and walked out the back door. The dark alley had never been brighter; Meeah and I were like a fire, lighting everything around us.

Meeah drove and I saw another view of her. Her attention was distracted by cars, buses, lights, turns and shifting gears. I watched her until we pulled back into her parking place behind the gallery.

She punched the security keypad and opened the door. I was carrying our day bags, so Meeah held the door for me. My eyes slowly adjusted to the dim light in the hall, but before I could do that, hot wet breath was on my neck. My arms were pulled down, bags hit the floor and more hot wet breath crawled up the back of my head.

"Tyloooowe!"

"Huh?"

"You wanna take a shower?"

"Ah huh." We made out like two desert animals fighting over the last drop of water in the high-noon heat as we made it to the bottom of the spiral staircase.

"The bathroom is right here. I'll bring you some towels." By now hot wet breath was all over my bare back.
I stood in front of the bathroom mirror breathing intensely in and out. I watched my chest expanding beyond its usual stretch. I removed my jeans and felt my thong underwear lose its frontal support from the wet thick weight. Meeah pushed open the door; she stared at me with towels in hand. I had nothing to hide, nothing to be ashamed of as I stood there with ninety-nine percent of my body naked, but I turned away. I slid the shower door open.

Then I felt my rear thong strap being dislodged from my cheeks; the soft touch of her finger made my heart start pounding, pumping the extra blood.

She reached around to turn on the water, and it became hot and hard instantly. As the water got hotter, steam entered my nasal passages. I was high, high on something.

The tight body suit that Meeah had on earlier got lost in our hallway to bathroom, teenage-like, heavy petting adventure. Now her bare breasts were on my back and her nipples drew figure eights below my shoulder blades. Her short stilettos kept her just tall enough to keep kissing my neck and for her hands to reach wherever. The I Dream of Genie pants were gone and a sheer sarong was tied around her waist. It fell to the floor. Now on my thigh I could feel her whole tan line area; I could feel her short, private velour forest texturing my skin.

She slapped me on my rear, first the right side, than the left. The pleasured pain shot a jolt of electrifying blood through my outer vein. That made my thong too tight for comfort.

"Tylooowe, you shower up and I'm going to do a few things and when you're done, you come up and I'll come down and take a quick shower." She picked up her sarong and tied it back around her waist as she exited the bathroom.
The relaxing hot water all over my body made me stand there and be rained into a dream state. I couldn't help but think a moment about what Meeah had said, that her husband had said she was a lousy lover. I knew that was not true. I knew from the first kiss she was a good lover. I knew from our entrance back into the gallery moments ago, to her just leaving me in the hot water that she was spontaneous and passionate; she was soft in heart and had a sensual touch.

There was some cocoa butter on the bathroom vanity; I oiled my body. My mind was fantasizing about my oiled body lying next to the woman in the room above my head. I had been staring at the mirror for some time, playing a movie daydream, when I heard Nina Simone's voice increasing in volume singing In My Solitude.

I wrapped a towel around my waist and walked out to a darkened room where I saw the ceiling mirrors reflecting a reddish light. Walking up to the top of stairs, I could see the light was coming from the fireplace. Two glasses of wine were on the piano stool. The wood floor glowed, reflecting a warm aura; my photographic mind started to kick in.

Meeah's voice called out from downstairs. "Tylowe, I'll be up in a sec. I'm going to jump in the shower."

Going back downstairs and all the way to the back door, I retrieved the bags I dropped earlier. I stopped by the half-open bathroom door and heard the shower running, Meeah singing along to Eric Benét's I'll Be There. That put a big smile on my face. I danced up the spiral stairs like a dancer in an old black-and-white movie musical. Back in the loft the music kept me dancing as I loaded some special low-light film in the camera.

"Oooh, boy." Meeah liked what she had walked in on. "Don't stop." Her voice teased as she started to work her body to another Eric Benét groove: Femininity.

I froze in place, not because I was embarrassed, but because her body was like molten hot bronze. Her alluring contours were gloved in a sheer, full body shawl. As she danced around and around me as if I were a campfire, sliding her shawl over her enticing, prancing body, exposing different exotic looks.

"What kind of woman are you? Come here," I begged.

"I am here. I can see you know that."

Now I had a reason to be embarrassed, but I wasn't. My towel had come loose with the added help of my extremely large erection. I wanted to jump her bones immediately, but I had to do something else that could only be done now. Any other time it would feel staged.

"Meeah, I want you to sit on the piano bench." Without hesitation she dropped her shawl and straddled the bench where the glow of the fire lit up her caramel skin. The firelight danced over her nipples on the fireplace side and left a 'dark side of the moon' effect on the side nearest me. With my camera in hand, I saw her rare beauty through its lens. Her femininity glowed with vivid intensity as she stared at the fire. I felt right then I knew all I ever needed to know about a woman. I shot pictures of her from every angle and then took a barstool from across the room and placed the camera on it and pointed it toward Meeah and the fire. I turned the camera's self-timer on and sat across from Meeah on the bench. The moment was perfect. I stared into her eyes and she looked into me; the camera clicked.

We took a few sips of wine and I went over where she had dropped her shawl and where my towel had fallen and placed them back on both of us. We danced slower than Aretha sang Ain't No Way. As the music faded into another song, Meeah pulled away; she picked up her glass of wine and slowly dripped the fruit of the vine down my chest. The waistband of my towel became soaked as I stood there, while she stared at me. I released the towel that was trying to weigh down my hardness but had lost the battle.

She handed me the glass and sank down to her knees. The wine had made its way down to my thickened penis and, "Ah... ah," became the cup she drank from. She drank the mixed human and berry wine like it was the last liquid on earth. "Ah... ah." With the heat of the fire, "Ah... ah" and the heat of her hands and lips, I became drunk. My vocal chords did strange jungle-like sounds; I had no control of them. "Oooah, wha, whoa, ooh."

I leaned over and rained wine slowly down her lower back. The wine trickled down and touched every place I wanted to be. I placed the glass on the bench and then placed my hands on her back. I slid my fingers all the way down to her rear spilt. She kept removing my juice that had slid down under me by lifting what was in her hands, her tongue kept me groaning. She teased and encouraged, "Yeah, baby, come on, come on now," she said sultry phases in between sultry licks and kisses. "Ah… huh, yeaaaah, oh baby."

She wrapped her forefinger and thumb around my drooling, mushrooming vein. "Ah… ah." With the right amount of tension, she stroked up and down the bulging head as if I were doing it myself, "ah… ah," but with her tongue doing a variety of things that had me humping air. "Oooah, ooh." I could not take it anymore; I wanted to taste her, her womanly one hundred proof intoxicant.

I lifted her up, stood her up, laid my finger on her softest spot and slid lightly inside her. She sucked in a short breath and her body jerked, a first-touch-gasm. Her wetness and my finger made a moistening sound. Another jerk came from her body as she drew in two quick breaths, and both her facial lips and secret lips opened wide, an air-gasm.

I kissed her tongue through her parted mouth and she sucked on my lips as I kept my finger in her. I pulled my lips from her mouth and she joined the church choir, each sound she made went higher up the scale as each note lasted longer than the one before.

Then I kissed her on her neck as I slid my finger up to her round marble of sensation. "Ah hah, I got you baby, come on, let me do this to yah." My voice was deep and gravelly with intensity.

Her voice was high and faint and with no control: "You doing, doing it, baby. I, I, I, I, oh babeeee!"

I kept circling her now protruding marble lightly as I walked around behind her. My lips worked my way under her hair to the curve of her neck, and I kissed her. She spread her legs while standing; I slid my finger into the depths of her.
Groaning "ughuh, ughuh" she pushed her ass into me. I pulled my hand from inside her, and slid my hands to her hips. My wet lips treated her like a Popsicle, my tongue licking her spine.

She moved her hips and upper body to the popping sound of the burning wood; it was a, lustful visual treat I treated her whole body as a tasty delight and kissed the small of her back, running my lips on the outer edge of the split of her ass and going all the way to her heels and her feet.

I kissed her toes one by one, her ankles, and up to her thighs. If there was music still playing all I could hear was high-pitched sighing. I was still behind her as I sat on the floor. It was warm and wet and slippery in spots. Was that her sweetness, or mine, maybe our juices were doing the nasty on the floor? She turned around and stared down. I laid my head back, she spilt her legs wider, and I reached around and put my hands on her ass and helped her squat down onto my face. She cupped her hand around my head. We were in sync.

An "Aaaaaaaaah" from her was an animal sound.

I leaned back after a while to take in a full breath. The fireplace burned bright red on her slightly rounded belly, and the light let me see the hair between her smooth inner thighs. The hair had dewdrops of clear sexual moisture. Her scent drew me back like an animal seeking that aromatic mating call. She was sweet, so sweet I went crazy with my own grunts and groans.

I teased her with kisses around the outside of her extreme wetness. Her lips below her hips were still closed but wetness was seeping through. My kisses caused those lips to part slowly and her juices slid down like melting Popsicle juice. I caught the slowly flowing stream with the tip of my tongue barely touching her skin. Her taste drove me wild. I had to take one long lick of her, right then and there. It brought gasps of wanting and needing; it brought shuddering from her body, a mini-gasm.

I parted her deep inside with my tongue and then spread it wide in her. I danced inside her lover's tunnel, shifting from side to side as her hips did a slow grind against my lips. She released my head a little from her firm hold and began to rub my bald head like a crystal ball. At the same time Meeah became the lead at the opera, several rhythmic up-the-scale notes echoed as her body shuddered on my face. She was having an orgasm that echoed throughout her whole body.

I pulled back and looked up at her. She stood over me as if deflated. Her body seemed to be like one big lung, breathing deep and heavy, as her head rocked from side to side.

Meeah smiled, shook her head at me and said, "Lay down," and I did as I was told. The top of my head faced the fire. Meeah stepped over me and added more fuel to the fire. She drank from a water bottle before she stepped one leg over me and looked down at my hard body; I knew what she was thinking by her expression.

I said, "Come on, baby."

She blinked her eyes, rotated her head from one side to the other, took in a deep breath and slowly squatted down on my hardness. She held herself in place for a long moment by bracing one hand on my thigh and the other on my navel. "Oh, baby, you feel good, come on now give it all to me, you can do it."

"That's easy for you to say," she said as she lowered herself a little more. Her eyes stayed open, but the brown circles rolled up behind her eyelids.

"Damn, baby," my mushrooming head wanted to whimper. Her prime, pink well-done insides came with no price on the menu; simply put, she felt good sliding down on my hardness.

"Ooooh," her voice wavered. "Having you in my mouth is one thing, but you're a big boy, baby." Her voice kept changing pitch.

I put my hands under her to help ease her down. Once down she let out a relieved breath and smiled with her tongue lodged in the corner of her mouth.

"See, you're okay," I teased.

"Yeah, I'm okay. Just let me sit here for moment," she said slowly while chuckling.

"You just want to sit there, huh?" I teased. My ass did a rolling up and around motion on the hardwood floor, trying to go deeper. I felt her insides starting to hold with a different tension, and the feeling made me want to stroke harder. Her thigh muscles became less rigid, and she met my stroke. Her groans and grunts were so carnally addicting, I pumped up and down in an effort to pull more reverberation from deep within her. We kept on and on, saying nasty shouts and whispers to each other. All within one motion we rolled over until she was on her back. I gazed down at her for a long moment and I turned her on her stomach with her ass up facing me. I grabbed pillows off the couch, propping her butt up in the air and for cushioning my knees. Her breasts spread on the floor and her arms stretched out in front of her as if she was reaching for the fire. I entered her from the rear, to sounds of groans and grunt. I danced inside her fire, keeping time with the deep funk of the music; we were in sync. Groove Theory sung "Ride." I was doing just that to her round, firm, brown behind. Her skin made squeaking sounds on the floor. The pillows under my knees got lost in our funky motion. I started getting floor burns, but the pain would have to wait, I was trying to release my liquid pressurized tension inside Meeah.

"Wait, wait, please, the floor is... Tylowe, let's get on the bed." We were short of breath. I was dripping as I stood up. I picked her up, and put her over my shoulder in caveman fashion. As I carried her over to the bed I bumped the coffee table, knocking over the little African warriors.

"Whoops, sorry."

"It's okay, Superman."

So much for Superman. At the most, she might have weighed 135 pounds but my ass needed a break. I lay on my back and she plopped her body next to me. With her head on my chest and her leg between mine, we stroked and caressed each other.

She rolled on top of me and easily into a military pushup position, locking her arms and looked down on me with a fierce look. She spread my legs wide with her feet and lowered her hips, but her arms stayed locked. I felt her sweet wet warmth encase my hardness. Her hips lowered more to take all of me in, and then she crossed her legs tight and her hips lifted up. The friction from her sparse hair around her lover tunnel had me ready to cum.

"So you in shape, huh?"

"I work out a little, swim a lot."

She kept her arms locked and let her pelvis climb up and down my high dive platform. She started closing her legs tighter and that increased the friction and pressure. "Oh, boy, look at your face, does it feel good?"

I grunted for an answer, and kept grunting. The stroke of the head of my dick against her tight opening and pubic hair had me on fire. The look of confidence was on her face; she knew she was in control. I was building up the urge to spurt inside her. Meeah's nasty up and down stroke and her wet inner heat provided the right friction. She was tight from tip to deep within.

"Ah...ah... shit!" I was erupting inside her. That treasured three to ten seconds a man feels when he cums is so much more intense when he doesn't have to work for it. Another long grunt; I put my palms on her back and pulled down so she couldn't move anymore. I was too sensitive as I whimpered.

"Look at that silly smile on your face," Meeah said as her nose traced my lips. She teased me. "Oh, Mister, I think your radiator hose busted. There's a lot of hot fluid down there."

Meeah slid down, and I felt her tongue suck lightly on my nipple. I kissed the top of her head. The long day started to challenge my eyes. The light from the fire started to dim. Her lips went still and I held onto her tightly while we drifted away.

Chapter Twenty

Daybreak. The light from the windows down below woke me with a little help from my bladder. I do not remember climbing under the sheets. The beautiful lines of Meeah's body were covered. We were on our sides with her backside tucked into my pelvis. Hair was in my face, and my arm was around her waist.

I slipped from under the sheets quietly, trying not to awaken her. As I walked around the bed, the wood floor reminded me of its late night adventure. I smiled.

I stretched, using the rail for support. I looked down at the art below while working out the kinks in my body. Then I looked back at a sleeping masterpiece. I stood in awe. I was not looking for love. I might even have closed my eyes to love before Meeah burned the feeling into my mind's eye. Sex with Meeah was great, but that alone doesn't make you fall in love. Something much deeper pulled and pushed me in, and I loved it.

I watched Meeah turn over. The covers molded and clung to her body like clay. I headed down to the bathroom, and spotted and picked up the poetry book by Alexandré Cornet. I thumbed through the pages for a moment. This one poem got my attention:

Sleep in my arms
Pressed against the warmth of feeling safe
Feeling needed
Feeling loved
She slept in my arms
I found her there in the morning light
Tired
Recovering from the night of closeness
Her forehead buried in my chest
I feel her exhaling into my heart
Sliding my palm lightly over tender features
I want to... all over again
I'm tired

I kiss her
Really care about her
I roll away I stare at her limp body
Still firm on my mind, her passion that tired me
I cover her up
I stroll away
Smiling
Thinking how lucky I am
I can't wait for you to awake
To share the day

Damn! I wish I had written that. I put the book down and made my way to the bathroom.

I hated taking a dump in someone else's bathroom with the thought they might come in after me, but I had to. I reached into the magazine rack in front of me. A copy of Hot Rod Bike, a magazine that featured custom Harleys, was a favorite. This is cool, I thought. I figured with the bad luck Meeah has had, she would have had a copy of "O," the Oprah Winfrey magazine, featuring Dr. Phil. I flipped through the pages backward as I always do. I looked at the front picture again and noticed the little subscription tag.

Elliot Piste
21657 Water Street
Vancouver, BC V6b
1B9 Canada

My stomach cramped; my bowels lost control. I reached for other magazines when I should have reached for toilet paper. Yes, there were other motorcycle magazines with his name.

I could not figure out what this meant, then it dawned on me. Piste in French meant Runway. I'll be damned! She was married to Elliot. I didn't believe it was possible, but what else could it mean? I sat there and sat and sat, until the seat started to carve a permanent ring on my ass.

How could this have happened? The doors to my heart had just opened up. Did Meeah know? My mind raced. Questions collided with each other inside my head. It wouldn't make sense that she knew. Why is that French piece of crap still in my ass after all these years? I grunted with full force. It all made sense what Meeah had been going through. It took an arrogant ass like him to use and abuse a woman like her.

I thought about little Mia; she was his blood, she deserves better than Elliot as a father. I sat there not feeling happy, but laughing anyway. The shit I was flushing deserved more than an Elliot. Meeah was still asleep in the room above my head. What was I supposed to do with her?

I stepped into the shower. Maybe I was dreaming, having a nightmare. Hot water might wake me up. I knew I was not dreaming. I just wanted to wash this ugly feeling away. I let the water pound my face, and wished Mike Tyson had just knocked me out; I'd feel better.

The water pressure dropped. I heard the toilet flush.

"Tylowe," Meeah's voice floated above the shower. She sounded happy. "I'll make you some coffee, or would you like to go to our café? Oh, I want you to know these motorcycle magazines are here because, well my hus—, well he has always had them sent here just to annoy me, I think. I toss most of them but, I keep a few, well, because I do like motorcycles. Do you ride? Because I can. Runway taught me back when he acted as if he wanted me. I'm sorry. You probably don't want to hear all that"

I knew she didn't have a clue. Oh man, what am I going to do? I turned the shower head to hard massage and let it pound on my head.

"Tylowe, are you okay?" She slid the shower door open and water misted into her hair and onto her face and breasts. I didn't answer her; still searching for the right way to deal with this. "You not talking to me this morning?" I didn't answer. She stopped smiling. "Look, if you just want to leave, I guess you have the right."

I stopped the water and slowly opened the glass door wider. Standing there with hot, wet skin and getting hotter knowing the naked truth, I asked, "Meeah, what is your last name?" My tone might have been hot, too. She moved back and gave me a quizzical stare.

"It's Runway, but in French it's Piste. I have always called my husband Runway. It was something my late dad always called him." She raised her eyebrows, puzzled. I blew out a pocket of air from my cheeks as if I was trying to blow out a row of candles in slow motion. "What's the problem? You wake up and realize I'm married? You knew that before we... What is the problem?"

I could not be angry with her; it was my choice to wake up here this morning, but I wanted to be mad. "Yeah, let's go over to the café and have some coffee, we need to talk."

She closed her eyes for a moment and then walked out of the bathroom.

She tossed the keys at me as we walked out the door. She never looked at me. At each turn, she just pointed the direction to go. I parked in about the same spot she had the first time we met. She jumped out and waited on the curb for me to come around.

"If you don't want to be here with me..."

I put my finger to her lips and put my other hand on her back to move her toward the café. She needed some reassuring, but I needed something too. I just didn't know what that was.

Coffee, chai spice tea and warm cinnamon bread was in front of us, but neither of us were eating or talking. I stared at every hair of hers blowing in the wind. She played in her tea; I stirred my coffee. I put too much sugar in. Nothing could sweeten what I had to say. I didn't know where to start. The café owner smiled in the background as if he was giving me a high five. If he owned the drama I owned, he would not be smiling, he'd close shop. I wondered if I should ask Meeah questions or tell her what I knew.

"Do you know your husband's friends, family, or much about his past history?"

"Some. Why do you ask?" I let a seagull flying by squawk.

"I know Elliot."

"How? From where?" Her voice sounded like she had dry ice stuck in her throat.

I told her a history, a complete life story, from A to Elliot and Elliot to Renee and Renee to Z-end. Four cups of coffee later, I had retold the same story I had told Suzy Q in the same spot just yesterday morning, but with more detail. When I was done, Meeah stared at her empty teacup. I needed water to dilute all the sugar upsetting my stomach. I was not feeling well for a number of reasons.

"No sense asking how this could be, but what now, Tylowe? You just gonna walk away? I understand if you walk away, really I do. I got some real life issues, don't I? I just want you to know, I had a lot going on in my life to be proud of at one time. Just when will this dark cloud named Elliot stop raining down on my life? I thought I was recovered, and I have been feeling good about me again. I see a good man like you, and I want you. Why is this happening?"

The harbor traffic demanded our attention with tugboats and ship horns. People came and went in the café. Life went on all around us as if we weren't there.

But we were there.

She spoke in a whisper, and I thought she said, "I have hope of having Mia back with me one day, and if not, she knows I love her." She fell silent and the seagulls screamed and wailed, filling the silence for a while.

I went to get some water,. I returned, and before I could sit back down, she stood up and spoke with her back to me. "I've walked into this same café nearly every morning for some time now, and then one day, Tylowe, you're in here."

She turned and looked at me. "Our conversation went from earth to heaven and back. I got lost in your presence, but it felt safe. I know this is some strange karma bull-do-do, and I never curse, but this so ef'd up!"

"You still haven't officially cursed. True, you have something different going on here, Meeah. Of all the men in the world, you and I have to deal with Elliot!"

My fear of what Meeah might have done with Elliot kept turning my stomach. I wanted to ask her if she took part in any of Elliot's freak shows. I'd been keeping myself from asking her, but I finally lost that battle. "You said you tried everything you could to please him. Did you really?"

"No!" She shook her head and didn't stop with once or twice. "No, he tried to set me up with that sick crap, too."

Then I went stupid and asked something even worse. "Well, I take it since Elliot is not around and you don't sleep with him, that there has been somebody else lighting your fire for you."

She licked her lips and then lifted her chin up high. She didn't speak, but her eyes had a message. "I'm sorry, I had no business asking you anything like that." I looked at the floor.

"You're right, you had no right, but since you went there, you satisfied me with some serious free style yourself, mister. I take it you practice your modus operandi sometimes, a few times, here and there, once in a while? Am I right? You've had or got lady friends, huh?" She answered my stupid question with questions. I did not want to answer her questions. It didn't matter; I didn't get a chance. She had more to say. "For the record, there is no one right now, and there hasn't been for a while, unless I count you, but it sounds like I shouldn't."

Check and checkmate. She fried my ass. The look on her face showed she was peeved and serious. Yet her beauty seemed to intensify, much like other women when they are angry.

Sometimes a woman can be so sexy when she's upset with a man. "I, ah, I apologize, again. Despite what's going on, you did not deserve my insecurities over something that doesn't matter. Two things are clear, though."

"Hmm, what are you talking about?"

"You will and can stick up for yourself now. And you blew my mind with the pushup thing last night."

She gave a small smile. "Life can make you dig your heels in, and a video will teach you a lot. I never really knew I could do it. You were the perfect person to find out if I could with. So please, tell me we're all right with us being together last night?"

I leaned forward and stared into her eyes then kissed her slowly. I sat back and let the breeze blow for a minute before I spoke. "We're cool, baby. But I guess the real issue at hand is, what now? You are married, and married to..."

"Hey, I don't want to be married to him, but if you feel you need to walk away... I don't want you to walk away. You said we shouldn't let what's right between us be outdone by what is wrong."

My thoughts went back and forth. How could such a beautiful city leave me with black clouds over my head? Yet the sky was clear before I picked up that magazine in the bathroom. I lost love in this city. Now I had found love. It didn't take four months or four days; it happened in twenty-four hours. Now that I love this woman, what do I do? Part of her life is being controlled by another man's evil ways.

"Tylowe, Tylowe." She could have been calling my name for hours, because my mind was traveling. "You know, when you're silent like this it doesn't frighten me, but I need you to share with me at this moment, please."

"Meeah, when you walked in here the other day, I was just reading a book and at peace with my life as it was. Yet I know

now, as we sit here, I realize I have unfinished business. It was strange at first you didn't want to know my name. But now, we know so much more. I have to believe we are both here for good reasons. God's got something up his sleeve, so let's just see where this is going. Let's play it by ear."

"Yeah, all right, but what do you mean you have unfinished business?"

"I don't want to sound insensitive, and I don't want you to feel like a possession, so hear me out."

"I'm listening."

"I love you, Meeah." Just at that moment, a big ship foghorn blew. People walking by would have thought we were mannequins in a store window. I stared at Meeah, waiting for the horn to stop, and her facial expression seemed to say, "Stop holding me in suspense."

"Like I said, Meeah, I love you. And it may be weird that I feel this way so soon. I feel it; I know it and I must act on it. I'm not sure how I'm going to go about this, but I'm going to do whatever I need to. That's who I am and what I'm about."

"You know, the day we met I walked out of here thinking you're a nice guy and in another life it might be meant for us to… Well, anyway, you know what I mean. So I had to laugh to myself knowing you were going to the school and would see my little girl. That was the main reason for not giving you my name. Then she tricked the both of us into meeting again. She's so cute. When she called for me to meet her at the pool, she said she hardly spoke to you or hadn't seen you around the school."

"Yes, Mia is something special and older than her age."
"And she finds me love." Meeah leaned forward in her chair and massaged my hand with a fingernail. A stronger breeze blew by, but this one was warmer. She lightly imprinted I love you in my

palm and then lifted my palm to the side of her face and caressed her cheek with it. She started an emotional rocking in her chair. "Will you let me love, will you let me love you with the best I have, Tylowe?

I nodded with a big smile.

"You said you did not want to sound insensitive and didn't want me to feel like a possession. What were you talking about? What is this unfinished business?"

"I can't make this sound pretty, and maybe it's wrong to think like this." I ground my teeth for a second before I spoke about being an avenging angel. "Elliot caused me to lose a love. I thought I would have that love to this day and all the days of my life." I looked out to the water, talking to myself as well as Meeah. "Part anger, part hurt; some things don't rot away, they eat away. I still close my eyes and see that day, that moment, and..." I stopped talking and kept looking at the water. I let more negative thoughts go in a circle and make me suddenly feel a bit depressed.

Meeah cut off my going nowhere blues. "And?" she prompted.

"And I want to change the way I feel about this."

"So let me guess, you want to take me away from him. Well, I don't belong to him! If you want me, let it be because you want me and no other reason, Tylowe. It's weird enough you and Elliot have history together. The last thing I need is to be mixed up in something I have no control of at all. That's all I've dealt with ever since I've known Elliot."

"Look, there is no doubt I want you, and I need you to help me get to another place in life."

"Well, this is not a plaything you're dealing with. Elliot is serious; he is a control freak. He doesn't like to lose at anything."

"I know, I know the man, I competed with him, I watched him compete in the sports and business worlds for many years. He has angles and moves. I hate to admit it, but at one time I admired him."

"So you two were college roommates, huh? Well, I bet you two were..."

I was not going to let her go there. "That was another time and place. I grew up, okay? You did not let me go down that street with you a little while ago. And for the record I don't have a workout partner. There is only you now."

Her tone was unnecessarily apologetic. "Tylowe, I just need to be in an honest situation. I want us to be up front. I think you know I need that, and I know you need it, too."
I didn't mean for her to hear my inner thoughts, but the words slipped out of my mouth. "Common ground, one enemy."

"So we would be taking a chance on each other. Well, you'd be taking a big chance on somebody like me. There are those who think I'm crazy, you know."

"I've heard your story, and that's my point. That arrogant ass can drive anyone crazy." I thought about what I had just said. "Ah, Meeah, I don't think you're crazy."
She laughed for the first time that morning. We both needed to laugh.

"Clean it up, you think I'm crazy. But at least you're the one now who's driving me crazy the right way." She blushed. "So you think I'm a pretty good lover, huh?"

"Hell, yeah! Yes, you were all the way live. I couldn't have asked for more; maybe, doubtfully, I don't know if I could have taken any more. That pushup thing, oh..."

"Stop, don't let anyone hear you." I started laughing, as her cheeks reddened. I was happy to let her know she had more than satisfied me.

She kept smiling, but our unfinished business still loomed over us like a drizzling black cloud in the middle of the blue sky. Even with all that was sweet and promising, a raven-colored French African dog dick stood in the way. I needed some alone time to sort all this out.

"Meeah, I should go by the school, and I need to get back to Seattle; I need to think." She sat silent. "I will not leave you hanging, okay? I know you don't really know if you can trust me because we are still new to each other. But just give me some time to work this out. Work with me, okay?"

"Do you have an idea what you are going to do?"

"No, and we will need to talk about everything you know about Elliot. Everything!"

Her face, still so beautiful, but distorted by a frown deep with tension. A very deep sigh, stronger than the breeze already blowing, released from her lung's depths. I got up and walked behind her chair. I started to massage her shoulders and leaned her head over to the side, nestled in my hand. Her trembling voice, rifled with fear, stated our major concern. "You have a plan? Do you have an idea what you are going to do?"

"Meeah, whatever I decide to do, it will include you being with me."

We sat silent for a while longer as the seagulls screamed. I held her by her hand, wet from wiped tears, as we walked back to the car. When we got to the car she turned around to face me. She kissed me and then leaned on me and whispered into my ear.

"Just for a while, let's go back to my place. I'm not ready to let you go." I rubbed the side of my face against hers and nodded.

"Tylowe, you need to remember one very important thing, I have a little girl, and she can't get hurt any more than she hurts now. So whatever you do, I mean, we do…"

I moved my face nose to nose with her. "It will be okay. It will. It will be okay. I won't let what's right be outdone by what's wrong." We headed back to the gallery to the tune of the wind and early morning traffic.

She opened the back door and walked away talking, "My faucet is dripping."

"What?

"I said my faucet is dripping."

I had no clue why she would be telling me a sink needed a new washer or a plumber right now. "I might be able to fix it. Do you have a hardware store nearby?"

She turned and burst into laughter. "Silly man." She fully faced me, unbuttoned her jeans as she rolled them down her thighs and wet her lips, teasing me. She took my hand and slid it into her fleshy faucet. It was sopping wet. She groaned and sighed. I watched and felt her twist, squeezing her thighs.

"Oh, now I know what you meant."

"Ah, do you think you can fix it? I think you already have the hard…" I stuffed my tongue in between her lips and she sucked on it as my finger caused the damn to break and her flow increased.

"Let's take this upstairs." I managed to lead her down the hall with my hand still in her pants. Along the way, Meeah made sounds that jungle animals would envy. Going up the stairs I started saying sexy, nasty things and making my own wild creature groans, because she had her hand in my pants. We stopped at the wood floor and both agreed to go right on to the bed.

We fell on the bed and somehow only a few items of clothing were left. Sexual heat had us going fast, until I saw wet eyes. They weren't tears of sadness, but tears of wonderment.

"I have never felt so wanted," she said. "How come I feel so much more than just you touching my body?" I understood her question was not for me to answer, but just to let her dwell in the amazing presence of being in love. "I feel you in every part of me. Please, Tylowe, don't let me be lonely, ever again."

Chapter Twenty-One

I was dreaming about being with the perfect woman, but perfect was on the other side of a wall that reaches too high to jump. There's no ladder to climb, and a crazed black Hell's Angel on a fire-breathing, out-of-control motorcycle is barreling down on my ass. How do I get over the wall to a safe place, a perfect world? The dream seemed never ending; Elliot kept coming at me.

Conversations from the ground floor woke me. My dream ended without me finding a way over the wall. I realized I was alone in the bed. I had been knocked out cold by intense sex. I was laying spread eagle covering the bed. The last thing I could remember? Her legs were tensing, my hips were slowing to a soft grind.

The clock in the headboard said 1:05 p.m. I should have been gone by then, but I wouldn't have changed a thing except for having to find a way over the Elliot barrier. After standing and stretching, I noticed those angled mirrors allowed you to see from the loft to the gallery floor, but I remembered seeing the angle didn't allow the gallery customers to see upward. The mirrors vision from the main floor only reflected the art. I saw a few people walking around looking at the art.

Grover Washington's horn increased in volume. I stretched a little more to the rhythm of the bass. I pulled my pants on, looked around for my other articles of clothing, and I made my way down to the bathroom to clean up.

Meeah met me at the door as I finished. "I turned up the music when I saw your shadow moving around." I kissed her on her forehead, and then teased her ear with lips and words. "Open for business?"

"Uh-huh."

"I've got to go. I have a number of things to do." I put my hands on her shoulders and squatted down a couple of inches to look in her eyes.

"I hope I'm on that list!" Concern was in her voice.

"Meeah, you're on top of the list. I've got to make it back over to the school and head back home."

"Home!" she repeated with a hollow voice. She led me out back to where her car was.

Meeah held me with an unstable heart as if it was on a ledge and could fall and break at any wrong word said while we stood next to her car. No long goodbye, a short kiss and she handed me her car keys. She told me how to get back. I was to leave her car at a parking garage a block from the school and she'd get a ride later to pick it up. I got in the car, she walked to the front of it and leaned on the hood. She pursed her lips to blow a kiss. All I could do was stare at her drop-dead gorgeous beauty.

I motioned for her come back to the car door. When she did, she spoke before I did.

"Call me soon?" There was some uncertainty in her voice. "I know all of this is crazy, even if there was no Elliot."

"Oh, why?"

"You and me so soon, so sudden, so intense. I'm so in love with you."

I raised my eyebrows. "So!" I smiled for her to know I was teasing.

"You and that smile; you think you're so funny." Her finger ran a course along my face.

"I love you, too. And I'll call, baby. But when I do, you'll have to tell me all you know; it will only help us." She nodded.

I started the car and she leaned over, brushed her lips back and forth against my ear lobe and whispered.

"Baby, could you write something for me and leave it for me to read when I pick up my car? I need another book marker with your heart prints." I felt her tongue slide into my ear; my foot revved the engine up too high.

~~~~~

I sat in Meeah's gold-colored chariot in the basement of the parking garage, with a pen in my hand. What to write? I wanted to say just the right words to let her to know the impact she had made on me. I wanted her to feel we were not just a passing moment. So many of the good things we feel in life are just moments in time. I did not feel that way about her. I had felt, and I'm sure she had felt in the past, that people sometimes gave us what we needed for the moment.

She and I were like an unfinished painting, forgotten in the back of a closet, only to be discovered and completed by the original artist. Like most great artists, their best work came after they had lived through trials and tribulations. The artists of the unfinished work of our lives would be the two of us. Words started to flow from my pen.

Brush Strokes of the life we live
Let us brush stroke a background of a life gone by
Like looking down in a valley and seeing what everyone has seen, but only you and I know the true story of how the river used to flow
Before there was a you and me being together, a background was started but not finished on the canvas of our life
Somehow we lost our canvas, but now there is you, and there is me, together.
Our canvas has been found
Now let us finish painting a background of love, past, present, and future
Let us brush stroke a background with a life to live
Like life on the streets we stroll, roads we're traveling, hills we walk and mountains we find ourselves climbing, let them be the background of a life we know now
Brush strokes

Dip our cerebral paintbrush into our souls and brush stroke a future river, a sea, an ocean of calm and the day of our glory has come
Brush Strokes
Pick colors; mixed colors, colors you and I can see
And when they are just right
We'll paint away them old blues
Dark blues, sad blues, painful blues, blue tears that fell from the sky that kept rivers running through our valley of blues
All in them old blues
They are a part of an old life, but still a part of you and me.
So we'll brush stroke them, into a corner
Let us make our canvas like a bed to rise from, to let us see sunrise blues, and sky blues and sunset blues that shine over you and me.
Let us paint a new dawning
Brush Strokes
Pick colors; mixed colors, colors you and I can see
And when they are just right
We'll paint green hues of greens
Earth tones of what is right
God has given us the green light to go forward, to be together, to love and to be loved
Let our brush go dry with each stroke to give us texture of an unrivaled life.
Brush strokes
Pick colors; mixed colors, colors you and I can see
And when they are just right
We'll paint yellows to blend in-between any and all colors to brighten our days
Brush strokes
Pick colors; mixed colors, colors you and I can see
And when they are just right
We'll paint red, hues of red
Heating up and bringing a warm fire that melts us into one
Let us brush stroke the making of you and me
On the outside
Your skin in shades gold, my skin in shades of bronze
Let us paint us as we are
Minds, hearts, and souls the color of diamonds, rubies, and pearls
Our passion is a color only you and I can see

Now as we brush stroke our way to the mountaintop
We look back and see the background from where we have come
And from that same peak we see a future river, a sea, an ocean to sail and
our paintbrush forever brush strokes a masterpiece of you and me

I left the poem on the seat and walked out into the sunlight. The afternoon heat was hotter than it had been since I'd been here. Sweat beads rolled down my face from the one-block walk from the parking garage to the school steps. My image of the school had changed dramatically in vision and feeling, since finding out so much. Meeah was the artist of such large works. That was focus of great magnitude. That's a major plus in any relationship. Yet the history of this place was not good. It was like Beauty and the Beast, but the beast was truly a beast.

I had to check my attitude at the top of the stairs. I did not want to show any ill will toward Tamara. I had to act as if everything was cool. For keeping Meeah and Mia apart, what could be her motivation? Was it just to have the school, or did she really think she was doing the right thing?

Of course, she could be under the influence of Elliot, too. But how could Tamara be thinking she's doing the right thing for little Mia?

Was it money? How much money? Was it just pure selfishness? I kept thinking it couldn't be that simple. Could there be things Meeah needed to tell me? I needed to know all and any of Tamara's angles. If Tamara was in communication with Elliot, she might mention my name. What would that do to the equation? I couldn't help but wonder.

Elliot. I knew what drove him. It had always been about ego. Money, Elliot likes money, but egotistical pleasures filled a mental bank account first. That much I could count on.

I had one more thought before I walked through the door. Mia was going to be wondering about her mother and I hoped she hadn't given it away with her enthusiasm. No sooner said, Mia called my name.

"Tylowe!" For sure she was excited. I put my finger to my mouth to hush a quickly approaching Mia. I looked around as I walked through the door. I saw no one else.

"Tylowe," she whispered. "Did you see… "

"Mia," I spoke in hushed tone, "Look, you have to keep all this to yourself; do you know what that means?" She nodded. "Now, how are you?"

"I'm fine." Her eyes were pleading.

"Mia," I leaned over and looked around again for Tamara. "Where is your grandmother?"

"She is teaching a class." Mia pointed down the hall.

I wanted to tell her that her mother and I are fine, and I cared a lot about her. I didn't. "Mia, when you get a chance, call your mother, but you need to act like everything is the same as it has been, okay?"

"Okay. I think ma is mad at you for something. Were you supposed to model today?"

"Oh, shhhh-it. You didn't hear me say that. Well, let me get this over with. What room is she in?"

"The room you were modeling in. Tylowe, you like my mom?"

"Yes. Now, go call your mom." I gave her a hug and kissed the top of her head and headed for the room of doom. I had spaced out. I knew I was supposed to model Monday, but somehow, someway, something got in my way. I laughed to myself. Tamara entered the hallway before I reached the room.

She stood in front of me, not showing any anger, and then she spoke in a slow, deliberate monotone. "The students were very disappointed that their prized model did not have enough respect for their talent to show up."

"I have no excuse for my unprofessional move. Is there anything I can —" She wanted to hear no more and cut me off.

"Well, Mr. Dandridge, I will not hold it against you. The students can work from the Polaroid pictures we took of you. It's just that you might end up with muscles in your face that are not there, or lack of muscle in your rump."

I stood in front of her hearing that I'm back to being called Mr. Dandridge, and was she insinuating someone might paint me with a flat ass? Okay, that was over the top!
Ouch. I stood and stared over her head trying to avoid eye contact. "Tamara, I guess I'm going to head down to the train station and head home tonight instead of tomorrow morning."

"I thought you needed to stay a few days longer. Didn't you have some other things you wanted to do? I may be upset with you for missing today, but you are still welcome in my house."

I thought about staying another day while listening to her. Meeah was like honey on my mind, thick and sweet. I wanted to hover around her nectar, but I needed a long-range plan.
"There are some things I need to get back to. Thanks for the offer. How about if I come back and do some modeling for free in a week or two?"

"Nothing is free; everything has a price, an old saying that comes true every time. But you can come back whenever you like."

"Cool. Would you mind calling me a cab while I pack? I really need to catch the last train."

I said my goodbye to Tamara and she handed me a check for the full amount. I tried to convince her to make the check for less, but she wouldn't. I almost felt bad. Almost.

Mia grabbed one of my bags and walked out to the street with me. "Be cool, and everything will work out fine. Contact your mom when you can. You like dreams to come true?"

"Huh?"

"Go rent the Wizard of Oz." She stood there blinking back tears.

"Don't cry, or you're gonna make me cry." I stuck my finger in her dimple and made her smile. We hugged and the cab took me away.

Chapter Twenty-Two

Crossing the border, heading home without the love of my life. Again. No tears in my eyes this time, but my brain was working overtime, reliving each moment with Meeah. I missed her with the same intense weight of the train rolling on these tracks. I had to find a way to make this dream have a happy ending.

I remember taking pictures of Mia at sunset and thinking I had lost out in being a father, but now I could be a part of this young girl's life. I knew she had a father and I really didn't know how Mia felt about Elliot. So I'd have to be careful and not try to replace the man. But, damn, he didn't care to be a real man. Something I could do was replace him as a husband to Meeah, and that would be sweet.

It didn't matter that he had been with her. I didn't know it before she lay in my arms. And it didn't matter now.
Staring. The window keeps changing scenes with the sun setting in the background. Everything had happened so fast. Slow this damn train down. My thoughts went back and forth, from good to bad and from happy to worried.

Getting involved with Elliot again may not be a good idea. Why would I risk so much for a woman who had only been in my presence a few days? No one answer made me secure with my decision to go forward. But for a love of my own, sacrifices would have to be made.

Meeah was so innocent and vulnerable, and with our histories having a common denominator, she knew I was just as vulnerable. She was someone to be scared for and someone to be scared with. She wasn't asking for anything other than love. I thought in order to fall in love, I would have to be friends with a woman for weeks or months. I thought I'd have to date someone for a long time before I knew I'd love her forever. Suddenly I see that isn't the case. I want her now and tomorrow and every day after that.

It turned dark while I was staring out the window. There were some lights here and there as the train rolled on, but my reflection was clearly visible in the dark. I continued to have silent conversations with my reflection. Whatever I decided to do about the woman I love, I'd have to be my own best friend, trusting in myself to do the right thing. I left for Vancouver in the dark, and I returned in the dark, as well. I was in the dark in more than one way. And I was a little scared.

It was not too late when I got off the train, so I made my way to Seahawks Stadium, right next to the train station and near where my motorcycle was parked. A good friend ran security, and I knew some of the coaches from back in earlier days. I could work out anytime, running on the field or pressing some weights in the weight room. The whirlpool and steam room had my name on it; my sore hip was still crying boo-hoo from Suzy Q acting like a linebacker and from erotic breakdancing with Meeah.

Hot water and steam relaxed me and helped slow the brain waves for a while. A few football players were still hanging around, working out for the coming preseason. I talked shop with the boys before I headed for my motorcycle.
Starting up my motorcycle and sitting there while it warmed up, my mind wandered. I started reliving my last motorcycle ride with Elliot. It angered me; I rode home too fast. I had to keep a cool head; I couldn't let raw emotions cause me to make a mistake.

Meeah couldn't wait. By the time I got home, she had called and left a message: "I love you" was all she said. That's all she needed to say. My ear was burning to hear her live, so I returned her call, but her answering machine teased me with her recorded voice. So I settled down and made myself at home in my own place. But it wasn't long before I found myself pacing and thinking about a game plan.

In the morning, I returned calls and settled down to do some work. I went into my darkroom and developed all the film I shot while in Vancouver. The pictures I took of Mia at sunset and later under the streetlights were astonishing. It was some of my best work, helped by Mia's natural emotions. I had to think about sending them out for others to view and publishing them.

I moved on to the photos of Mia's mother, the woman I am now in love with. In the darkroom, the red light could not hide the fire developing on paper. Fire. Two perfect bodies silhouetted by yellow and red flames, I felt myself breathing deep. The shadows of Meeah and I on the floor captured lovers making love. Consuming desire burned through every detail; I got lost in the picture and started reliving every moment. The phone rang, bringing me back to the present.

"Hello. Oh, baby, I miss you, too. I returned your call last night when I got in." Meeah told me she was able to see Mia last night. Tamara had let them go to dinner and a movie. It was a rare occasion. It was a happy time for the most part. The two of them had spoken at length about feelings; the feelings that Meeah and I shared. That part the girls enjoyed. It had been a difficult discussion at times, Meeah said. She was a young girl who had a mom and dad, but strained relationships in many ways. Elliot had pampered Mia with material things, but with no real emotional attachment. He rarely spent time with her; yet he was her father.

I did not waste any time in downloading more information from Meeah, as she had to open the gallery in only an hour. I asked her to tell me all the details left out of our previous conversations, obscure knowledge, public and private, personal and business. Unnoticed, Meeah had watched Elliot's actions, trying to figure out things he might not have wanted her know. She had knowledge of things that had my head spinning in circles. She just did not know what his actions meant. My grandmother said, "Knowing what you know and knowing what it means are two different things." What Elliot had been doing, and what he might be involved in, went deep into a world Meeah knew nothing of.

I took notes and tied ends together. Elliot's world was deep, dark and full of webs of deceit. It was no wonder when Meeah first told me about *her husband* Runway, and I didn't put two and two together. She never mentioned his motorcycle enterprise and that might have caused me to ask more questions early. His world had grown to heights way beyond expanding motorcycle dealerships. He was involved in importing art, liquor, cars and motorcycles from Russia and other places.

Meeah recounted to me her early travels with him to many places in the U.K. and Russia and the people he kept company with. Often she was sent to another room while Elliot and these business people talked. Nevertheless, she would listen from other rooms and in a naive way, she knew that Elliot might have been doing something illegal, like tax evasion.

I listened to her tell me what she thought, and she even threatened him by informing him at one time she knew he was skipping out on import taxes. She thought that would make him stop playing and humping around with other women and make him pay more attention to her and Mia.

Instead, he laughed her off and became abusive and threatening. She took time to complete her story about taking too many sleeping pills. In one of Elliot's abusive nights, she found herself feeling very depressed. She just wanted to go to sleep. That one night sent her life into a downward spiral. This explained the full force of Elliot's arrogance in taking away any control she might have. All the legal things that happened to take the school and Mia away from her were really being done in order for him to keep doing whatever he had going on.

She thought Tamara's participation in all this was because Elliot had convinced her it was the best thing for everyone. But she also thought her mom may not have liked how far it had gone.

I had homework to do. I thought I knew what was really going on, and what I needed to do about it.

"Meeah, you keep doing what you're doing, baby. I'll be back up there soon to see you, really, I mean soon, in a week or two, okay?" She didn't respond, there was just air on the line, until I said, "Everything will work out, baby, I do love you."

"I love you, too."

Hanging up the phone, I got a queasy feeling in my stomach. If I failed, people would get hurt; most of all Mia, and Meeah would be left with nothing. We might end up losing each other.

~~~~~

Ten days later, my motorcycle's engine was revving down the road toward Vancouver on the freeway of hope, hope that I wouldn't screw up. I'd done my research and made a plan, even though I had to keep changing it as I received more information. I wasn't changing lanes anymore, I was accelerating toward an end.

I had talked to Meeah every night, and one thing was for sure: she believed in me now. When I first left from her place, I had to keep reassuring her everything would be fine. Now she had verbally been letting me know she had faith in me. I was hearing the things that keep a man and a woman together, believing in each other.

I passed by the state patrol going over the speed limit. He didn't pull me over and I kept going the same speed. I had a mission of risks and sacrifices ahead. Meeah didn't know much of my plan, because she needed to be focused on one thing: getting Elliot to come to town.

I had made some professional and some non-professional contacts to help me in my quest. To find out what Elliot had been involved in, I had to enlist others to help. However, that could lead to risk for them. So I had to make it their cause, too, and I had to make it worth it for them.

Riding along, my thoughts bounced around in my helmet. Slow traffic at times broke my concentration. Once I was clear of traffic and cruising down the highway again, I continued to have a conversation with the walls of my helmet. My conversation was interrupted again, a hostile chill making me shake in my hot riding leather, when another rider pulled up alongside me. A black man of extremely dark hue nodded to acknowledge our bond as motorcycle riders and brother riders. At the same time, I nodded, it hit me, he resembled Elliot behind his helmet, although I knew that was not him on that motorcycle. My BMW had a custom race built motor with a turbo. I used the extra horsepower to race away from my fellow brother rider after he rode next to me for only a minute or two. I couldn't take it; I was freakin' inside my helmet. He might have thought it was odd that I would speed away from him so fast. Life for me had become real odd.

My motorcycle was loaded down with clothes and other things I might need. I knew it would prompt the border folks to ask a lot of questions if I wasn't lucky. I wasn't lucky. The Canadian border patrol had me pull over at their inspection station, and they took a look at everything I had. I hoped it was not a sign of things to come. The fellow brother rider looked over to me and gave me a look that might have said, "That's what you get" as he passed through the border without a problem.

I had booked a room at the Rivera Hotel, the place of my greatest heartbreak. Everything must change. The hotel was on Robson Street, which had become the place to be. Crowds of shoppers filled blocks of shops and eateries. Anything and everything from high dollar quality to giving away your good money for cheap tourist crap was on that people-burdened street. Traffic lights and cars impeded me. I wanted to get to my room and let Meeah know I was back and then take a nap.

It hurt staying in that hotel again. The memories were painful but it was something I had to do.

I had to kill an old demon, and facing haunted ground was a start. I wanted to wipe away the emotional bloodstains left splattered on the walls.

Chapter Twenty-Three

I ordered my second Canadian beer while waiting for Meeah to show. She was thirty-five minutes late. Maybe she had some late customers. Fifty minutes later, I called her private line at the gallery.

"Hello." I listened to the voice say "hello" twice before I hung up. There was no mistaking who answered. Elliot's deep French accent was just as recognizable as it always had been. I ordered a shot of tequila and another beer. My plan was in effect, but I got that queasy feeling again. He needed to be here, but I wondered was he forcing himself on Meeah. Damn!

~~~~

I should have been too nervous to sleep, but after three, or maybe was it five, shots of tequila and three beers I was drooling on my pillow. The phone rang. The clock-radio said it was 1 a.m. I didn't say hello into the phone, just waited to hear a voice.

"Babe, it's me, I'm sorry I couldn't meet you for dinner, I was…"

"I know Elliot was at your place."

"I know."

"You know, I know, you know. He answered your private line, you know, the one that's in your upstairs room." Her silence became eerie so I spoke again. "Just be straight with me and tell me where we are."

"Tylowe, I was not home when he came here." She spoke with a few deep breaths between her words. "Look, Tylowe, I got him to come here like you asked. Now you're going to have to believe me, I wouldn't have anything to do with him.

"How did you get him to come?" I was trying to maintain an even tone in the midst of all the liquor swirling in my head. I had awakened with a bit of an attitude.

"I called him and told him I was over on the north side by his dealership and said I thought I saw two of his mechanics or at least two of his female freaks in his blue mechanic's uniforms, riding crazy. I knew he would hate to hear that. He's so anal and such a control freak. You know that."

"Yes, I know.

"My mom told me to come take Mia out. I told you she lets me spend some time with Mia every once in a while. That's where I was, okay? And with him being in town, I really should spend all the time I can with her."

"You're right."

"I thought about bringing Mia to my dinner date with you, but decided otherwise. I don't want to confuse her, with her father being in town and then seeing you, too. I think that would be too much for her to comprehend. That might lead her to say the wrong thing, at the wrong time, in front of the wrong person. I can't let her get hurt, Tylowe."

"Okay, all right, we're in deep here. I have to ask where is…"

"Tylowe, I will not let him touch me ever again. Besides, he doesn't want me. I don't please him, remember? He's got wanna-be porn star pussy waiting for him all over this city." Her voice sounded like she had tasted something awful. "Most of all, Tylowe, I would never sleep with him. I love you, I want to be with you; yes, we are in deep."

"So you don't know where he is?"

"Not here." She was losing patience.

"I have to ask for other reasons, Meeah. I need to stay on top of everything."

"He came by when I was not here. Ms. Lynn left me a note saying he came here, walked around and left. She would not try to stop him from looking around and I wouldn't want her to. He left a note giving me a number to call."

"Would there be anything around that dropped information into his hands?"

"No, I left nothing here for him to see. I told you he comes here acting like he owns everything, so I leave nothing for him to think about at any time."

"I really wanted to see you earlier, but in time. Baby, you've done a good job of getting him to come here. Now Saturday night at around 7 p.m., I need you to get him to meet you at the Sho-Jo art gallery on Kingsway Street. Maybe you could tell him there is a painting or something there you think he might want to buy. Then while you're there, spend time away from him. Like maybe keep going to the bathroom, or talking to others away from him."

"Why? What are you going to do?"

"I'm going to help him with his image and let his nature follow its course. Hopefully it will lead him in the direction I want him to go. You know he thinks he's God's gift to women. And for now that's all I want you to know, okay?"

"Well, Tylowe, you need to trust me and I trust you."

"It's all good. I'll page you from now on. Oh, I almost forgot, Meeah, Sunday night I need your mother to be out of the school for a couple of hours. I need for you to make it happen."

"Let me get this right: you want me to get Elliot to come to Sho-Jo Art Gallery Saturday night and my mom to be out of her place for a couple of hours Sunday night?"

I repeated what she had said earlier. "You trust me and I trust you."

"Image, huh? I don't understand how his image is going to change things for us to be together. I know you want revenge for the pain he caused you, and I want to be free of him, but…"

"Meeah, listen, baby, he gets what he gets and we get each other. Yes, there is some underlying shit behind all this, but we will have everything we should have always had."

"Which is what?"

I did my best Luther Vandross singing imitation. "It's love. Now let's fight with all we got, it's too late to turn back now."

She laughed. "You must be sleepy; singing, if that's what you call it, and what you just said is plain corny."

"Yes, I'm sleepy, and you're in love with my corny ass, right?"

"Yes, I am. Now go to sleep, baby. Good night."

After we hung up, I wanted to call Meeah back and have her come to the hotel, but I played it safe. I could see us making love out on the balcony with her gripping the rail while we enjoyed the view of the harbor at night. I lay there in bed dreaming about her feel, her scent, her everything. My body was begging for her, but my hands could not come close to her touch. I went to sleep frustrated, but with only a plan in hand.

Chapter Twenty-Four

I finalized my plans by calling all my contacts the next morning while eating breakfast. I didn't have coffee; I didn't need any more jitters. I had so many things going on it was like preparing a ten-course meal of activity. The kitchen was hot, and being mentally sharp was paramount to keeping me from burning down the house.

One of my contacts was Ms. Julia from The Blue, The Black and Tan Nile Café. She was more than happy to help Meeah. I had talked to her several times while I was back in Seattle. As I felt when I first encountered her, she was filled with knowledge. Ms. Julia helped with some very interesting information about strange things that happened at the school. Very troubling to her was an African man, Elliot, who was in her words, "Not noble, not honorable. He does not know how to love a queen."

The information she had was some of the biggest help in my operation. If Elliot was doing what I thought he was doing, I knew he could be a danger to anyone standing nearby.

I headed out for a meeting. My agent-lawyer had connections in Canada and knew some people who could help Meeah with her legal entanglement. My agent set up a conference call to a law firm in Vancouver that could handle complicated business deals. One of the main partners in the firm was a gentleman named Rockwell Barker. He was intrigued with the story I told him. I felt he was interested in me as a person, too. That was important to me, given how much was on the line. Before we got into a lot of detail about Meeah and her legal issues, we had a conversation about life in general. He gave me the impression of someone with a high I.Q. who was not into showing off his intelligence just for the hell of it.

I walked through huge frosted-glass doors and across a marble floor on the thirty-second floor. Rockwell Barker was waiting for me. He looked like a young fifty in a jogging suit and had the look of an ex-jock.

"Mr. Dandridge, I'm glad you made it. If you hadn't, I'd be stuck golfing."

"Stuck?" I laughed. "I'm glad to see you in person, Mr. Barker." We shook hands.

"Hey, call me Rock, that's what my friends call me, and yes, stuck is the word. I do the golfing thing because it's about all I can do with the old knees will let me do. So I act like it's a sport and lose money betting per hole against my hacking friends."

I laughed. "Meeting with me did you double duty!"

"Meaning what?"

"Well, you don't lose any money on the golf course today and you make some money by taking my case." We both laughed.

He showed me to his office. The old school song You're Still a Young Man by Tower of Power was playing.

"For the record, sometimes a case comes through our office that we feel is more than a money maker. This is one of those times, Mr. Dandridge. We will not be charging any firm fees, just outside costs. We'd like to be about what's right, and when we can, we want to change what is wrong in this world.

"Call me Tylowe."

"Also, Tylowe, we at this firm try to benefit our standings in the city. The firm that represented Meeah's husband has a dubious rep. We've come against them in the past and underestimated their way of applying the law. We have a chance to expose them and help you and your lady friend."

"All I want to do is help the woman I love. If you guys make other things happen, well, I guess it's good for everybody."

"Now, as we discussed about your friend Meeah, I have good news, only if..." He stopped in mid-speech, pressed his lips tight and looked over his eyeglasses at a document.

"Good news if what?"

"Well, good, but slick lawyers may have put her in a bind as far as her mental health was at one time, but they have not stayed current on her evaluations. She was admitted for an accidental overdose of sleeping pills and it was not proved to the court that she was acting irrationally. So she can have removed any court orders if we can provide new evaluations. I have the right people already setting up all the ins and outs of that part. Would she submit to our doctors evaluating her?"

"Yes, I'm sure she would, but you make it sound like there are other issues."

"Nothing is as easy as it sounds. If Meeah is as competent as you feel she is, then there will be no problem having the court return the custody of her daughter to her. There is no record of Meeah being a bad mother, and she is living within the mainstream of society."

"Then what is the problem?" I was a little rattled, and I guess I was showing it.

"Listen, Tylowe, stay calm. The problem we may have is having her financial holdings returned to her and the school. Without Mr. Piste giving up his rights willingly, we are in for a court battle, unless he is committing crimes involving the school. Even then, it's no slam-dunk. The financial situation could get nasty."

"Nasty it will be, just like he likes it."

"What are you saying? I don't understand what you mean."

"Just thinking out loud. Could you have all the documents ready for him to sign if he doesn't want to go to court?"

"You sound so serious, Tylowe!"

"I am!"

"I'll have them ready by Monday at the end of the business day. Tylowe, please don't resort to any violence or threats upon Mr. Piste. I can't support you in those kinds of actions."

"Rock, in the States we have this saying: 'It's all good.' Trust me, life is too short for me to end up in somebody's jail."
We finished our business and went down to a lounge on the ground floor to have a beer. While there, Meeah called me on my cell. I told her the good news about her legal freedom being on the near horizon. The part that mattered the most to her was Mia being with her full-time, and she was ready to talk to any doctor right now.

"Baby, I need you to act cool until the time is right, and you will know when."

She said okay and told me she had Elliot ready to meet her at the gallery that night. I reminded her of what to do, but added she should bring Ms. Julia with her as an escort.
"Tylowe, I hate that you're this close and I haven't seen you yet. When will I see you?"

I heard Meeah's playful yet desirable voice and felt I should respond, but I still had the lawyer sitting next to me. "Hold on a second, babe," I turned to Rock. "Rock, I'm sorry, I have to go out in the hall to finish this call."

"No, no, hey, I'm headed out. We'll talk Monday,"

"Okay, we'll talk Monday." We shook hands and he left.

"Meeah, I'm back. Baby, we'll be together soon. I miss you so, so bad, too."

"Keep talking to me so that I know this is real. I want this dream to never end."

"Meeah, write this down:

Clear to me you are the life in my world
Much of that life rests in my heart
So waking
Seeing you or not seeing you
Brings no fear
The morning haze clouds my vision
Yet you are a beacon of light, leading me to places I need to be
So blessed to be with you my dear
No matter where you are
I am nearer to you than the air we breathe

"Believe in that. I have to go now. You do your thing tonight. Call Ms. Julia."

"I love you."

Ms. Julia would help be my eyes for part one of my plan. She would report to me in order for part two of my scheme to take place. I would be at my hotel room setting up another part of the plan.

I felt smug about what I had set up and the possible outcome. Knowing a snake can peel out of its skin but is still a snake, I felt I had Elliot by his balls, if a snake had balls.
I set up by 7:30 p.m. and waited for a phone call. At 9:30 the phone rang.

"I believe he is true to his degenerate ways. I saw him being tempted by the poison fruit."

"Thank you, Ms. Julia, I'll talk to you tomorrow." I waited a while longer. The phone rang again at 11:05 p.m.

"Meeah, baby, I need to keep this line open. We'll talk soon, okay? I'm glad you're home. Get some sleep." Ten minutes later the phone rang again.

"All right, be safe, have fun and keep your head high, and no one will know it's you. As much as possible let your friend do all the work." Everything was in place. It was happening, it was coming together; the freaks were coming out at night.

Chapter Twenty-Five

At 8 a.m. there was knock on my room door. I answered. Suzy Q walked by me and slapped my butt as she passed by.

I said, "Yuck, don't touch me after touching Elliot's nasty ass."

"Oh, I can't get a hug after I did some dirty work for you? And I mean dirty." We laughed, we hugged and she handed me the videotape.

"Oh, you had some pleasure with your work." She stuck her tongue out mockingly. I said, "Ooh, keep that in your mouth. I don't know where you been putting that."

"Put the tape in, silly, and you'll see."

The plan had worked.

While at the art gallery, Elliot's charm caught him in a trick bag. I had set it up so that my friend Suzy Q and a friend of hers would seduce him into a freaky human sandwich. I slid the tape into the VCR. I placed a video camera the night before in the same room where he had done me wrong twelve years earlier.

Ms. Julia called and said he was flirting with Suzy Q and a funny-looking lady friend at the gallery. Suzy Q was waving a nasty finger his way and he wanted to sniff. She told him she and her friend were staying at the Riviera Hotel.

A hidden camera was waiting for him in the room. I went down and turned it on right before they got to the hotel when Suzy called and said he was following them to hotel. Right away, I could see on tape why Suzy Q would say I would find it very interesting. Interesting was an understatement. A woman at least two inches taller than Elliot was all over him, taking off his clothes and going down on him just as soon as they got in the room. That meant she had to be 6-foot-5 and she had flat sandals on, not heels. Plus, this woman was ugly!

"Suzy, where did you find this friend? I'm glad you and me didn't party like this."

"Stop, that's not nice. That's my friend, Lenora. She's a nice girl who likes a party when she can get in on one."

"When she can get in on a party is right! I've seen better faces on iodine bottles, skull and cross bones. I can't watch this, anyway."

"You need to keep watching. This is better than you wanted. Just wait or fast forward."

I pushed the fast forward button. "Suzy, I hope you didn't have to let him in you, and I see you kept your face out of this, but you do have a nice butt when it's naked and not tackling me."

"I'm glad you like, but, nah, I didn't have to do too much. Plus, I don't like a man in me all that much; I'd rather be the one leading the charge. Anyway, no matter what I wanted, Elliot found something more interesting, as you can see." Suzy started laughing crazily while looking at my expression.

"Shhhh…it, it's a maaaaan!" Elliot was fully engaged with a he-she and deep into it, so to speak. I stopped the VCR and hit eject. "I'm not having breakfast this morning. I knew he was a freak, but this is more than I bargained for." I stood there shaking my head and chuckling. "I know he doesn't want anyone to see this, especially his investors and board members."

"Who knows? Maybe they're into all that."

"Maybe, but there are some straight-laced public figures, some important people Elliot is dealing with, and no way in hell do they want to deal with this."

"Sounds like your plan is working. Now you're going with me to the folks for breakfast, right? I told my dad that you needed to talk to him. Oh, by the way, my dad thinks he remembers you when you played football back in the day." She kept giggling in front of me and covered her mouth for a second and looked up at me with a sheepish grin. "Oh, Lenora's real name is Leonard."

"What's so funny?" I said

"You did tell me you and Elliot were roommates back in college, right?" She popped me on my butt again and headed for the door.

I said, "Don't even think some bullshit like that. I like mine soft and wet, not hard or limp with an ashes' butt."

"Okay, okay, I was just teasing," she laughed as we walked out the door.

"Hey, remember I got your butt on tape here being a freak. Don't make me blackmail you with your own folks."
"Shit, honey, I tell me mum everything I do. I think I get my nature from her. Mum thinks it's so romantic about you and Meeah; she's going to like you."

"What about your dad?"

"My dad? Hell, he's all about his Dudley Do-Right job, sports and women. I catch him looking at women all the time."

"Think he plays around?"

"Hell, no. He may work for the law, but me mum's the real law. She'd kill him with his own gun."

"Where the hell are you taking me? I do want to come out of there alive."

"They're good people; it's just that dad wanted a boy, and since I act like one, he's starting to accept my lifestyle."

"Hey, Suzy, thanks for helping me out like this. I'm sure when you said if I ever needed anything just ask, last night was not on the list of things you had in mind."

"Hey, I got my freak on watching and ordering the both of them around. You didn't see the part where I broke out the whips."

"Damn and I slept through all that."

"I told them to bite the pillow, no screaming."

"You're all right with me."

"I want to be there for you to help it happen."
I gave her a return slap on her butt before I handed her a helmet and we got on my motorcycle.

She said, "Is that the kind of slap on the butt, like when guys play sports and they're doing their bonding thing?

"Yeah, you can call it that."

"Yeah, it felt like it."

Suzy's parents lived about an hour outside the city. Wheeling into a huge circular driveway, we passed horses walking around what appeared to be a small track. Just like in the movies, Mother and Father were sitting out front on a huge plantation-type porch sipping tea.
I never know how people who don't look like me will react when I pull off my helmet, when I have a black face and their very white daughter is on the back of my bike.
Suzy Q's parents greeted me like family. We had breakfast, then sat around visiting and later walked the grounds. After a

while, mom and daughter went off to do a little shopping. I reminded Suzy that the motorcycle couldn't carry lamps and tables.

Dad-Dudley-Do-Right and I moved to his den; we talked and talked until there wasn't any more to talk about. He acted relaxed when Suzy and his wife were around, but that changed when they left. He was tightly wound, peculiar, suspicious and overly inquisitive. Well, he was a cop. I made headway with him by the end, and he spent time on the phone making some calls on my behalf.

The women returned, and Suzy and I headed back to the city. I had another part of my plan to enact.

~~~~~

At 6 p.m., I called Meeah. "Hey, baby, everything okay? I miss you, too. He did come by today? How long did he stay, and what did he want? He wanted to spend time with his wife? Well, did you tell him where to get off? I'm glad you were too busy to listen to his bullshit. So, Tamara, I mean your mom, will be over at your place in about hour. Oh, you're making dinner for her and Mia? Good. Can you cook? Well, we never got to that part of our relationship." We laughed and she reminded me I didn't know a lot of things about her. "I know all I need to know and, that is I love you. Call me later."

I entered the school through the front door at 7:30 p.m. I knew there were evening classes in session. Those classes started at 7 and I hoped everyone was in class and not in the hall. I needed to get in and out without being seen. If someone did recognize me I would have had to say I was here to see Tamara. But that might tip my hand if Elliot came by the school and Tamara by chance told him that she knew a Tylowe Dandridge.

I crept down the well-lit hall until I reached the room where I had borrowed the bike before. Ms. Julia said when she taught at the school, Elliot had kept the room off limits. Mia was allowed to get her bike, but Ms. Julia had gone into the room thinking there were art supplies in there for her to use, and Elliot became angry and told her to stay out. She said she thought there had to be more to the room because strange men had accompanied Elliot in there. When I was here last time, I hadn't paid much attention to the room. There was the fancy bike rack with just a few bikes, although it would hold at least twenty. I had thought it odd when I first borrowed a bike.

I was staring at the fancy bike rack and the few bikes when it caught my attention there was a floor door under the rack. A recessed, pull-up latch, accessible when you slid the rack on wheels to the side. It took some work but I uncovered and opened the door. I felt good about my private eye skills, but luck was on my side. Fifteen minutes had gone by as I walked down some stairs. I was sweating; this was mentally harder than I thought it would be. The stairs went twenty feet down into a street-level basement with darkened-out windows.

I had this little-ass flashlight that didn't provide much light but it was enough to see cars, motorcycles and many fancy bike racks a few feet in front of me. I walked down the middle of the dark floor between small narrow aisles. It was packed tight with Russian motorcycles. Why was he storing all this stuff here? If my research was right, his ass was grass and I was the big dog shitting on that grass.

At one end of the building, a huge door opened to the street. A big truck could back in; this must be on the backside of the school, a side I had not seen. I kept looking, thinking, I'd find the "Weapons of Mass Destruction," if nothing else. I made my way to the other end, seeing exotic motorcycles and a few cars. Back in Seattle, I done research on the Internet and knew Elliot was importing cars and motorcycles to the United States, but I thought more was going on. Some of his Russian investors were suspected of some serious crimes. Importing Russian motorcycles is no crime in itself, but the crime could be the reasons they were importing.

As I pointed my flashlight around a crate, knife-like eyes were staring at me. Shit! My lungs sucked air I couldn't breathe; my knees felt like there were stuck in dried cement stuck. I froze in place, but my heart was racing. I told myself "I'm not scared," but a rat is a rat, and he was a big ass rat. It was over there and I was ten feet away, and one of us needed to leave. I picked up a tire-iron from the top of a crate, it was made for changing motorcycle tires, and it was about eight inches long and looked like a slim, old-fashioned bottle opener. It was too small for me to go over there and try to hit the rodent. If I had thrown it, it might have made too much noise.

I flashed the light on and off at the rat and he crept away. I held onto the tire iron just in case. I looked at it a bit closer because it looked a little different than the type I have. It had Russian writing on it, or something I thought was Russian. It had something else on it. Something white and powdery, like baking soda. Might it be drugs? At least I wanted it to be. I didn't know what kind it was; it was never my game to be around when the "get high candy" came out. It could be cocaine, heroin, or baking powder; maybe something else. I pulled out my cell phone.

"Hello, it's Tylowe Dandridge. How do I tell the difference between cocaine, heroin and other similar substances? A bitter taste and the other will numb my tongue? Will it hurt me to taste it? Thank goodness. Yes, sir, I'll leave it. Thank you, I've got to go."

I dabbed the smallest amount on my tongue. It tasted awful. I assumed it was heroin. I kneeled down next to a motorcycle that was on a flat. I took a good look at the rim of the tire. There were more powdery traces on the rim. I squeezed the tire on the motorcycle, and it had something hard in the center of it that squeezed and separated away. The tire had been cut, and even more of the white substance came out. Elliot must be transporting drugs in the wheels of these motorcycles and cars, maybe in other things down here, too.
This was the reason Elliot kept Meeah at arm's length from having any control of the school. This was why his big money and crooked lawyers fought her. He only wanted the school to hide this poison under his own daughter's bed; well it's under the school and living quarters. He had to go. Did Tamara know what was going on? I had to believe no way.
I put the tire iron back and got back to the stairs when the street bay doors made a noise as if they were opening. My ass jumped

over almost all the stairs; I closed the door behind me, put the bike rack back and got the hell out of there.

Chapter Twenty-Six

I rode my motorcycle along the shore drive seawall before I returned to the hotel. My adventures as secret agent man had my brain running figure eights from information overload. I started back to my room, but stopped and walked across the street to the Five Star Hotel. At the top of the hotel was a lounge in circular revolving room with a panoramic view of the city. I sat at a table by the window and watched the city view change in slow motion. I ordered a beer even though I really didn't want a drink. The lounge took almost an hour to go all the way around, and I had not finished the beer by the end of the first circuit. I had calls to make. Some of the calls I wanted to make, and some I didn't; my stomach bubbled with anxiety. I was changing the lives of people who mattered to me and a person I used to care about as a friend. Now that I had the upper hand, I started having second thoughts. Was I doing the right thing?

No doubt little Mia should be millions of miles away from this madness, for what lies underneath where she sleeps. That was one reason I had to do the right thing. I sat there disoriented from my realizations. I was so gung-ho to do Elliot in even before I actually had seen with my own eyes the dirt he was doing. He could spend most of the rest of his life in a six-by-nine cement box with bars because of my sleuthing efforts.

Another hour, another half a beer, far from drunk but my head was spinning around and around, and I kept sitting there watching the city blinking at me. I asked myself a few questions. Why was my ego not satisfied like I thought it would be? And why is it that revenge does not feel sweet?

Mentally exhausted, three hours later I headed for my room. I skipped taking the elevator and walked every stair on my way up to the eleventh floor; I needed more time for my soul to become at peace with my mind. I ran some bath water. Hot water and hot times; letting everything soak in might let some things float away.

Men are known for holding in their emotions in front of others in most cases, but we cry. My tears rolled, dropped, dripped and plopped into the hot water of the bath I'd drawn. I was naked beyond naked. I was in love and had really been missing love in my life more than I ever knew. Though I had known love before, it had slapped me harder than a whale's tail. But, Meeah had made me feel that being in love for even one moment makes life worth living. She had touched me and reached past my guard with her need for love and the ability to give it. Yet, what I was going through to have her love, putting another man in harm's way, caused me pain. After the bath water became colder than my tears, I climbed out. As I dried off in front of the mirror, I noticed lines across my forehead, worry lines.

A knock on my room door made the lines ease. Her smile, her pretty-brown eyes, the faint brown freckles on the bridge of her nose; my pretty woman had come to see me. I couldn't take being without her another second; I needed her. She came over just as soon as she could after I called.

I opened the door naked and still slightly wet. I pressed my body against her tightly to let her feel me through her clothes. As I stood back to look at her again, she started to remove her clothes without taking her eyes off of me. We watched each other until she was able to press her naked body to mine.

I walked backward away from her and she followed. In the bathroom, again I started to shave my head. Meeah teased me with her fingers. She finger-painted my body, reaching between her legs and deep inside her own wet flesh. She then painted my lips, too. She rested her chin on my shoulder and her naked body pressed against my damp skin. She took the razor from my hand and began to shave white lather off my copper dome. At a turtle's pace, she caressed my head with the razor stroke after stroke. She was removing stress and stubble. We moved about each other without saying a word. Even though I was silent, she knew I needed her there.

After she had finished shaving me, she applied cocoa butter lotion to every nook and cranny, every curve and crevice. After she finished catering to my body, she sat on the bathroom vanity. I watched her body double in the mirror. It was double vision of a woman, a good woman, as good as a woman can get.

She sat sideways leaning against the mirror. Her inner thigh was over the edge of the sink. Her other foot was on the floor. She pushed up on her toes to help spread her legs wide. With her eyes locked with mine as she smoothed shaving cream between her thighs like frosting on a cake. Her lathering motion escalated my body standing at attention.

She stared at my body reacting. Her hips slowly rolled and switched around. Her mouth opened in a perfect circle as she ran her tongue to the edge and around. Her breathing was silent but deep.

More blood rose from my feet and injected into my pelvis area. It was pure excitement watching her breasts go up and out, making her nipples scream, "suck me." With a hand full of lather she wrapped her hand around my dripping erection, and pleasure tortured me. A long, clear, thick stream of life oozed down onto her thigh and it rolled down her leg, and then stretched into a long stream onto her toes. I moved in closer, resting my squirming ball sac on Meeah's leg.

Releasing the head of my penis, she cupped and caressed my balls. Then she reached for the razor and held it up for me. I knew what she wanted. Slowly pulling myself out of her cupped hand, I turned the water on and adjusted the temperature until I had it just hot enough.

She tilted her pelvis forward and up, and I began to shave her. Every time the warm water ran over her inner thighs, her body shook. Her nipples extended a bit and became rounder and firmer. Now I could hear her breathing hard. I finished shaving her smooth as a baby's butt. I rinsed her thoroughly and dried her completely. Every time I finger tested to make sure she was dry, my finger came back slippery wet.

She spoke in a whisper, "Can I make that your regular job?"

"Hey, this is a nice job to have. I'll be all over it, sweetheart. "

We made it to the bed.

"Baby, put it in now!"

"I will, baby, but let me taste it first. Let me lick that sweet juice."

"Ooh, babeeee, please, I need to feel you. Now. I need you close, in me close, please!"

"Okay." I still went down on her and licked the kitty, like a cat licks his paw for ten, twenty, thirty seconds just to watch her squirm. Then I slid deep inside her hot tasty wetness with one motion. Spreading inside her, while embracing her body, we lay still. We just needed to be as close as we could get.

Three minutes or so passed and we were still lying still, with her nails lightly pushing into my ass; she slapped my ass hard.

"What's that for?"

"Because you cheated and didn't put it in right away when I asked you to. Now move that ass!"

My hips waved into her like the ocean rushing in, and I rolled my hips up and almost out of her freshly shaved kitty. She joined me and soon we were like a full moon high tide rushing in and splashing on the shore. We turned into athletes and our hips quickened. I was hitting deep and hard inside her. Grunts matched our drive, as I lifted her legs and pushed her knees down next to her breasts. We became nose to nose as I kept hitting deep inside her. Meeah's eyes opened wide with each deep thrust; our pupils locked, we looked into the eye of the storm that was in us.

Her hand pulled our heads closer and, lips locked, we both opened wide. Our tongues danced a nasty dance. We let lusting hunger drive us to a place we could feed our needs. I felt my balls slamming against her rear, while her hand reached between us, and she found her clit. I felt her hand vibrate against my pelvic hair. Her legs jerked, and her toes curled and feet shook. I spread her legs even wider and lifted my chest up and humped fast. I found the right place, the right pace, I started to feel pressure building; we were almost there with jungle-drum intensity. The vibrations increased from her fingers on her clit. A hissing sound from her mouth sounded like a tire going flat.

My hips slowed to a stop for a long second, followed by short, light thrusts. I released my pleasure pressure liquid into Meeah's inferno. I growled and then whimpered.

Meeah tucked her chin into her neck and her face grimaced in intense orgasm. Her teeth clamped and a long lung full of air escaped through her nose. Her face relaxed, but her body jerked a few seconds. I wrapped my arms around her tight; it felt like she was melting in my embrace.

I was still moderately hard and thick inside her. I waited for my hardness to dissipate and then rolled us onto our sides. Her eyelashes closed against my neck like a gentle kiss.

An hour or so later she lifted her head and reached for the nightstand light and clicked it off. Our lips met in the dark; we kissed, filling our need for more emotional closeness. Still not sleepy, we talked all through the night or we made love again and again, not with our bodies, but with the things we said from our hearts.

Chapter Twenty-Seven

After breakfast in my room, she left with the last of the plan in full detail. She gave me many mental ego strokes for being a man with a plan. It made me reflect on my life of many successes, not just the failed attempts at success in finding a lasting relationship. Meeah made it real clear we both had found what the lonely dream was made of.

"Tylowe, every woman would want a man like you. You're laying it on the line in each one of the moves you make for me and Mia. I will do all I can do for you and me forever. I will be there for you no matter what. I believe in you."

She gave me Elliot's cell phone number. A twisted knot cramped in my stomach. My first choice was to contact him face to face, and if that weren't possible, I would call him. If I had to call him, I wanted to call him from his place of legal business, instead of using his cell phone number. I didn't want him to ask how I got his number. So calling from his motorcycle shop would make it seem like I was looking him up. Maybe he would be there; if he were in, I'd have to act like it was good to see him just to get him to do what I needed. I rode my motorcycle over the Lions Gate Bridge to the north side of the city to E P European Motorcycles, the property Elliot and I once looked at for his business when we had been friends.

I wanted to fool him into a meeting at the lawyer's office later. I'd tell him we had an old college teammate who works there, and we could surprise him. I was sure he would be stunned to hear from me. He might even think I had finally forgiven him for the dirt he threw on me that will never wash off.

From the time he ruined my life with Renee and until now, I always kept in mind that a man will make many mistakes in life; he will hurt and sin against others in many ways. Within a man's life span he hopes to be forgiven, but that can only happen if he has risen above his past weaknesses.

Elliot's crimes of erotic selfishness and an immoral lifestyle were what had led to his fate. Who knows, he might even have wanted to apologize for the past. It would be way too late; his grass was way too brown to turn green ever again. But I could act like it was cool for a minute, and let him brag about his business and his life. He would not have a clue about what I knew.

I turned into the parking lot and was greeted by an employee as I dismounted.

"Hello, welcome to E P European Motorcycles," a woman said. "I can tell by your custom racing exhaust and the rumble of the motor you have a custom BMW high-performance motor on your bike."

"Yes, I have one of the few BMW racer motors being ridden on the street."

"You're from the States I see. Are you here to order some custom parts? We have one of the largest inventories in existence of high-performance racing and custom parts for your bike."

I took a closer look at the woman. Her blazer jacket said her name and that she was the sales manager. I scanned her face and thought I knew her.

"No, I'm here to talk to Elliot Piste. Is he in?"

"No, but he might be in later. Do I know you? We've met before, haven't we?"

"Well, you do look familiar, but I can't recall from where." I looked at her nametag again. Her very large breasts made her nametag almost lay flat like on a table. Then I realized she was the young girl from years ago who was the waitress at the marina where Elliot and I had stopped while we were out riding. She was not a young girl in the looks department anymore, but she still had her best assets, and that was the reason Elliot had taken notice of her in the first place.

"How long have you been working here?"

"Oh, I've been here ever since we opened twelve years ago."

"Did you start out as the sales manager?"

"No, I started out as information desk receptionist." I smiled and held back a laugh.

"Is it possible to phone Elliot?"

"You're a personal friend?" she asked as she led me inside; there was a huge poster of Elliot with blurred motorcycles going by. He had no shirt on and his sweating back was exposed. It was hanging over the receptionist desk.

"Yeah, we go back a long way. He will be surprised to see me. That big black-and-white photo over on the wall of him over there?"

"Oh, yeah, we all love that picture of him after a race, peeling out of his race leathers and standing by his bike."
"Well, I took that picture of him about twenty years ago."

"Oh, wow, you guys do go back a ways." She dialed a number and spoke into the phone. "Hey, boss, you have an old friend here... the one who took the photo of you racing back in the day... Well, stupid me, never asked his name. " She handed me the phone.

"Elliot," I hesitated for a two count before I said, " It's me, Tylowe."

"Tylowe?" His deep French accent turned my stomach for the second time that week. "Tylowe, my Tylowe? Well, well, my old friend, you're at my motorcycle dealership? You're in Vancouver. It's been a long time. How are you?"

"I'm doing fine. Hey, an old college teammate of ours is also in town. We should meet. Can we meet at 3 p.m.?" I was not about wasting time with him.

"Yes, I'd be glad to meet you. Frankly, I'm very surprised to be hearing from you. You know I tried for many years to..." I cut him off.

"Hey, that's in the past. Here's the address. I'll see you at 3."

"Who is our old college friend? Good timing. I really don't spend a lot of time here in Vancouver."

"Oh, it's one of the guys, and he wants to surprise you. And, yes, I guess I am lucky you are in town."

"Yes, my friend, it will be good to see you again."
"Yeah, I'll see you later." I hung up in a hurry. I left in a hurry. A hurry to go somewhere, where didn't matter. I just needed to move fast in any direction.

~~~~~

I sat with Rockwell, on the thirty-second floor in a meeting room. We had been there since 2 p.m. He was reconfirming some details and making a phone call; timing was everything.

At 3:10 p.m. Elliot walked through open double doors. He looked the same, but had a question mark on his face. He looked at Rockwell to see if he recognized him as the teammate from the past.

"Tylowe, good to see you, ma man." He walked toward me, and I wasn't sure if I was going to shake his hand or let him hug me. Just then Meeah walked in from the other room where she had been waiting.

"Come on in, baby," I said. Tamara walked in behind her. She had a shocked look on face. She had been waiting with Meeah in the other room, having been misled. Mia was at the gallery with Ms. Lynn. Tamara had been told another woman from her husband's past life wanted to turn over some of his artwork for a small fee. It had happened in the past. Then when the time was right she would see what was really up.

"What is this? How do you know Tylowe?" Elliot spoke to Meeah, but I spoke to him and Tamara.

"You two need to sit down," I said. My words were met with stunned silence. Rockwell asked them to sit again a moment later. Tamara sat down, but Elliot split his glares between Meeah and me. As I sat down across from Tamara, Meeah came and sat down next to me. The table was long and oval; it took up a lot of space. Space was needed; tension brewed. Elliot still kept standing on the other side of the room.

"Mr. Piste," Rockwell began, "apparently Mr. Dandridge has something here for you to watch. But as an officer of the court, just in case there is something said or done between you and him, like a bribe or blackmail, I can't be a party to anything unethical. So I'm leaving the room for a moment." Rockwell left the room.

"What could you have to show me, and what are you doing with my wife?" Elliot demanded. It seemed his chest size expanded. I stood and walked over to the video machine and monitor at the other end of the table. I wasn't worried about a fist fight. A few punches thrown and his ass would still be grass. Besides, I would have taken a lot of pleasure in slapping the black off of him.

"The question is, Elliot, what are you doing to Meeah, and what have you been doing to your daughter? And what are you doing, period?"

"What are these questions, and who in the fuck are you to ask me anything? Meeah, how do you know this man? If you have anything to do with this, I'll put your ass back in the loony bin."

Meeah turned her head from him, but with pride. She did not fear him anymore. Tamara's eyes went into a piercing blaze, looking like she was trying to put some voodoo curse on Elliot.

Elliot spoke loudly, like he was in control, "You are in my life trying to do what? Oh, maybe you think you can try to get even for a bad day in your life by being in my business. That must be it. This is about you leaving your woman many years ago because she was doing something freaky with another woman. I'm leaving!" Elliot announced and made like he was going to walk.

The tape started to play and the he-she and Elliot were having sex. Suzy Q, in a leather face hood, was spanking Elliot with a belt. There was full exposure of Elliot having sex with a man-wanna-be-woman. Elliot heard the sound from the monitor, and stopped in mid-stride. Tamara turned her head and, with her eyes like a welder's fire, she still had not said a thing.

I said, "Elliot, I'm not going to go around and around and fight with you. Copies of this tape will be sent to all your associates, the legal ones and the not so legal. You have one option."

He shouted, "Meeah, where do you know him from? And fuck you and your option, Tylowe. You don't know what you are getting into; stay out of my way. You and our days are long past."

"Elliot, put yourself in the here and now. That was then, this is now, and you are going to step out of everybody's life. You're going to sign over everything to Meeah and your daughter." The tape was playing, and he had to watch because I was standing next to the monitor. Tamara kept looking the other way. But she was a part of this.

She finally spoke. "He knows Meeah because of me."

"You put them together after all I have done for you?" Elliot spoke to the back of Tamara's head.

Tamara spun around in her chair and spoke to Elliot. "You have just ruined any happiness civilized people could have. At first you made it seem like it was the right thing to do for Mia, but you are no father, like you are no husband." Her statements caught me off guard. I had been thinking she was in full compliance with his past actions.

"Oh, you had no problem, old lady, when you gained control of the school!"

"I may have been partly to blame for what is wrong by thinking I was doing something right, but you are the devil, and I don't want to be a part of your sins no more. Meeah, I am sorry, my daughter."

"Tamara, how can you say you are the reason Meeah and I are together?"

"Tylowe, I know a few things about Mr. Sin over here."

"Shut up! I took care of you, old fool!" Elliot shouted at Tamara and walked toward me. We stood black iris to brown iris, I cocked my head a bit as if to say, "I dare you," and held up a writing pen. It sounded like he might have been having an orgasm on the tape that was still playing.

I said, "You need to sign." He turned and walked out of the room.

Tamara watched Elliot leave the room and started to tell her side of a story. "I knew of you, Tylowe, from Elliot getting drunk one night with my husband. They were exchanging lies and truths. They had become so drunk that they forgot I was nearby. I overheard Elliot tell of his long friendship with you and that you had helped him get his career started with the photos you took of him. I heard him tell Meeah's dad about what had happened, and without knowing you I felt sick for you.

"This woman you loved broke your heart, you trusted her to be there for you and only for you. I thought about your story and wondered did you ever forgive the woman. I wondered did you two get back together. I imagined the pain of a friend and your lover hardening your soul. I remember Elliot saying that you, the poor fool, didn't know the half of it.

"Because of your photography work being known here and there, I was able to find and follow your life. You seem to be one very interesting person. As an artist I sensed emotion that could not be explained when I saw your photos.

"It's amazing my grandbaby taught me to use the Internet and ended up contacting you. I did not think about you and my daughter connecting. But you do have magic in your soul. Mia took to you so well and so fast, and she has a mind all of her own to have what she wants, and well, here you are.

"As for me, how did I lose... I never wanted to be such a burden after my husband died. He gave everything to Meeah, and what she didn't get his whores did. He didn't leave me much except a past life of me supporting his life, the good and the bad.

"When Elliot first approached me about taking control of the school, it seemed to be the right thing to do. Then he made my baby out to be insane. I went along with his plan, but I guess even then I knew it was wrong. It just got out of control. I, I, I'm so sorry, Meeah."

Meeah got up, but did not go over to her mother; she went to the window. Tamara got up and went over and stood by her, but faced me and spoke to me.

"So many things have happened between Meeah and me and Elliot and Mia. It has been splitting me in two, but I just did not know what to do. You coming here and needing to go to the pool. I knew Mia would try to see her mother when you took her swimming." Tamara turned and faced Meeah and stroked her cheek with the back of her hand. "Baby, I knew Mia always saw you whenever I was not with her when she went out; I knew this.

"Maybe powers much greater than me let things fall into place. I did not stop Mia from going to the pool even though that meant Tylowe would meet you. I had no idea what would become of such a meeting. Tylowe, I don't know if you're serious about my daughter, if you care about her, love her or if you are just helping her because that's the kind of man you are. But I hope you don't let her down like I have."

Meeah turned and looked out the window and spoke to her mother. "You can't imagine the pain you have buried in me."

"No, my dear, but I prayed even if you and Mia ran away, the two of you would at least be happier than you were."

"I thought about running away from all of this with my daughter. But I care about what kind of life I can give her and did not want her having to hide out and live in fear of us being found."

"I know my dear. You have every right to…"

I cut them both off. "Tamara, I'm not so sure about your motivations in all of this. I'm trying to understand what part in all of this you do play. Elliot is mixed up in the criminal underworld, and it is about to take him down. It matters a whole lot what you know and don't know. You are at risk because the police are involved." Her head jerked and her eyes squinted.

"Yes, I hope for your sake you can prove you are only a part of what you have been saying. I'm in a "Catch-22" with you. Tamara, you saying you felt sorry for me when you heard what that snake and my ex-fiancée did has got me involved with Elliot again. And that has opened a wound that maybe I didn't need to open. But your drama has let me find love again. I do love Meeah no matter what, but you have been playing with our lives."

Tamara's hand stroked her own wet cheeks, and her words became slow. "Tylowe, I know nothing of anything criminal. I may have hurt and hindered my two girls, but I would not knowingly put them at risk. All that really matters is that my daughter has found the kind of love that you have apparently put on the line. I prayed so much the other night after Meeah and I had dinner. I had never seen her so happy and I knew it was love. And Tylowe, my Meeah will never hurt you."

"I don't know, Mom, if I can deal with you right now, but I want Mia with me."

"She is your daughter; she will be with you, and I will not stand in the way. If you choose to have me in your life, I will be blessed; if not, I guess it is what I was supposed to have." Tamara's Jamaican accent sounded remorseful.

Meeah reached for Tamara like her mother was a little child in pain. "You are my mother."

The big double wood doors opened. A small crowd of people walked in. Rockwell, a studious-looking lady in a black pinstripe suit, Suzy Q's detective dad, and two blue uniformed police officers holding a handcuffed Elliot between them.

The studious-looking lady spoke. "Mister Dandridge, I'm Deputy Prosecutor McCallum. You have helped solved a major drug ring with your information. We raided the basement of the school an hour ago. We are very grateful to you."

"Raided the school?" Tamara shouted.

"Yes, and I assume you are Ms. Kraft. You run the school, right?

"Yes, that is right."

"Well, you seem to be in the dark about Mr. Piste's activities. Our investigation as of right now clears you of any wrongdoing, but we will need to talk to you.

"Elliot Piste may end up spending many, many years in jail along with his criminal allies. It seems he is more than ready to be quite forthcoming with the fact we raided all of his associates' places of business throughout Canada. We have recovered a major load of drugs."

I looked at Elliot, his chin bowed so deeply into his chest it looked like he was pushing his chest into his back. I turned to Meeah; she and her mother were still holding each other, they did not want to look at him.

Prosecutor McCallum spoke some more. "Is there anything we can do for you? All the Canadian government agencies that will be involved in this matter will be eternally grateful to you, Mr. Dandridge. When your lawyer called me, he said you might have some other problems I could help with. I've known Rockwell for some time; you have chosen a good man."

"Well, I do have some issues. Could we speak in private for a moment?" She waved her finger for me to follow her out to the hall. Elliot's eyes seemed to be focused on his handcuffs as I walked by.

In the hall, I told her about the school and that it really belonged to Meeah. I let her know I thought Tamara didn't know she was being used to hide drugs. The Prosecutor agreed there was no knowledge of any involvement on Tamara's part and doubted they would be pursuing her for any charges. Most of all, I wanted all of Elliot's business holdings to go to Meeah, and not be confiscated by the government. She told me if it could be worked out she would help in any way to make that happen. The school was good for the city. The motorcycle business would have to be restructured, but she felt my lawyer could work out the details.

"I want to marry the woman inside as soon as possible, but she is married to Elliot."

"We can fast track a divorce in about a week, if they have been living apart. I know a judge who can move it up on his calendar. But if Mr. Piste contests, it could be up to a year or more. Elliot would have to sign off but I have an idea."

Elliot and I stared at each other as I passed by.

Prosecutor McCallum spoke to Elliot, "You, sir, are most likely going to spend the rest of your days in prison. If not, you're going to be a very old man when you get out. I might be willing to save you a few years. So let me get right to the point. If you were willing to give the young lady a fast track divorce, I'd be willing to work with you on a plea bargain and sentence length."

"What the hell are you doing, Tylowe? Look, what kind of man are you trying to steal my wife and daughter? When you had a woman before who liked women more than you…"

I was glad he was handcuffed. I might have been the one going to jail for choking the shit out of him.

Meeah screamed at him from across the room. "You're no kind of husband or father, you son of bitch! You had drugs underneath our daughter's roof."

He said, "So you like the flawed hero here to be a father?"

"What the hell? You call me a flawed hero? What are you on? I'm doing the right thing and always have. You still go around hurting everyone in your path."

He laughed bitterly. "You want to steal my child, and you don't even take care of your own. Oh, you hurt people, my man."

"My own?" He wasn't making any sense and a tiny chuckle escaped my lips.

"Yes, my flawed hero. You have a child, a daughter, you fool. You see, you played like such a hurt little bitch when your woman, Renee, crossed your line in the sand and had fun with my bitch." The contempt in his voice was taunting me.

I looked around the room. Meeah looked to me for an answer to Elliot's accusation. He continued with his version of my history.

"You see, she tried to tell you she was pregnant with your child, but you walked out of the room that day. You wouldn't listen to anything she had to say. Let's see, your daughter would be maybe eleven or twelve now. The saddest part of all, Mr. Hero, her mother, the woman who made you cry, died some years ago."

"How do you know all this?"

"Oh, I kept my bitch around for a while and they used to talk and she went to see her when she had the baby. And I even sent her some money because I felt sorry for her and you." He laughed a nasty laugh.

I wanted to kick the shit out of him, but now I had other concerns.

"You lie! I saw her several years ago. She was married and the child with her was not mine; she would have told me."

"Believe what you want to believe. Just think about it. If you think you want to raise my child, what kind of father are you?"

Meeah screamed at him again, "A hell of a lot better than you could ever be. Give me my divorce and go to hell! You have children all over this world that you don't care about, you son of a bitch!" Meeah headed in Elliot's direction, and I'm sure she was going to kick him in his crotch, but I stopped her and turned her back around. The room became pin-drop quiet. Meeah turned and screamed at him again.

"You didn't even take time to see Mia this time, but your sick, foul ass was doing a man in the ass and treating him like a woman." She laughed, but it was filled with pain. "I don't want your evil to be around Mia, ever. If Tylowe has a child, he will be a hell of a father, and I'll be right there with him."

The prosecutor spoke up. "Mr. Piste, you have been read your rights, and you have the right to an attorney, but my offer of a plea bargain is only on the table until you have met with him by tomorrow noon. But it is a take it or leave it deal."

"I'll sign." His chin bowed back into his chest.

~~~~~~

As people filed out of the room, Meeah and I stayed behind, emotionally drained. She rested against my back as she held me. I looked out the window as if it were a TV screen. I watched the replay of the day that I walked out on Renee. She did want to tell me something, but I wanted to hear no more from her. She hurt me, and I just thought she was going to beg me to forgive her. Maybe Elliot was lying? I changed the window TV screen to where I last saw her. Renee and a child with a man I thought was her husband. I remember thinking she had something to say, but what? The child looked like her, and I thought the child to be young; not the age of a child she and I could have produced. Elliot had to be lying.

"Tylowe, I know you're confused." Meeah's hand stroked my back. "If you have a child, I will be with you and help you through this." I heard her heart speaking through her lips. Thirty-two floors up, I felt like I was in outer space. Lack of emotional gravity had me drifting in another world.

Chapter Twenty-Eight

Two weeks later Mia was calling my name. "Tylowe, you remember when I asked you if you met the perfect woman, would you make her happy?"

"Yeah, I remember." I sat in my chair nervous because I had a question to ask.

We were sitting at dinner, the two of them with Tamara and myself.

We were taking our time and taking turns explaining to Mia about the changes that were occurring. When there was no more to say about her biological father's demise, and other related subjects, I could see she was okay; she was extremely happy she was going to be with her mother. It's what she had wanted all along. She even started calling Tamara "Grandma."

It was strange territory for all of us. Tamara had already prepped Mia before we met for dinner. I let her know we all had a lot to learn, and it might not always be easy, but I would always be there for her. Mia had got up from her seat and came over to me and nearly hugged the air out of me and said, "If you met the perfect woman, would you make her happy?"

So that's when I asked the question. "Will you marry me, Meeah? And Mia, will you let me be like a dad to you?"

Meeah's eyes widened. "Tylowe, it will take some time for all the legal stuff to be straightened out."
"It's handled. You should be able to sign most of the basic documents next week."

"Mom, say yes." Mia moved in between us, put her arms around our shoulders.
"No," Meeah said, and my eyes blinked in slow motion.

"I want to be the one to ask you. Will you marry me, Tylowe? And will you be a father to my baby girl?"

"You two, I mean you three, are so beautiful together." Tamara wept as she spoke, and the tears fell down to the cleavage between her breasts. "Please be happier than I was. I loved your father, Meeah, but he never let me be enough for him. I became bitter and things became distorted. I lost what was important, seeing my family happy." She barely got the words out.

"Ma, a lot has happened. It makes me sad how the past has been, but we have time to learn, you and me, how to be mother and daughter." Tamara continued to weep.

"Tylowe, will you marry me?" Meeah asked

"Yes, I will." Mia about squeezed our heads off. Until I knew for sure I decided not to tell Mia that I might have a daughter who would be near her age. If I did have a child, what would lie ahead? Would there be a place for me in my child's life? Elliot said Renee had died. Damn. What if he was telling the truth?

My feelings swirled in my head and my heart like dust in the wind. It saddened me if it was true the mother of my child had left this earth. It saddened me that I once loved her.

Meeah spent some time being the good woman she is by letting me know it was okay: I should feel some emotion. She told me: If ever you have loved someone, no matter how it ended, no matter how long ago, you will reflect on what they meant to you at that point and time in your life.

~~~~~

The prosecutor called two days later, and she had the information I requested. She pushed her deal with Elliot to the hilt: if he ever wanted to see the free world again, he had to give up any information he had about me having a child. She told him it had to be good information or no deal.

She had a name and an address. Simone, the woman Elliot was with many years ago and the one I found Renee with in bed. She had knowledge of my child.

She lived in Chicago; I flew out that same day. This was strictly a hands-on investigation. Meeah and Mia came with me. They were my support team, even though Mia just thought we were going on a vacation. I did call before I flew out, and an elderly sounding lady answered and informed me Simone was at work and would be home late. I did not leave my name.

We flew in and a limousine taxi took us to the address. It was late, but I could not sleep another day without knowing something.

I had Meeah and Mia wait in the taxi. I rang the doorbell of a large house in a very nice neighborhood and a man answered. The man had been with Renee the day I last saw her. I had assumed he was married to her and the father of the child I saw that day.

"Hello."

I took a deep breath before I spoke. "Hi, my name is Tylowe Dandridge and…"

"Tylowe Dandridge? Come in. You're Tylowe Dandridge, please come in." He seemed to be almost happy I was at his door. I stepped into the house, but what had I stepped into?

He spoke to me like an old friend. "The day has finally come that you are here. There is no way we would ever know when, but we thought one day you would come."

"What are you talking about?"

"Well, before we get into all that, would you like who you have in the taxi to come in? All are welcome on this happy day."

Talking about being confused, this man's happy dialogue was like putting a black hood over my head and leading me to a secret hiding place.

"Look, I'm sorry, but I'm here to get some information. I've been told that a Simone lives here. Who are you?"

His eyebrows drew close together and he smiled. He pointed for me to go around a doorway. In the living room I saw an elderly lady and Simone sitting on a couch. Her face still had its ultra-fine qualities with maturity added. When she saw me, she looked like she had just seen a ghost.

"Tylowe, oh my God! Tylowe."

"Okay, Simone, I'm here because I got messed up with Elliot again. He has gotten himself into some serious trouble with the law. In the midst of it all he has said I had a child, and you would know all about it. I came here, and I see Renee's husband answering the door like he's happy to see me. Somebody needs to clarify what's going on."

"My name is Jerome, and I am not Renee's husband." He extended his hand and I shook it. He spoke to Simone. "I don't think he knows much of anything."

"You're right. I don't know much of anything, so please tell me something." Simone came over to me and hesitantly reached to hug me. I let her.

"Tylowe, Renee passed away," Simone said. "She's been gone for about three years now. She passed away from brain cancer. You have a daughter, a very beautiful, smart daughter, and she knows all about you." Her voice choked out the words.

"Where is she, who is she living with?" My eyes were giving me a problem. I wanted to keep them dry, and they didn't want to. "This is my brother, and this my mother, Ms. Ivory."

"Good evening, Ms. Ivory. I'm sorry to enter your home like this."

"Young man, it is a very good day that you are here." The elderly woman had a British accent, and I remembered that Simone was from England.

"Your daughter is upstairs; she lives here with us." There was a long silence, and my legs felt weak, I sat down in a chair.

"Tylowe, let me tell you the story, and if you want, we can wake her up so you can meet her. She knows about you and one day she was going to come look for you, if you never... Well, you're here, so let me tell you all that has happened."

I spoke with feeble vocal chords. "I need to get someone who is in the taxi, and send the taxi on its way."

"Let me take care of it. I'll take care of the taxi and have your people come in," Jerome said. I could see now that he and Simone were related.

Simone sat across from me in a chair and started to tell me a story. Renee left the hotel as I did twelve years ago, with a broken heart that she shouldered all on her own. She never blamed me or hated me for giving up on her. She knew it was asking a lot of me to deal with the crazy maze of events of that day.

She was pregnant with my child, and she tried to tell me that day, that moment, but it was not to be. She wanted any part of me she could have. She did love me, but she just had issues with past feelings of being with a woman. She never lied to me about it, but she lived a lie by never telling me.

As she was telling me the story Meeah and Mia came in. Jerome was carrying Mia, who was asleep.

Ms. Ivory spoke up. "These people are going to stay here tonight. We have plenty of spare rooms. Take the baby up to the room next to mine, and take their luggage to the room next to that one." Meeah smiled at Ms. Ivory, and looked at me. I nodded.

Simone continued. "Renee never had another man in her life; she just lived to raise her child." At first she had hoped I would come back into her life. Then she thought it might hurt me again by having had my child and not having told me sooner. I asked Simone about the day I saw Renee with Jerome and I thought he was her husband.

"Jerome was being a big brother to Renee and an uncle to your daughter."

"What is my daughter's name?"

"Tylowe your daughter's name is, Tyreene Pearlene Dandridge."

"But we call her Pearl, and she's a beautiful, wonderful girl, too," Ms. Ivory added.

"Tylowe, what's up with Elliot? And who is your lady friend? Are they your wife and daughter?" I wanted her to finish telling me about my daughter, especially how she came to be living here. I remembered Renee was an only child and her mother and father were fairly old, so maybe that had something to do with my daughter being with Simone's family.

I told Simone the short version of Elliot and our recent history. Then I told her who Meeah was and what she was to me now. She told me that she kept seeing Elliot for some time after what happened in the hotel room that day.

"I was just stupid, just weak, thinking he was a great guy who one day would settle down and only be with me. I've put my insane times behind me. I guess you want to know why your daughter is here."

"Yes, tell me."

Simone went on to tell me how Renee could not be with another man after me. She tried and she just could never get her emotional feelings going in the right direction. Renee and Simone stayed good friends, even though for a while Renee stayed away because Simone was still involved with Elliot.

Jerome and Meeah came into the room after they put luggage away and put Mia to bed. Ms. Ivory spoke to Meeah.

"Honey, come on over and sit next to me. You're a beautiful woman." Jerome said he would get us something to drink and he left the room.

"Tylowe, you're going to hate me, but the truth is, Renee and I became lovers, real, in-love lovers. Neither one of us had what it took, emotionally, to be with a man after what we had been through. After you and Renee went your separate ways, and I had enough of Elliot's bull-crap, we needed to be needed. You may think it's just about strange sex, but we needed love, and we lived for each other to her end. She had someone to love her to her grave. I have no regrets. So hate me for what made our world go around, but that is how and why your daughter is here with me."

"I don't hate you, Simone. What will be will be."

"Amen!" Ms. Ivory's few words carried a lot of weight.

"Tell me about my daughter."

"Well…"

A sleepy young voice entered the room. "Mama Simone, I can't sleep 'cause there was noise up there." Near the bottom of the stairs stood Renee's beauty, only many years younger. It was my daughter, Tyreene Pearlene Dandridge. I looked at her in amazement. I looked over at Simone and she smiled and nodded her head. I looked at Meeah and she stood up and walked behind me and put her hands on my shoulders.

Simone said, "Let me take her back upstairs and talk to her a bit, and then you should come up and talk to her." I nodded. She walked my daughter back up the stairs, and I think I took my first breath since I had been in the house.

When Simone came back and told me what room she was in, I asked Meeah if she wanted to go up with me.

She said, "I'll do anything with you or for you, honey, but this will only happen once in your life and in her life. This time is just for you and her. This is the birth of your child, just a little delayed." She gave me a smile that pushed my confidence up a notch. It was enough to get me up the stairs.
I knocked on the door, expecting to be asked in, but the door opened and arms wrapped around me. My own flesh and blood, Tyreene Pearlene Dandridge buried her head deep into my chest. She held me like a lifeline; she squeezed me tight. I could now blame her for my eyes having that "can't stay dry feeling" again.

She spoke first. It was a good thing, because I didn't know what to say. "My mother said you might come one day, and Mama Simone said you would, too. I was going to look for you when I grew up." Looking over her head I could see on the top of her dresser, pictures of Renee and me together at different times when we were a couple.

It became apparent Renee never wanted to drive a wedge into what we had created.

"Honey, I would have come sooner if I had known." We were standing in the doorway of her room, and I walked her over to the edge of her bed and we sat.

"Mom said you might not know, Dad. Can I call you Dad? Where do you live? Do I have any brothers or a sister? Are you married? Will I have another mommy?"

"Tyreene, we have so much to talk about, but you need some sleep and I have traveled a long way today. So we will talk all day tomorrow and every day. You are just as pretty as your mother."

We sat on the edge of her bed just staring at each other. With her hair pulled back into a long ponytail, I could see me in her, along with Renee's perfection. I could see she had my widow's peak at the top of her forehead, and I kissed her there.

"Goodnight, Tyreene Pearlene Dandridge."

"Night, Daddy." Her smile imprinted itself in my eyes. When my day has come and gone, and I am laid to rest, the one thing I will see from under the ground, and through the sky, will be the memory of the first time I saw Tyreene Pearlene's smile.

Downstairs, Meeah and Simone were in conversation along with Jerome and Ms. Ivory. They all fell silent when I walked in.

"She is something else. Thank you, Simone, for helping her be that."

Simone stood and spoke with many words in between shedding tears and trying to control her nervousness.

"Tylowe, I want you to know Renee and I spoke about this day if it came; she put it in her will, and Tyreene knows. If you were to come into her life, and if you wanted to raise her, she is to be with you. I only ask that you let her be a part of my life, my mother's and my brother's. She has been a part of our family and we love her. I knew this day could come, but it shocks me so much now that it has happened."

Her last words barely made it out of her mouth before I walked over to her, hugged her and said, "There's room for all of us. My daughter seems to have a real big heart with room for all of us, okay? I do want you to know, though, I want to be with my daughter."

Ms. Ivory spoke up, "Well, everything is going to be all right. I would like to say a prayer, give thanks for this day. Someone help me, and let us hold hands and pray." We all bowed our heads and held hands, and I had my own personal thanks for all God had blessed me with.

POSTSCRIPT

Four years later, I found myself crossing back over the border again headed to Vancouver. My wife and my two daughters and I were on two motorcycles.

Meeah and I, with Tyreene now fifteen almost sixteen, as she is so quick to say, on the back of Meeah's motorcycle. On the back of mine is Mia who is fourteen now.

The girls have developed an undying love for each other. You would think they had been raised together all their lives; they are sisters in spirit and love. They honor Meeah and me as if we had been their parents from day one.

Mia, like her mother and grandparents, became a very good artist. She is a photographer with a great eye and has already won some local and national awards. Tyreene is a freshman starter on her high school varsity basketball team. And she is very good.

Happy? We are, but we have had some problems with adjustments, as expected. One of the reasons we are headed up to Vancouver from Seattle, where we live, is to see Tamara. She has suffered the last two years from some serious health issues. We make sure she gets the best medical care and keep loving her; she seems to be getting better. She lives in a very nice retirement community, where she teaches art.

Adjustments. All of a sudden, I was a man with three females in the same house. Talking about swimming in the shark tank, I'm adjusting; we have a big house, a dog and the activities the girls are involved in.

I've learned to say where I'm going, and when I'll be back, but I'm still getting used to hearing, "Take the girls with you, and pick up this and that." Oh, and now boys are calling my house.

Business is good. Ms. Julia runs the school, and in the basement of the school, we set up a free drug detox center. We had the basement remodeled into a beautiful, comfortable place to be, with one-way windows to the world to look out, but the world can't look in. Up until this time, my friend Suzy Q had been running the center for us, but today we are going to her graduation. She is graduating from the Royal Canadian Mounted Police Academy.

Income is rolling in from every direction. The school and gallery continue to flourish, and Meeah buys up-and-coming artists' work from around the world. Ms. Lynn is the manager and still part owner; Tamara helps out, with some part-time help. Sometimes Meeah and I stay upstairs in the gallery when we bring the girls up to see their grandmother. We still find a way to blow each other's mind. For sure, our love life, mentally and physically, will never get old.

The takeover of EP European Motorcycles went okay after we purged some criminals from within the business. We changed the name to "All World Motorcycle" and we carry brands of motorcycles from all over the world.

Good things have happened to me from out of nowhere, a big a deal happened. I sent a photo layout of those pictures I had taken of Mia at sunset and nighttime to Photographer's Digest. They liked what they saw and asked me to use those photos and take some more of other child models and do a photo book of pictures of children at night. It became a bestseller. I'm in demand for my work again, but I work when I want to. I have a family to tend to.

The girls fly back to Chicago to spend time with Simone and her family whenever time permits. Sometimes I go and take Tyreene to her mother's gravesite. We both have a talk with her. I tell her thanks for keeping her love for me alive through our daughter. So who knows what would have been if... well, who knows? How we handle losing love has everything to do with finding love.

So life is good. It's as if someone had painted a perfect picture of me, and all those near me now, and how we would find a wonderful life. We all paint pictures of what we want to see and feel, and the final brush strokes would be the strokes of a masterpiece.

THE END

Questions and thoughts from the Brush Strokes

1. Tylowe had shut down from the thought of being in love after he had been hurt from love. Do you feel it helped him or hurt him before he met Meeah?

2. People in the background worked for him and against him. Have you been that person on either side, and how did it workout for you?

3. A chance meeting is it fate, or do we work toward a chance meeting unknowingly?

4. Would love make you put it all on the line to make it right for someone else and for yourself?

5. Has a friend who was endeared to you been slimly and you knew it, but you excused their behavior because you felt they would not do dirt to you?

6. Tylowe had love and hurt in his heart for his ex-fiancé, what effects do you think it played in his future?

7. Tylowe also found out his ex-fiancé never stopped loving him in the end for the fact she placed her with someone who take care of his daughter until he could be located, and what she named his daughter. Do you keep love alive in ways that you can't stop loving that someone who may have hurt you, but it's hard to admit?

8. Would you have hit/punched Elliot when giving a chance?

9. Do you have that one friend who is so very different, (such as Suzy Q) and you don't care what others have to say or feel and show you no shame, and you are willing to defend who they are to anyone?

10. Can you see Brush Strokes as all-time movie you would watch more than once, as in seasonally?

About The Author

"Brush Strokes" by Alvin L.A. Horn aka Alvin Lloyd Alexander Horn, this is my debut novel.

I finished this project and headed out the door to my thirty-year high school reunion. Most of that night, old classmates asked, "Do you still write poetry?"

One classmate said, "Hey, man, I know it's been thirty years, but I'm still mad at you for writing a love letter to the girl I married. She kept asking me to write love letters after that."

I said, "Well, write her a love letter and spice up the old relationship."

"I can't because she left me for a writer a few years ago."

~~~~~

I started writing poetry and love letters back in the day, and now here is my first novel. I can say it wasn't easy. I have started three other books and life kept writing a period, and an end of that chapter in my life. Some of those chapters needed to end and others I wish never did. In all chapters of my life, I was earning a living. Other chapters had me raising a handsome son and a beautiful daughter. The chapters that rerun on in my head and heart are the long Romantic Blues verses with fine-intelligent-sexy-my-best-friend-at-the-time-almost-and-should-have-been-my-soulmates-forever-lovers.

What are the Romantic Blues? My definition is: Loving and missing someone, even if it's only a minute or a lifetime.

~~~~~

I was born in Seattle, under the bluest skies there ever were. I do love Houston, Hot-lanta, Vegas, Vancouver B.C., and most parts of California. I work in education and coach high school sports.

Oh, I have too many hobbies, but I love to cruise in my classic cars. That means I need time to restore them. I love being on my 45-foot houseboat, but that means I need time to maintain it. I should head down to Pike Place Market to buy some fresh shrimp and then sauté them in real butter, but that means I have to do more sit ups. Maybe I should play my bass, or write a love song on the guitar, or play the piano and sing a song called Romantic Blues. Nah, I need to finish writing ... But first I need to tune my motorcycle and then I have to go out for test spin.

Hope to see you online or in a bookstore soon.

~~~~~

The first thing I should have said: OUR CREATOR blesses us and we can do what we need to do with him being in our lives. Thanks, Bigmama, for keeping that truth in my ear and the word in my eyes.

Look me up on my website: www.alvinhorn.com

Alvin L.A. Horn – aka Alvin Lloyd Alexander Horn

Other books written by the Alvin L.A. Horn between the first edition of Brush Stroke and the second edition:

Perfect Circle, and One Safe Place, published by Simon and Schuster and Zane-Strebor Publishing

Books with the author's writings in compilations:

Pillow Talk in the Heat of the Night and, The Soul of a Man 2: Make Me Wanna Holler, published by, Peace in the Storm Publishing

.

For the re-release of Brush Strokes, I have added bonus. I added a short story of emotional love for to enjoy.

LOVE IN THE STORM

Chapter One

MISSING
I'm missing you
It may sound silly, but
I miss being near you, even though I have not been near you
I know you, but then again, I don't
Have I not noticed you?
I'm missing you now
Boom … boom!
Was I not supposed to notice you?
I'm ready to push everything aside
Did you look at me…with that look, and I gave you that same look back,
but time and place made us walk away?
I'm calling out to you now
Yes, I do think of you
I'm missing you
I'm missing a kiss we never had
I am missing your magic touch I never felt
It must be magic, because I'm feeling you in my dreams
I feel your
Lips so soft, so warm, so tasty, because you know how to kiss me
Cheeks touch like feathers while we whisper in each other's ear, listening
from what comes from deep within
Hands making a finger trail over my breast—your chest, and from you I
feel the earth move
I'm thinking of you from head to toe
Even though we have never met

I'm missing you
Boom ... boom!
I'm missing visualizing you moving into me and your scent
Even though we have never...made love
I'm missing you
Boom ... boom!
I've been waiting for a man like you
I've been waiting to ride alongside you
Going around the world
Maybe tasting wine in the vineyards of Spain
Maybe hiking a mountain in Kenya
Maybe riding the A-train to a Harlem book fair
Maybe strolling on the beach in Monterey
Maybe as Prince serenades us, while we sit in the front row, and Sade
closes the show by blowing us a kiss
Maybe all our dreams come true
Even though we have never met
Damn, I missing you
Boom ... boom!
But most of all I am missing hearing your voice
The voice I hear in my dreams; it awakes me to a full alarm
I'm wanting and missing you
Do you hear me calling out your name?
I don't even know your name
I'm tossing and turning in my sleep...missing you
I hope you're missing me in all the same ways too
I'll keep waiting, please keep waiting for me
Until we meet I'll never...ever...get over missing you

~~~~~

It's June, 2012

    That's the poem I wrote as Boom...boom bombs went off in February of 1991. I heard the sounds of distant scud missiles landing in the desert as I was writing in my journal. I remembered smiling into the wind, and the sweeping sand was either sticking to, or pricking my skin. I wished, and wanted, I could have gotten lost in those historical biblical lands of beauty that Christ and his disciples ventured. All the things that happened there...turned everything beautifully ugly, and dreadfully inspiring.

That was some twenty years ago.

Now, I'm flying across the country headed to the East Coast for a medical conference; and while I'm there, I will be able to do a few pleasurable things, including taking in the nightlife. I've heard of some good spoken word lounges that I want to go to, and maybe I'll even get up and read a little of my works. So while I feel the flight turbulence jostling my nerves, I'm trying to calm myself by reading my old poems.

Boom...boom, explosions of the time as I was writing poems send jolts of joy and pain that I'll never escape. I wrote to fight the fear of misguided antiquated weapons of destruction that rarely hit the target, but they hit my nerves daily.

Boom...boom, was an annoyance as I was camped in a war zone in 1991. Every once in a while, the annoyance of Boom...boom bombs hits somewhere hurtful to all of us, as the Iraqis got lucky and hit some unlucky U.S. soldier.

I was there to help, save, heal, and suffer. Helicopter turbine blades pushed hot, sticky air and sand onto my skin. I laugh, and still think my skin was sweet, but maybe a bit salty as I tried to maintain any sense of my femininity. I kept some of the hot air off of me by pinning up my hair to help me feel the slightest cooling along my hairline. It was against military regulations. I knew. I was also wearing my uniform collar wide open as if it was another minor cooling effect; but yet, it was another military regulation failure. I knew. My cleavage was exposed as if I was in a classy jazz lounge wearing my favorite black dress, but I had on thick green canvas-feeling type shirts. Yes, there was a chance I'd be written up, but the other choice was the danger of heat exhaustion. Dammit, I'm a woman, and I liked looking down in between my cleavage and seeing my chained gold cross with Jesus tucked away tight—safe.

I was far from America shores, sand fleas, and birdbath wash-ups which came along with dry skin in a tent city, war zone base. I fought to feel like a woman, and I always fought to survive with the tools God instilled in me.

Most of the male soldiers went without shirts, which was

also against regulations; but when it's hot as hell, and they're men, well...they wrote the rules. A few of the boys broke the unsanctioned military freedom, just to flaunt their boot camp All-American muscles.

Often a breeze flowed in the arid air from the compression that followed minutes after each boom...boom. A hot breeze, yes, but any breeze was welcome. The sky was a rainbow of three colors: sun hot yellow, brown, and black smoke, with the smell of burning oil turning the whites of eyes red.

Routinely, I'd go out back behind the camp about a hundred meters, and sit behind an old broke-down truck, and bow my head to pray and read my little mini Bible that I kept in my shirt pocket. I'd look to the heavens, but the intense sun was the devil to my already dry eyes.

Boom...boom.

Rotor blades would make an oncoming swirling swishing sound, signaling time to stuff my journal deep into my rear pocket so not to lose it, and I haven't lost it, I have it twenty years later. I'd take off running as helicopters would start landing, seemly seconds after every half second, as they unloaded soldiers in need of medical attention. A few soldiers flew in and flew out quickly, as they were beyond any help a medic-doctor could administer. Some flights lifted a few lifeless bodies zipped away in bags with dog tags displaying name, rank, and serial number. Chaplains sent prayers up through swirling turbine blades carrying bodies, returning living souls back to the U.S....to grieve. There were soldiers that rarely carried any weapon other than a pencil; they pushed paper to journey along with body bags. I watched and heard that long zipper noise close up the end of a life.

I didn't carry a gun. My weapons were surgical tools used to cut and sew human bodies to help fix their wounds.

"You're in the army now."

The slogan was a clear reality for me, a young female medic, at the time. I volunteered; honored to serve in Operation Desert Storm. My only comfort was that the bombs were far away, at least that's what I had been told.

Boom...boom.

Some people scrambled, most didn't, simply because they didn't know what to do. Bravery and scared actions come from the same place in the heart. When you see one action, you can mistake it for another action. Heroes can come from dark alleys of no explanation of bad people doing good things, and good people doing nothing in the mist of confusion.

TV and newspapers need heroes; but the truth is in the hellhole of life or death, it's just about staying alive. A hero is someone who lived when they should have died from their actions, or they did die from trying to live. Now, hear me when I say, if you wake up in the morning, you don't know what you will do from one moment to the next moment in the face of fear.

Another boom...boom, and I'd wait for a warm percussion-breeze to blow in from miles away into the medical tent. No matter the conditions, I would pour my heart into my job to help those in need, while trying to avoid most personal connections. Why, because soldiers die in wars. 'Catch-22', everyone needs personal connections in the minefields of not knowing who will be there one day, and maybe gone the next. Within my medical unit, I added some comfort to those in need of needing to be home; some more than others.

Boom...boom. There was no comfort, no matter how far those bombs were away. Where were the gas masks? Maybe the next bomb would have sent poisonous gas floating in with the warm breeze.

I'm smiling at my reflection in the airplane window, with the red pillow clouds as background. I was told often that my engaging personality was heighted by my outward beauty that others saw as a desert oasis in a desert that had no retreat. Yet, I refused any special treatment, because if ugly rumors spread of how I got this or she got that, it would pierce me as deep as any killing machine. The same ranking soldiers who would sex me down in some nasty tent or backroom, would cover their ass instead of protecting me.

The new army was the same as the old when it came and comes to enlisted women drawing unwanted attention, but I didn't let the males and their sexual innuendoes and flirtations, interfere with my life-saving work. Daily, young and older soldiers flirted with me, but for the most part, they kept it moving. I always tried to get them to see that they needed to show some grace and humanity in middle of all that pain, death, and destruction of the human body and soul. If shaming them into behaving worked...oh well, so be it.

If one of those boys stepped too far down into a gutter foxhole, I went militaristic on his ass, throwing verbal bombs of embarrassment that his momma would feel back in the good old U. S. of A. I ended up teaching a few soldier boys of fortune exactly what would happen if he touched the wrong triggers attached to my body, or how a bomb could go off inside me and blow his ego to hell.

Boom...boom.

Sirens screamed in the distant night back twenty plus years ago.

Chapter Two

Bobbie Rasheen is my name. I was nicked nicknamed Bobbie Pen by some GIs because I always had a writing pen in my hair, breaking a regulation. My personal regulation: I lived to breathe my thoughts and feelings on paper, and for others to hear or read those thoughts. My poetry was my survival of sanity in a crazy world. In a world that takes young men and women like me to die in wars of ignorance; but it was our honor to serve and then go back home the next day…cut our grass, play with our kids, and make love to lovers. I shake my head because none of that made sense.

I just couldn't get too close to people over there; they might not be there the next day for whatever reason. The deepest feeling I had, I just didn't want to get too close to any of the men. I had lost men in my life. It seems that all women do, is lose men. My momma lost my daddy. Well, actually, she left him when I was in the fifth grade, and that's the same as losing. She basically told me that my daddy brought home everything but a paycheck. All I can remember is my daddy loved me and played chess with me. He wrote me letters and poems almost every day, and he and I would read them while I sat in his lap. I will never understand that he didn't bring home a paycheck, because when we, I mean…when my momma lost my daddy by moving away, we were even poorer.

She never really told me about the "other things" that daddy brought home, but it might have something to do with Verdine Jackson. Momma told me, *I'm never to marry him, date him, or even think of him in anyway kind of way.* I do think he's cute, though; even to this day, and people say we look so much alike. Verdine's momma, she told him the same thing, that we are never to date; but she went even more hardcore by flat out saying that he was not to have sex with me or even think about it.

Verdine and I talked about what we really knew, but grown folk couldn't admit; we had to be sister and brother of different mothers, but the same daddy.

Anyway, Grandma lost a bunch of men too, so had most of the women at my church, and most of the women in my hood had lost their men. With me losing as I had, and then being in that war with men around...ah no. I kept my distance.

I did have two male friends; two GIs I had come to know fairly well as they watched out for me. Delvin Thomas and Roylyn Graham mostly did security work while waiting for orders to go out to the battlefield.

During the times when the boom...booms were silent, we all sat around enjoying poetry writing, or reciting in round circles of duos and trios, or playing cards and spinning neighborhood tales. Occasionally, we had Bible study when our unspoken fears overrode everything else.

The two became good friends in boot camp, and were able to stay in the same unit once they were deployed to Iraq. Roylyn was from Washington D.C.; he's always the outspoken one on most subjects. He had gone to college for a few years before joining the army. It appeared to me that Roylyn joined the army not from any sense of duty or need of a job; I think he joined to see the world from any angle he could.

Roylyn had an almost rough-tough guy persona about him, but he was very creative and insightful. He had a tone of voice from the earth's core of deep, smooth, and gave me hot feelings if I let my mind go there. He had a chiseled faced that made him handsome and sexy, with the body of a tall sprinter; maybe even, almost dangerous. Often his demeanor was something like a protector.

Delvin was from the other Washington...Seattle Washington, and he was more reserve and soft spoken; shy. He was sweet like a momma's boy, almost tending to anyone's needs when given a chance. I had to turn away from him sometimes, because he had the features of my grandmother's idol, Sam Cooke; fine and beautiful. Delvin was fine and beautiful.

The two argued like brothers, but forgave and moved on like the best of any family. They'd fight together against anything, or any man, that tried to come between them. They were the friends that I chose to be close too, even though I knew it was against my better judgment; but those two fought together as a duo against three other soldiers in the dark desert one night. They defended my honor. Prior to coming to my defense, they had only said hello to me in the weeks prior.

I can still hear their voices, remember what we said, and everything that happen then. How could I not?

Chapter Three

1991, It Was Late Winter in America – Cold Times, But Hot Times in Iraq:

"Bobbie, what do you think about the fact that people were constantly at war in the Bible? I mean…when I think about it, maybe by letting war be an option, it is God's way of testing people's resolve or cleansing the earth. Does that make sense?" Delvin asked.

I thought about what he said for a minute while the wind kicked up the sand and made it swirl. "God sends His people into war to defeat sin as in the promise land. He gave victory to the people if they were righteous. If they weren't, He let them be defeated."

I held my Bible out if someone wanted to read.

Roylyn shook his head and said, "Nah, Bobbie Pen, I know that's a way of looking at it, but that don't fit into what's going on here. This is about oil. This is about a big mouth dictator who the Pres' wants to show 'em he's from Texas of the United States." Roylyn mocked a southern drawl, speaking like a White from Texas, while laughing as he continued on. "This is about how war creates jobs back home, and how fat cats get even more obese and greasy while us…young, gifted, and Black cats put our butts on the line. There are no weapons of mass destruction over here."

"Man, chill with all that," Delvin put his finger to his mouth in a hushing motion. "Let someone overhear you, and twist up all you say, and call you a traitor. This is still, the "Man's'army. The least that would happen, you'll find your ass on the front line with the quickness," Delvin stared hard at Roylyn when he spoke.

"We have opinions and they should be respected; but some of these gun-ho-wanna-be-soldiers-of-ignorance will shoot you in back when they hear an opinion against their redneck patriotism. Yes, be careful."

"You two are right," Roylyn said, as he nodded to both me

and Delvin. He knew that you have to watch your back when you have strong opinions.

Even I, who helps to save the life of idiots…I have to watch what I do and say with some of these, by-the-letter military folks of no culture or human soul. It's just crazy all the things we have to put up with and survive.

Chapter Four

Boom…boom.

I've been up helping handle one medical emergency after another for eighteen hours. I finally get a break to get some sleep, but I'm tightly wound up from the horrors of wounds and death, and I can't sleep. I walk the grounds, and sit out in the cool of the nighttime desert. Lighting a candle out behind the old broke down truck, I block out some of the wind. I sit on a rock and write in my poetry journal.

Knowing things run deeper than the blue of the water at the dockside,
I have chosen to dive deeper than you can see from the surface
For most, I know the fear of the unknown is not worth knowing the
unknown
They say
I have what I need, I have what I want, and personally, I'm doing fine
I wonder do they really…do they really believe what they say?
I do know, most skim the surface of information, not wanting the mental
waves to get rough
Me, I have dipped my toes in the deep waters of knowledge
And yes, the water was cold
Until my mental heat waves flowed through my pen and made the water
boil from wanting knowledge, my pen caught fire
I did not drown from the onslaught of realizations
There are treasures in the history of understanding my past, present, and
my future
There is no pain, or injury, that I can't survive from, if I know the truth
Yet, I have not lost my sense of humor; but surely, could have
It did not jade me, I did not let it blade me
The truth has opened many new seas and oceans
I now have mental comfort of knowing I can swim ashore from the deep
waters of knowing
I write these words that float on
Words carved in stone my sit on the bottom, but the words still exist
Letters etched with my eyes seek sails to you to make you aware

Thoughts flowed in my heart's ink, flies to you
Most of all, knowing what lies under the surface will help you, and I
stand above with a clear vision of the future

The sound of approaching steps draws my immediate attention.

"Hey lady, what cha' doin' out here?" a man laughed.

He's either Black, or Hispanic, or both; and huge. His voice is sick with evil...I can tell.

"You know, maybe one of them Iraqis might come kidnap you, little lady. You got more curves than these sandy hills, and they might want to torture you and flatten you out."
He laughs again, with two others giggling as if he had really said something funny.
Boom...boom.
Three American soldiers – almost out of uniform, jackboots, army gym shorts and T-shirts – encircled around me in mincing stances.
I'm straight out of Hunters Point in San Francisco, Californian. I'll fight! I've seen dead-killed young men growing up in the ghetto by the Bay. The street battles of my youth, were the mental minefield of keeping my sanity, and keeping my morality the best I can. I had lost friends in my teenage years. I had lost my college sweetheart to a drive-by.
That day, I was standing next to him when he was gunned down. I was almost able to save him, by ripping off my blouse and stuffing it into his wound, but my sweetheart died in my arms in the pollution of the violent fog of the inner-city war. I took the battle to the killer after that.
The killer was a thug that I had rebuffed in front of my boyfriend just days before. The ignorance of pulling a trigger seemed to be his only response. My sweetheart wasn't even in the ground yet when I hunted that punk-ass thug down who killed dreams, and made me lose part of my future. I hunted him down, along with the help of a cousin. I found him in a club sitting in a corner booth. I surprised him, and bum-rushed him with an artist

scalpel and stuck him in the side of his neck. I avoided hitting anything vital, and I told him that if he moved even an inch, I would slice an artery, and he would die gurgling in his own blood.

One might wonder if I'm violent. I felt like a dog cornered…with that punk-ass thug walking around smirking at the pain he had laced my soul with. He made me attack him. You can judge me if you must.

Anyway with my artist scalpel stuck in the side of his neck, I whispered in his ear. "Now, so…you wanted to get next to me, well here I am. You stole from me, you whimpering bitch. You stole what I can never get back. You stole the man who loved me, and now I'm going to slice your freedom. But it will never be enough because of the bullshit you live is always short lived anyway. Selling drugs and killing folks just because you can…well, it has no pension plan. But you will get free meals and a room with other stupid men who will be your lovers.

"You know I will never understand why any man would live a life that could take away a lifetime of feeling the softness or taste of a woman like me, and trade it to be housed with thousands of other men!" I kissed him on the side of his face and said softly, "A lifetime without a woman." I laughed in his ear and kissed him again on the side of his face as I handed him a pen and pad and told him to write in complete detail what he had done, and whom he had done it with. I had to slightly push my hand against his neck with that scalpel to remind him of what I could within a heartbeat. I had him write all the dealers and drug pushers he had done business with, up and down the food chain.

My cousin, an undercover DEA agent, walked up just as I pulled the scalpel out of the thug's neck. My cousin handed the thug a Band-Aid and arrested him. The criminal justice system as it is, let him go because his confession might have been coerced. It didn't matter in the end for him. He had snitched on his fellow thugs, and he was dead within a day of being back on the streets.

The revenge did nothing to ease my pain of losing the man I loved. We were young lovers making plans for our future. Just days before he was murdered, we had moved in together, with a wedding date marked on the calendar. Just days after he was murdered, I laid flowers on his casket, and got home and marked the calendar of the week; the week I was expecting the birth of our child.

I became a single mother in one of the ways ghetto warfare creates war babies. I was determined not to be a victim of my circumstances, and sought an education in the medical field to save lives and to make a good life for my child. I completed two years of college, but the stress of paying for college and raising a child left me overwhelmed. With the help of my dead lover's parents — the grandparents of my child, I entered the army for training and future benefits of schooling. My child is in good hands while I'm in the hands of Uncle Sam.

Now, soldier-thugs want to gang rape my physical soul and lay my body out in the desert night. There are hustlers everywhere, and someone had hustled liquor into the bellies of some cowards. Lust to shoot and kill, and lust to take and plunder, increased with cheap whisky courage.

I stood and eyed my options; it would not be easy. I wouldn't call for help. I prayed aloud for the soldier-thugs to hear paraphrasing Psalms 23, "Yea, though I walk through the valley of the shadow of death, I will fear no evil, for Thou art with me; Thy rod and Thy staff, they comfort me. Thou preparest a table before me in the presence of mine enemies."

I pulled a surgeon's scalpel out of my hair.
Boom…boom.
I went right at the biggest one who had spoken to me. I caught him in the face, and sliced him deep and long. He felt pain down to the hell I was trying to send him to. He groaned in enraged hate and hurt. He swung hard, grazing the top of my head. I ducked and started to run, but one of the other thugs grabbed me. I stabbed him in the ass, and we all went down into the desert sand, joining the sand fleas. All three men grabbed, slapped, and punched me. Wanting to live for my child, I fought the best I could.

The big boy wrestled the scalpel from my hand, and he stabbed me in the chest. My mini Bible absorbed the penetration. The Bible saved my life.

I could not fight hard enough to keep the soldier thugs from sexually penetrating me. When, when, when, when...they finished, they stood me up and let me pull my pants up. The big one told me to walk out into the desert. As they were following me, I overheard them whispering that they had to kill me, and then bury me in the desert. I started to run. It caught them off guard. I had to get my journal, and the Bible that saved my life so I circled back in that direction. Just as I got to the old broke truck, I heard bone-breaking explosions going on behind me. I turned my head to see the three soldier-thugs receiving intense pain and losing conciseness quickly.

Delvin Thomas and Roylyn Graham brought life to me as they beat the ugly off my rapists. They, too, besides my Bible, saved my life. They pounded the thugs unmercifully into the desert sand. I walked back to the scene of the ass whopping. The big boy lay in the fetal position; out cold. He had dropped the surgeon's scalpel next to his body. I kicked open his legs and stabbed the thug in the testicles. *Are you judging me again? I know this is twice you know of that I have become violent to the pain of losing something I can't get back.* I stabbed the other two in the privates as well. You can judge me if you must.

Boom...boom

We didn't kill the three thugs; they ended up needing surgeries and dragging their tails between their legs and other wounded appendages. Lies are often told on the battlefield, and Purple Heart award lies were told of some Iraqis capturing them in the desert and beating them. CNN News painted them as heroes for escaping with wounds they will be forever marked with, and living to tell about.

The real heroes...we had our lives, the truth, and friendship as our Medal of Honor. You wonder why I would not report the rape...give me a moment...please...I came over to save lives. I came over here to receive training and school credit for my future education, so that I can feed my son who is back at home waiting for his momma. It is a sacrifice I'm going to make to give my child a better life. I didn't want to be a part of any trial or the court martial of those thugs, and bring unwanted attention to my life and my child's world. Could those thugs attack another woman? Doubtful; they are injure in such a way that I can't even write about it…you might judge me.

After beating down the enemy within their own army, Delvin and Roylyn became my big brothers, or sometimes I was the big sister.

I tested myself for diseases. I'm clean. I don't think Delvin or Roylyn know the full extent of the attack on me, and we didn't, and don't talk about it.

Chapter Five

"Bobbie, you always leave me in awe of your deftness of your thoughts that flow from your pen to what comes out of your mouth. When you recite your words, it's so Gil Scott-Heron like."

"Delvin, you have great thoughts. Try letting go of what doesn't sound right when you speak your poetry. What matters is that you write and speak from your heart."

We, the three of us, are into a regular routine of sitting, and writing, and reciting. For Delvin to recite his words, never seemed to work. The poems and subjects he spoke about were good, but his spoken word lacked poetic flow. I encourage Delvin to keep honing his craft. One thing Delvin did, is hum. He would walk around and hum. Whenever he was reading, or we had prayer service, he would hum in the most beautiful way. He never sung, but he might as well have; it sounded so pleasing.

Now Roylyn, he's more confident in his speech and poetry. Whether he's being funny, or reciting something serious, he expresses himself well. Roylyn does have a dirty mind. He always says sexual things that I accept from him, that I don't accept from others. I, having a curvy figure, entice enough unwanted verbal attention from the other GIs; but Roylyn made me laugh with his tongue-in-cheek sexual innuendo.

I want both of them in a theoretically scandalous way. I can enjoy an internal mental romance of being near two handsome men in this nasty war zone, and still be able to keep my panties on.

NO, don't judge me with the thought that I'm just a horny young hood-rat girl playing fast and loose. Even though I think about sex all the time, I have only been with one man, my son's father. My heart wraps around the feeling that love will never be a part of my life in the way I had wanted it to be. I feel the same way about sex. I only want to be with someone who truly cares about me. Maybe I'm naïve, just being twenty-one years old, and in time, maybe life experiences will change how I feel.

I have a child, and not many men I have come across are really willing to love you if you have a child. I've seen it all too many times in my short life. Men look at me...they see me as simple housewife material and a bedmate. They don't see me as a woman who wants love, and wants to give love. Men already have taken the position of thinking that I need a man, and they don't value me as a woman who seeks a career. Simply having a man care for me is just not good enough for me to share my life and my son's life. My mom and grandmother felt that same way. I just don't see the value in love when all the love I know either controls you, or gets lost, or love dies. So this is why I'm over here wanting something better for myself, and going it alone, if I must, I will; go it alone.

My son's father, my fiancé, he loved me. He was my soul mate; but he's gone, and now my duty is to raise my son. I'm not saying I'll never let a man touch me, but most likely it will be a far cry from the feeling I had with my fiancé. I doubt if another man will ever touch my soul.

Through the weeks of knowing human destruction was coming, I'm wishing for an end of the war before it gets bad. I'm becoming scared, and I can see the fear in many eyes, including Delvin and Roylyn; it's bringing us closer. We spend time shielding each other emotionally from the harsh realities of Operation Desert Storm by writing poetry.

Delvin recited a poem about coffee one day because we drunk so much of it:

"Coffee
Got me up
Going down
She
Brown sugar soul
Creamy and thick
My lips to the rim
Tongue stirring her brew
Alluring scent going up my nose
Addicted to her energy
I woke-up with her on my mind
Love hearing her percolate

I want her all day
Love me some coffee
And coffee loves me
Cause I adore her
I would never sue her for spilling in my lap
I expect her to be hot"

Delvin has started reading sensual type poetry to me, often when Roylyn is not around. I feel like he is starting to have a crush on me. Love in a war zone is potentially a misguided mission, leading to an emotional Boom...boom, and you already know how I feel about getting too close to any man. Being isolated in a war zone is not a lovers' holiday, and it's sure not a place to expose feelings. There are just too many reasons to avoid putting myself in that position to have a romance. I can't, and I won't, let a man get close.

Delvin gathered his courage the other day and kissed me on my cheek. I tried to play it off as a brotherly kiss, but he handed me a poem with touching words:

Seeing you, seeing me
I want to be everywhere you'll be
Doing with you, being done by you
My love is a work of art being designed by you
Please commission me to be your carpenter, your painter, your driver,
Your fisherman, your everything man

I was caught off guard. I didn't know how to respond. There's nothing worse than rebuffing a man's feelings, and then trying to still be friends with him. I don't want to lose his friendship. I need both him and Roylyn; they are my safety net of stability.

The two of them had taken on the role of uncle to my son back in the states. They both wrote letters, and sent them back for my son's grandparents to read to him, and we all took pictures together and sent them back for my son to see.

I'm looking forward to being back with my son, and to one-day driving from San Francisco to Seattle so my son can see Delvin, his play uncle. After that trip, I wanted to ride a train with my son across the country to go see Roylyn, his other play uncle. For sure, I wanted my son to meet the guys who protected his momma.

Often, the three of us find ourselves on different shifts or outposts, so sometimes we spend time in one-on-one moments. One day I might hang with in the morning, and later in the day or night I might hang out with Roylyn.

Roylyn comes across as if he doesn't care about much in life, but he does. He's the type of man that hides his emotions; aka, the *bad boy* image. I have to laugh to myself when we get into long dialogues, because he doesn't realize that after a while, he has dropped his tough veneer and becomes intensely open about his feelings. He never comes on to me directly, but he jokes in a way I think is his way of flirting without committing to his real thoughts. Sometimes he jokes too much, but hey, he's a man.

Roylyn and I are chilling out behind and old truck and a rock right now, after I have been in six surgeries in a row, and after another night where I couldn't sleep because I was so wound-up.

"Bobbie Pen, check out my old school player rap."

"Sure, Mr. Pimp of Desert Storm."

"Hey, you never know what I was supposed to be. I don't know who my father is, so maybe my old school rap was passed down through a talent gene."

"Roylyn, boy, let me hear this rap from back in some old player polyester wearing man."

He obliged:
> Okay, okay. *Damn, you're fine*
> *Can I have a minute of your time?*
> *I spotted you the minute I walked into the room*
> *It was the way you carried yourself*
> *With that inviting smile and confident sex appeal*
> *I can tell you're a creature of the night*

So I want to spend the night with you
I'm sure your sensuality increases with the stillness of the night
Dancing like a gypsy around a campfire light
I imagine sheer silk covering exposed perfect beauty
Might you have warm, moist treasures behind those tempting lips?
And ooh baby, I see your firm, but rather large, buttocks
I'm watching you
Walk that walk, baby gurl
Tease me with sexy hot talk in my ear
I want to be with you
Whatever the cost
You wanna know about me?
I'm a super freak
The one that you have been waiting for
I'll do ya first class all over that sweet body
Now come on with it honey, give me the good stuff
I'll pull your hair from the back, spread you wide like a painting on the
wall and much, much more
Just close the door
It's about just you and me being free
Do me right, baby
No limits, no boundaries
Wide open
Damn, you're fine
Your booty has the shape of the hook of a clothes hanger
You got my eyes hanging and swinging
I want to be in a dark closest with your booty, doing things to your booty
in the dark so nobody would ever know I did certain things such as...
Can I have a minute of your time?
Let me tell ya what's on my mind
Ah yeah, keep on smiling
You and me… will be ticking and tocking
You and me… are perfect timing
Can I have a minute of your time?"

I'm sitting here amused, cracking up, and kind of honored, I think. "Roylyn you've got a dirty mind. I hope you're not one of those old men sitting at the end of a bar, waiting for a young girl to come in so you can use them old lines on her."

"Stop laughing at me, it just might work."

Roylyn might have meant some of what he was rapping. We laughed in the middle of the midnight sky of a faraway land. Many miles away from bars with drunks, streetlights flickering that can't hide addicts in the shadows, old Cadillacs, and broken-down pimps and old whores. Roylyn's old school rap made me miss home and dodging death on the street life I know.

Sometimes I sit out here and wonder if I did the right thing by joining the army, and being so far away from my son. Dead-end street life, and dead-end love kind of forced my hand to leave and seek an upgrade of my life through benefits I pay for by being here. I'm scared knowing I may never see my son, and my son might not ever see his momma again. As it is, I had to leave him at such an early point in his life. I fear I did the wrong thing leaving, knowing that he will never see his father—his dead daddy who was gunned downed in the ghetto by the Bay. The same ghetto I want to get back to just to be with my son.

Would I have been better off to stay, and possible stay poor, with no way out of repeating a cycle of women like me; losing men through all the various nasty means there are?

Boom...boom.

It's not the wanting to give and share my love, but love itself; the coming and leaving and dying that seems to be attached like a slave is chained. The pain to survive is attached like tentacles to my soul. After watching love die in my arms, and then come out of my womb, I had enough! Love for me has been twins of different mothers: God's love, and the devil's hate.

Chapter Six

I'm a part of trying to heal so many wounds that come from falls and accidents, which happens more than direct war wounds. I stay busy and go days with rest. It seems to have affected my body as I am so tired, but I can't sleep; but my body sure wants to go in shutdown mode. My mind shoots missiles of worry that I can't dodge. The only thing that feels good is that I have Delvin and Roylyn here, close to me, in the nasty killing heat.

The two of them are starting to play the *Dozens* on each other more than usual though. I think some kind of jealousy exists between them. Maybe it was over whom is receiving more of my attention. I just know for sure that they both care for me in their own special way.

Boom...boom war is intensifying, we are bombing Bagdad, and there is some fight coming back from a soon-to-be defeated dictator. He is launching bombs in any direction the Iraqis can point them in. Delvin and Roylyn both got their orders that they were going to be deployed to another area, closer to danger. We all sat down, with many of the other solders about to go to battle, and had prayer service. Then the three of us had our own private prayer service. It is a comfort to know that my best friends over here are God-fearing men; far from religious, but we understand from where we came from, and where we wanted to go within the hands of the Lord.

Another long day, and into the night...I have been in the medical tent doing everything I can trying to stay cool in heated times of trying to help men in pain from their wounds. I get a break; I head out to my spot to write. Delvin is already there. He has a candle burning, and I see dry tears on his face.

Boom...boom.

"Delvin, what's going on? Tell me; please tell me."

I look at him, and he seems almost like a lost little boy. He had been crying for a long time. Layers of an ashy face made of tears, look like dry riverbeds on his light autumn brown skin.

"You, me, all of us...this may be the last time we may see each other," he fears is expressed with deep breaths. "Any day now, I'm going into battle, and my mother might lose me her son, and lose the chance of her having grandchildren. I might be all but forgotten in ten years if I die over here. I don't want to be some name on a plaque on some memorial wall, and be countered as a number. To think...I may die and never really have felt the love of a woman. As far as I know of, a woman has never been in love with me, and I have never felt the love of a woman. You, yourself...you told Roylyn and me that you don't know how a man could give up the right to ever feel a woman. Well, if I die, it will be without me ever having felt a woman."

He stared through me and onto the dark desert. Boom...boom, in the far distance, a red flash in the sky beamed like taillights. I had to ask. "Delvin, are you telling me that you have never been with a woman? You are..."

"Yes Bobbie, I am a twenty-two-year-old Black male virgin. Sounds..."

I couldn't let him finish saying something negative when there was no need. "Don't sound like anything wrong at all, so don't say anything to defend something that's not wrong. This war is wrong. My child's father being dead is wrong, and then the reason I had to make a decision to leave my child and come over here may be wrong. Anyone who has ever had a broken heart is feeling wronged. You and a woman never being together, is not wrong. It has no bearing on you being a man."

"Bobbie...how ironic it can be that I'm over here to possible kill other men, and if their women or children happen to be in the line of fire, it's okay. But in the sand storms of this paradoxical funk, if I kill him, I'm taking something from another man that I have never had, and may never feel if he kills me."

"Paradoxical? Delvin, you're talking like you've been reading Roylyn's poetry." He looked at me as if he was embarrassed that I found him naked. "You and Roylyn, and me...we are all over here with thousands of other men and women fighting with our lives on the line in the most dangerous situations.

"We have to have faith in God, His will, will be done. I'm scared with every heartbeat that I will never see my son again. Fear is real every time I hear Boom…boom. No one should judge you, and if anyone did and I knew about, I would stick a needle of something painful in them to make them feel the same pain you feel in your heart; but much worse. Whatever the reason, whether by choice, or you have not found the woman you wanted to share yourself with, it doesn't matter."

His speech struggled to say, "Scared."

"If you want to tell me why you're scared, Delvin, you can. I will not judge you for something a whole lot of people should be – a virgin, instead of making babies they will not, or cannot raise. Many people should be abstinent from creating a child if they are not willing to make the sacrifices needed." I put my finger on his chest, over his heart. "If your heart isn't in it, don't do it. You'll always be closer to your soul, and farther away from self-inflicted pain."

The tracks of tears under his eyes cracked when he spoke. "It just didn't happen for me in high school; as you know, some guys lie about the conquests. I had no conquests. After high school, and going right into the Job Core, it didn't happen there, but it could have many times over. If you know anything about many of those kids, the girls are doing the boys like birds shit on cars, no matter the make or model, or how broke down. Then right before we shipped out, I was seeing this girl, and when we got to *that* point one night, I was there…with her…we were all hot and ready to go. She was in bed, naked, and I came out of the shower and she almost screamed. She said, "No, there's no way you're going to put that in me."

My eyes felt like I had pushed them open wider than possible. He's been mortified by whatever happened. The look on his face was of embarrassment. My initial thoughts were maybe he was damaged by a birth defect down there, or I've been told some men can be crooked down there and it can hurt a woman.

The pain in his face said he needed understanding that he had not been given. I reached out to hug him, but he pulled back. "Delvin, it's okay."

I moved into his space and pulled him in slow. We held tight. A rush of my own pain slapped me back to the last contact of a man's body being that close. Those thugs who took me into the dirt of the desert and sweated their nasty foul in me, I had pushed the thoughts away the best I could. Being in Delvin's arms, I realized I was still not whole, and how could I be? I had the fear of being in a war zone as my therapy of distraction. I cried inside. I felt my face touching wet on his chest. I was crying on the outside, and even that hurt because of the dry air. I wished a hurricane could wash away what had happened.

In Delvin's arms, after seconds or a minute, my pain began to feel so far away for the moment. I hoped he felt the same. *God let it be…let it be right with Thee.* Delvin held me tighter every few seconds.

Boom…boom.

Another far flash of an eruption of emotional lava ran between me and Delvin. The close hug of a good man and his musk…passion sparkled like fireworks. I knew I missed a man; I knew. I knew the pain of missing love, but going without physical passion; I knew it was something I was lying to myself about not wanting. Maybe I needed. I did desire. Delvin needed in so many ways that I, as a woman, could never understand. I would be alleviating a problem right here and now, while inside his arms.

I eased back and stared into his eyes, they were like lasers that held me unsure of what I wanted to do. I unbutton my shirt, while staring at his chest expanding in deep breaths. I released my bra, wet from sweat. He saw quickly the firming of my expanding dark nipples. I'm leading him to the back of the truck. The canvas canopy top gave us privacy and room, but was far from a nice bed with a romantic surrounding. It didn't matter. We did have a candle.

I unbuttoned his shirt. His chest, I had seen before when we all sat around trying to cool off; but now, I wanted to kiss and lick. I had sexual experience and he did not. I'm leading him. I place my lips on his face and slowly start to kiss it. His salt is almost sweet; it was human pain being washed away. I kiss his lips and our breath was cool, but still hot breaths intensified our desire. Our lips fight for control; we both lost. I make my way out of my boots, pants, and panties. Nothing sexy about army undergarments, but it doesn't matter as I feel his huge hands on my ass. He's lifting me, and I wrap my legs around his waist. He's suckles on my breasts as I kiss his head. He's pulling my nipples into long gumdrops. Oh my, it feels so good to be touched and handled tenderly.

He put me down, and I turn away to make a pile of all we had, and I sit on the nest. He's standing between my legs and his pants drop. He pulls down his boxers.

Boom…boom.

The light from the candle highlighted a human cannon. I had felt his hard erection against my leg when he was holding me, but…oh my, oh my, oh my; he is so thick, and pretty long too. Oh my, he is so-so thick. Breathing in the desert heat was hard enough at times, but now I'm suffocating with *what am I going to do with that?*

Shoot, I had had a baby, and I'm still seeing something I having to think twice…no, three times, about. Another woman had told him no, but I'm not going to decline. I'm going to try.

He got down on his knees, and I sit up to kiss him. I'm touching myself. I am wet enough to make a lake. I circle my clit. It makes me hotter, and maybe more prepared to take him in. I'm so horny. I almost had an orgasm from the thought of his huge manhood going inside me, but there was still the thought of it not being easy. I spread my wetness over his wide mushroomed head. The candlelight shadow of my hand, and the feel of the weight of his manhood, make my hips hump upward. I'm in animalistic control…out of control. He's groaning from me stroking and squeezing tightly on the head of his manhood. He's exhaling grunts with each stroke.

I'm trying to make him cum in my hand to avoid taking him in me. Yet, I want him inside me. I need him to wash away the violation I had dealt with. My hand cannot fully go around his shaft. I start guiding him into my throbbing, aching, wetness. I'm shocked; it only hurt a little. There is more pleasure than pain as I slowly keep guiding him in. It feels good as the pain eases away. I'm reaching around, pushing my fingers into his firm ass, and pulling him in. I lie back and start humping my hips upward. He joins me in a nasty rhythm. I want to cry out with pleasure. We might be erasing bad and replacing good for the both of us. We kept humping.

Boom...boom went off in the distance. I think I'm seeing stars. He went too deep, and I pushed my hand into his chest to hold him. He pulled out and that...wow, feels so good.

I make him flip on his back for me to ride him. I want to control how deep he can go in me. I squat down, rising up on my toes, and his manhood found its place. I let just two inches go in and out, teasing my G-spot. I feel myself wetting as it feels like he's throbbing. I'm wheezing in this heat. My lungs are burning. He feels massively thick inside me, but I had to keep the groove going from him. His virgin skills show, but I'm showing him how to swim in my rivers of current, and he's learning to stroke me just right.

I put one hand on his chest and leaned forward. I told him to hold my behind. I loved the feel of his strong hot hands on my ass. I'm rubbing my clit in a circling motion. "Oh shit!" I almost scream too loud. I was about to cum, and damn that rare occurrence happened...we came together. With him already filling me up with his girth, it might have added pressure to me feeling a warm, hard, pressurized squirting inside me. His grunt might have come from the tombs of pyramids; it almost echoed.

Unfortunately, we were not in a five-star hotel; we were not even in a fleabag motel. We had been *doing the do* with sand fleas on the ground about four feet away, so no cuddling in the back of a broke down army truck. We pick ourselves up and start to move before someone comes looking for us. We hold each other not wanting to leave, but we must.

Chapter Seven

Tension gone, I'm smiling as I assist in surgeries. The thugs who took ugly turns in me no longer held me in check. I feel like a queen who did not surrender to the evil sorcerers of violation that had me feeling as if I never wanted to be touched by a man again. I took my body back from their violence.

In some ways, I feel that by sharing my body with Delvin, I saved two people. His fear was real in that he needed to feel like a complete sexual being, *a real man*, before he possibly gave his manly body to this war.

Noontime, I see Roylyn, and he's in good spirits despite the fact that any day now, he and Delvin will be near the front line. He has another sexually funny poem to recite to me, and he makes me laugh. I kind of feel funny…like I'm hiding something from him; but then again, what happened between me and Delvin is just a moment of liberation that we had shared.

Roylyn, I know, has feelings for me; but unlike Delvin, Roylyn hides in his tough exterior, and uses sexual innuendos as his way of telling me likes me. He's not like that all the time. Roylyn is profound in thought about the world and social views. Knowledge is sexy too. He and I connect in that way, and I don't connect on the level with Delvin. The bottom line for me though is, I have two men who protect me. They are blankets of warmth needed in this wartime chill.

By the end of the day, I haven't seen Delvin, but it was not too unusual to go a day without seeing one of them if either of them were on different duties.

Another day, and I don't see him.

Another day, and I had not seen him by noon. I asked Roylyn about him.

"Bobbie Pen, he didn't tell you? He chose to go out on a short detail, one he didn't have to go on. The detail is dangerous, but he should be back late tomorrow."

Roylyn and I had Bible study with a couple of other

soldiers, it was strange without Delvin. I'm feeling so good, but becoming a little worried. I tell Roylyn that when Delvin comes in, for him to tell Delvin that I want to see him. Roylyn didn't want to tell him, but I knew that he would. Simply because I asked him to. The jealously between Delvin and Roylyn is not that thick. I'm sure Roylyn doesn't know what had happened with me and Delvin. I think his actions would be different if he knew.

Late night, I'm out by the old truck. "Hey Bobbie, how are you?" his voice is sweet to my ears.

"Well, I thought you might have swum back to the states to cool off from us getting too hot for you," my words respond with the slightest mixture of sarcasm and seduction.

He smiles that Sam Cooke smile, and takes a while to speak, "Thank you, for you." He laughs. "You were gentle with me."

I'm laughing aloud; real loud. "Delvin, if anything, you were gentle with me. You could hurt a woman with all that down there. Take your time with a woman. Kiss her all over, and go down on her. Then pull out that cannon while under the covers, and ease it in her before she sees it, you'll be fine. After you have been with her, she'll already know she can handle you."

"Sounds like you and I might not be doing...us again."

His face is dead serious, and I'm not a poker player; I can't hide my facial expression. I not sure what my expression is saying, but I'm sure he did not like what he saw.

"Delvin, I don't know what we need to do, but for now, get up and see another day...if that happens."

"I hear ya, but I..."

"Hey, what you guys out here doing...making love under the moonlight light?"

Roylyn is approaching; he's cutting into something thick and, an undeniable predicament. Releasing stress with Delvin has brought about another kind of stress.

I was attracted to Delvin, and we connected in so many ways. I liked him; our personalities fused well. Maybe I'm avoiding his mental touch coming inside me because I made a rule in my heart. My brain had gone through the same pain as my heart; they were same side of, *never again*. There is no civil war in me. I know I'm doing the right thing. When this war is over, his need, and whatever residual affects it's having on me, will go away, just like love seems to do.

Delvin and Roylyn were staring at me. I had to walk away from the both of them.

Boom…boom.

Chapter Eight

Now, here I am in 2012. Some twenty plus years have passed, and I look back at February 1991. This plane is hitting turbulences, and instantly, fear hits me. I don't want to go back to that time, but I know I can't just revisit most of that period in my life and not let you know it all.

I look out this window and see white pillow-top clouds. I begin to wish angels would take me away from this fear. The fear I feel whenever I think back to the moments of knowing I needed to clear the air with Delvin, even though I didn't know exactly what I was clearing up with him. What seemed like such a good idea at the time of our passion in the desert heat, had become an *emotional-minefield.* Roylyn and Delvin...I had walked away from them, and have not spoken to either of them since.

As I walk down the corridor of this plane headed to the restroom, I see rows of people I'll never know, and who will never know me. They remind me of the wounded numbers that piled up as I stayed busy laying healing hands those days in Operation Desert Storm. Faces of the wounded were just numbers of people who, most likely, I would never see again. I worked long, hard hours in that medical tent when I could have taken breaks; but I didn't in an effort to avoid Delvin and Roylyn. We all had to maintain our friendship in that crazy place. I understood the need for human interaction, but when it goes over the soul-line it becomes as dangerous as a sniper ready to take you out.

Walking down a plane's corridor, you end up touching people who you will never touch again. You'll never know the connection that might have been made, or what their life story is, or will be. Right before I head into the plane's restroom, I see a beautiful young Black man sitting in his seat, looking out the window. I have to stop and wait, went in the restroom ahead of me, so I stand here. The young man turns and looks at me. I must be staring at him. He appears to be in his early twenties. He smiles, and I nod to acknowledge him. His soft baby face tells me he has a world ahead of him that can swallow him up. His face reminds me of the young faces Delvin and Roylyn had; I'm reminded of them, and that time in my young life.

Avoiding Delvin was not the right thing to do. I knew I needed to tell him to hold his feelings in check. I needed to tell him that we couldn't make decisions of the heart until we were on the other side of the world. We needed to be in a place where there were no bombs of fear chasing us into making decisions out of the fear of need, or fear of dying. Funny – but not funny some ten years later after Operation Desert Storm – a plane, just like the plane I'm flying in now, became a bomb and took down three-thousand people on American soil.

In February of 1991, after days of not talking to my friends, I finally got the courage to face Delvin. I had just one day to sit down with the both of them; not at the same time though. All our troops from around our area were amassing, preparing to leave to push into Iraq.

I also needed to be clear with Roylyn too. I may have been wrong about his intentions; maybe he was always joking with me, and had no serious meaning to his flirtatious poems. But, I had to get away from that place to see anyone in my future. Number one thing I needed was to get home to my son. I needed to come home and make my son my first and only priority; then, in time, maybe I could think about a man being in my life.

Finally, in the plane's bathroom, I'm washing my hands as if I'm about to operate. I can't wash away pain. I stare in the mirror. A knock on the restroom door…

Boom…boom.

A scud missile dropped in a training area just outside our camp compound. War reached a place that was predicted; the coverage was outside our zone.

The impact hit like a fireball from HELL! Delvin and Roylyn felt the impact. Delvin was dead! His nightmare of what he didn't want to happen, came to be in so many ways.

Roylyn was hurt so badly. They had to fly him out to a hospital in Israel in hopes of saving him. I was stunned. Mortified. Chaos was in the face of, *I had to do my job. I was a soldier.* I was a surgical nurse dropped in a war zone to help; not to be a victim of my grief. I sobbed all the while, while helping in the surgeries I was a part of. This was not Biblical war, and I was not a person in the Bible lying out on the ground wailing.

I had told myself not to get close to anyone. Why? Soldier die in wars, but those weren't just soldiers, they were my friends. I was falling apart; I acted like a walking zombie. I saw Delvin's body bag. "God is this real," is all I could say, and hear in the mist of my own screams inside my head. I also realized another man was dead whom I happened to have had some feelings for. *Was it me? Was I the common denominator that love will die?* My soul went on life support.

As for the person who keeps knocking on this airplane's restroom door, I guess I'm done looking in the mirror. Sitting back in my seat, I need a break from going back in time. I put on my headphones. Oh…what do I hear? Diana Ross and the Supremes sing "Reflections."

Boom…boom.

Reflections of days later, when most of the damage you could visualize was gone. When dead bodies had been flown away, and the wounded we were able to help had also flown away, I was able to retire to my barracks. I always went out by the broken-down truck to unwind. That place had turned into a pit of quicksand; I was raped there, and made love there. Everything that was near that spot was a sinkhole of hurt.

I went on the other side of camp near where the scud missile dropped outside our compound; there weren't many places to find solace at that time and place. I craned my necked toward the sky in every direction, and tried to see the stars. The sky looked like my soul felt, dark. I bowed my head, and I and prayed with so much intensity that I felt my body shaking. I know people saw me out there looking as if I was at the Wailing Wall in Jerusalem with such movement. I'm surprised no one came to see if I was sane. Who wouldn't be possessed with mental annihilation after such pain and destruction? I prayed for Delvin's family, and for the children he wanted to have. I prayed for Roylyn; the reports were that he was on life support originally, but that he came through, but is severely wounded. They said he would never be the same in functionally being able to care for himself. I tried getting a message to him, but what came back was he could not talk, could not see, he could not do anything anymore but breathe.

I prayed for God to let a missile hit me and take me away. Then I realized God put me on this earth to do His will. I had a son who counted on me to come back, if at all I could. Thinking I wanted to die, I was being selfish. I finally headed to my tent that night. I did need some sleep, even though I knew sleep would bring nightmares.

As I am sky high in this airplane now, and look out this airplane window, what happened back then plays back like a movie in this window, as if it's live from twenty years ago.

When I got to my tent, on my bed sat a small box with the words written, *For Bobbie Pen*. I opened the box to find it stuffed with poems and letters, all addressed to me.
The first letter:

Dear Bobbie, I don't have the skills to say words in a flow as you do when you write or speak. I can only write what I feel. I love you for your style, grace, tenderness, and most of all, your caring heart. You didn't have to do anything for me or with me, but you did. Most of all, you listened to me. I only hope I made you feel like a woman in this mess they sent us to. Maybe one day I'll be more than just a friend, as I feel you want to tell me we should be, or maybe I'm just hoping. Bobbie, the reason I...

Delvin had read my mind. He knew what I was going to tell him. I could not read all the writing, the piece of paper was faded and torn. He must have written this when he went out on that patrol, and was gone for a couple of days.

I read the other letters and poems. I did that for hours, all through that night. Delvin's words made me fall deeply in love; but he was dead. His poems and letters were so intense, and filled with passion. He had to have been writing two or three poems and letters a day, there were so many. I was no longer sleepy that night. I was tranquilized into falling in crazy love, knowing I would never have a chance to share my love with Delvin.

I can still feel the weight of those tears that flushed the desert dust out of my eyes. I still feel the weight of the sorrow I felt back then. I was screaming inside as I sat on my bed and whimpering aloud when I read:

If you could
If you could feel my emotion
If only you could feel the effects of you on me
If you could
You would not wonder if I care about you
You would know
You would feel the warmth of my breath, of my exhale, as my heart
pounds
Look into my eyes, my eyes will not lie to you
Get lost in my embrace, as I pull your life into me
If you could
Hear the sounds I cannot hold back
Let my voice enter into your soul, I sing euphoric joy unto you
Gaze upon me, all you see is yours
You will know, I do care about you
If you could
You would not wonder if I care about you

I screamed that night in low volumes, as I knew I would never be able to look into his eyes again. I might as well have been blind.

I had to leave the tent and walk about. I took the last poem with me and walked into the desert. First light, gave me enough light to read. His words chained his heart to me forever. He addressed it as to be a wedding vow to me, hopefully for him to read to me at the altar one day. He had plans for us.

My Woman
She holds my secrets
She holds all of me
My woman knows the pleasures of my mind, and the fantasies of my soul
She judges me not for having desires of more than I have
All I have is for her
My wants, and desires, she is all I need
Her being the woman she is, encourages me to complete my life as it
should be
She understands the completeness of this man does not come all from her,
But I am encouraged by her

With her by my side, I am a better man
There is no hiding the love that comes from her mind, body, and soul.
She brings out the best in me, to be a man standing tall, firm, and
compassionate
My hands are busy, my mind is innovating, and my body races for time,
To spend more time with her
She is proud of me, I am proud of her
I love her
We found in each other, trust
I will always do what I must do to have such a privilege of loving her
My woman is sensual and beautiful
But her body alone will not do it all
I seek love, honesty, and her loving emotions
I seek my love to be king
She is my queen
My woman, and I do not let pride hide our weaknesses
Our weaknesses make me more of a man, and her a woman
We are there to do for each other, what the other cannot do
This woman is real to the core with a heart that gives
In return, I want to help her, and enjoy her
She gives me no reason to fear her
My woman will be there for me
We are accepting of one's need to forgive in order to receive forgiveness
Accepting God to bring about real happiness in a spiritual union
I am the man for her; she makes me feel it in my heart
She wants the man in me
She loves me, and craves me
I love her total being
Her hands to her feet, from her eyes to her lips, and to her sighs to her
mind
I long for the sight of her moving around me
The woman crawls all through my mind non-stop
She and I, likeness, sameness, stimulating conversations, exchanging
views, and experiences
Beauty, passion, and simple pleasures, a common goal
My woman
I love you
I'm here to be your man forever

He said, forever…forever…forever; but he was gone before
he had a chance to give me forever.

Chapter Nine

I left from the war emotionally injured, my soul ripped wide open. I had met a man who loved me within his death. Delvin loved me, Bobbie Rasheen; and to this day, I still feel his love. Some days it feels like a dream, but as I talk to you, I know it's real and forever a dream alive in me, as he is my soul mate.

When I got back to the Bay Area and saw my son, I knew I would fight to the death for him. I missed him and loved him. In some ways, I had fought to get back to my son to honor what I believe his father would have done for us. When I had a chance to just go to sleep with my son in my arms, I'm sure I almost squeezed the life out of him with the new life I was bringing home to him.

When I got back to the states, I was just starting to show. I was at least six months pregnant. My period was still in full affect most of that time. My medical knowledge did not alert me that something was wrong, or should I say, *alive in me*, until I was at least four months pregnant. I had no noticeable signs when I was re-stationed to a medical aircraft carrier. The food there was much better and richer, and I ate and ate; but the mornings were hellish with my stomach being queasy. Even then, I thought maybe I was just getting seasick. Pregnancy was the furthest thing from my mind. I knew I had had unprotected sex, twice; but it still did not register in my mind. *I haven't asked you in a while, but are you judging me…again?*

Denial is a powerful drug, and I told myself no, even when my face was getting slightly rounder, as well as my behind. I had been pregnant before, and with that pregnancy, I did not know until three months had passed.

There was an older female doctor aboard the aircraft carrier who I knew was hiding a secret life in the order of, *don't ask don't tell*, even though anyone with any awareness would know. I simple told her I needed a test. She didn't say a word as she nodded, and later in that day, handed me a pee test strip.

Another war raged inside me. Not the issues of should I have another child, but good and evil clashed in days and weeks, with years to come. I had been raped, and I had made love to Delvin. A difference in time and hurt and life I could not pin down conception of the seed growing inside me. All I could pray for my child was the product of making love.

I did not see a doctor following learning about my pregnancy; I hid it well. It would have been a military big brouhaha that on top of everything else, I could not handle anymore.

Boom…boom.

I was going to be a single mother of two, and their fathers were dead; or dead to me. If I wanted to know who the father was of my second child, I guess I could have known, but it was to be God's will; His will be done.

The benefit of knowing? Well, the pain was already bad enough and could get worse if the sperm came from an evil seed. Did my child need to know? Would it benefit my child if the ejaculate contributors were…well, remember I was raped by three men, so *NO*, it would not help my child to know. If I was to be a responsible parent to protect my child, it would be better to believe a man who loved me was the father, even though he might not be. *Are you judging me again? How many times are you going to do this?* Walk in my boots then, or my heels now. Tell me how it feels.

The sun setting and the nightlights down below, gather as cities on the East Coast are so close. It is red in the disappearing horizon. It has been stressful talking about my past. I need to write some poetry to feel whole. I'll finish telling you my story as it has been for me since coming back from the war, after I write a poem.

Pillows in the sky
Billowing
Red pillows
Above me
Passing through
Then me on top floating above

Alone with my thoughts
Watching the nightline coming
The last of the daytime
Soon to be dark
I'm flying
Gazing out the window
A thinly visible reflection of me I see
Red pillows a backdrop in a fantasy of you and me
Reflecting
Racing
My heart has already landed
Love grounded
Seeing God's rays of light glowing along pillows in the sky
Skyline fading
Anticipating the sight of you
In my dreams
You are the one
I'm floating across pillows in the sky
As dark approaches, light disappears
Stars start guiding my pen to paper
Remembering love
Knowing you are floating in the sky with wings of your loving spirit
I lay my head on a pillow and only think of you
While floating on pillows in the sky

I finished school. I am a doctor now. I raised a wonderful educated son who is a fighter pilot in the air force. He has done one tour of duty. My son – his name is Fearsom, and he was protective of his sibling and me from day one. I tried hard to keep him as a boy, but he molded into a young man fast. He had, and has, a leader's aptitude of responsibility at an early age.

I was financially able to move out of the hood after I became a doctor, but I chose to stay in the hood and set an example. At least my children's friends had role models in my children. Our home was homework central for all kids. I feel good about the fact that there are kids doing well because I stayed in the hood. Other parents had an example of someone who got involved in their children's schools.

I helped set up a youth scholarship program with backing

from doctors, hospitals, and other medical facilities, to help promote low-income children become educated and work in the medical fields in the Bay Areas. I named the Scholarship Fear-None-Heal-All, after my son's slain father, the man I was going to marry. His name was Fearnone, and he was in a training program to be fireman medic at the time he was slain.

I have raised a wonderful daughter who has just finished her freshman year in college at Howard University. She thinks she wants to be a lawyer. Her mind is sharp, she's witty, and extremely beautiful.

I told you at the beginning...I'm headed to a medical conference, and I'm looking forward to doing other pleasurable things. Well, I'll be hanging out with my daughter. She's a marvelously talented poet and vocalist. She often mixes her spoken word with song. Her name is Roberta Delroy Rasheen. Her middle name, Delroy is in honor of the two men I once knew—a mix of their two names, Delvin and Roylyn.

Twenty years have passed, and even though I have gone about my life, I have never lost my feelings for the young men who protected me during wartime. A few men have come into my life, and maybe they wanted me for all I am and want, but none could touch and surpass the feelings that lingered from my past. I date periodically, but no one, as I said, has aroused my inner spirit. I'm doing well, but I believe I'll never feel the kind of feelings I had once read on notes of paper; those feelings have never waned.

Now in my forties, my babies are grown; and they are still growing into fine, caring people. I smile at the thought that my son might be flying this jetliner one day soon, and my daughter could a Supreme Court Justice within my lifetime. I'm in the airport now, and I see my daughter, Roberta Delroy Rasheen.

Chapter Ten

Two days later, the medical conference is over, and now I'm

spending time with Roberta Delroy Rasheen. We are all over the Capitol shopping, eating, and being mommy and daughter. Just girls hanging out. Later tonight, she has talked me and into doing a duo spoken word performance; she has arranged a poem that I wrote and recited to both my son and daughter the last time we were all together. We have practiced, and I'm looking forward to it.

Club True Word & Soul

What a classic old theater converted into a lounge. Brick walls, tiered hardwood floors, with just two steps going up to the stage; this place is beautiful. My daughter has been coming here to perform. She's good, I know, but my pride is booming; everyone keeps coming up to her and telling her that can't wait to hear her because she always brings the house down.

The band playing behind the poets has this smooth, funky, groove going on. I love it, and the poets are following words like feathers floating in the air. I'm in metaphoric heaven. The place is packed from wall to wall, and they give so much love to the poets. Oh, we're up next.

"Club True Word, welcome a favorite to the stage, along with her mother. Wow here we go folks...Roberta Delroy Rasheen, and her mother Bobbie Rasheen."

My daughter stepped to microphone with me standing beside her, and she spoke to the audience. "Hello everybody, I love coming here to perform, but tonight has a special meaning for me. I have my mother to help me."

The crowd clapped and gave their vocal approval. I felt nervous, but in the same manner as I have tried to be a mountain of force in my children's lives, they have been sold rocks of joy for me. So I know I can deliver. Roberta Delroy Rasheen starts to hum and sing just one line from an Earth Wind and Fire song called "Devotion."

"Thru devotion, blessed are the children," she hums the song and sings that one line, filtering in and out when I start to recite my poem.

They are mine
Before anyone can claim them

I am the first and last, after God
When all others fail
My love is here for my own
They might fall down, and no matter whatever, or whenever, I'll be there

My daughter brings a down-home gospel feel to her humming, and keeps singing that one line: "Thru devotion, blessed are the children."

I recite on:

I stay on a journey as I'm always learning how to love them just as
they are
I see me
I see me, in them
They are mine
I am theirs
I have carried them
I have birthed them
I'm not perfect, as no one can claim, so there have been times I have failed
them
It's only been a lesson in life for them to be better
Everyone fails at one time or another
I taught them God Forgives, as we all should

My daughter keeps humming and singing that one line: "Thru devotion, blessed are the children."

I recite on:

If my heart…is the only heart to keep them alive
My last days will be happy days knowing they will live on with my heart
Beating in their souls
As they go along their own path
In the back of their mind, my voice will help lead them, guide them
Our souls are connected through more than just
They know what I have said, and will say, because I love them
One day they will raise their own
And they are mine too, by the way I have shined a lasting light of love
Right now, and always, and long after the ground has consumed me,
they are mine
No one can come between what they mean to me, and what I mean to
them
Not even me

They are mine

My daughter sang that one line, one more time with jazzy long notes:
"Thru devotion, blessed are the children."

The crowd loved us; they stood and clapped. My daughter encouraged me to take a bow. I was a bit embarrassed by all the attention everyone paid us as we exited backstage. I thought we would go back to our seats, but Roberta led me behind the curtain. We were handed water. I hugged my daughter; mostly because I got through it, I didn't mess her up, and I could take a deep breath finally.

We sat on some stools. I admired my beautiful daughter, and the blessing of having done what we shared. The curtains blocked the sound of the announcer a bit, and my daughter started talking to me at the same time. Another poet graced the stage.

Robertastopped talking, and I could hear the poet; and he was exceedingly good. I got off my stool to get a better view. The poet was a man with dark glasses who sat on a stool as he recited. He was tall, bald, and very good-looking. I could tell he was blind by his movements. He spoke with a rich warm voice. I turned my head. I'm sure I looked like a poodle in amazement.

Boom...boom.

It was Roylyn. Roylyn Graham was sitting out there on that stage where I was just standing. Twenty plus years ago, I last saw him. He was sitting where I was standing just moments ago with my daughter. Seeing Roylyn brought into vision Delvin, as I can almost imagine seeing the two of them laughing and talking to me.

I heard that Roylyn had survived the bombing, but was in really bad shape. I was told he was almost in need of hour-by-hour care. Reports came back that he might not live long, and I did not want to know when he died, if he died. It would just have added to what I already knew was the worst time in my life.

For a long time, I gave thought to looking him up, but I chose to remember him as he was before the Boom...boom. In many ways, I never wanted to find him and not see Delvin at the same time; it would be a reminder of the man that loved me. In many ways, the two were one in how we had met, and all we had gone through.

I'm twenty feet away, no longer twenty years away from him. My daughter is right next to me, and her middle name is part of his name. I look at my daughter. She's smiling. Her smile is like the cat that ate the parakeet, and is now caught. I want to ask her what is going on, but I can't find the words. I want to know is there some kind of connection between her and Roylyn, but I don't. My mouth is dry. My lungs feel hot. I feel sweat around my body. My heart rate is up, and I know my pulse is showing in any vein close to my skin.

I'm looking at Roylyn and I might be dreaming, but my daughter is rubbing my back, so I know I'm awake. I look at him, he is alive, and as far as I can see, Roylyn is just blind, and at ease with himself, with a sweet flow of words. He's reciting an erotic poem:

The curve of her arch, the slow turn of her heel
Straps of leather turn me on
Turn me out, as I lick the tip of her five toes, as a cat licks his paw
Nice and slow
I look up to the long, shapely flow
Calves, knees, thighs, posterior
Sensuous lines
She's
Lying
Spreading
Round and just wide enough
Just like I want
I choose one leg
I run my tongue from the bottom of her foot
Toward the inside of her arch, and up behind her knee and her thigh
My eyes open wide
My nose flares and draws in all her womanly goodness and all her
womanly scents
My lips get there, and kiss

Women in the audience are loud voicing long, "oohs" and "ahhs," along with a few, "Baby talk to me. I can feel ya." The chants roam throughout the crowd. Excitement is in the air. His voice still had that smooth, hot molten tone.

He recited on:

She feels my kisses like there is nothing better
I keep kissing her high and low
I start back down her other thigh
I reach to touch where my lips have been as I travel to where I started,
only it's the other curve of her arch, the tips of the other five toes

I'm sitting with my daughter, and even though we talk about the moon, the sun, and the shape of a fine man's behind, this here is strange for me. It's baffling as I hear him, or to hear any man, recite with the erotic intensity he is putting into his flow. He has emotionally stimulated me and confused me by what I see and feel. If ever there was an overdose of, *all too much, all so sudden...*this is it.

I'm happy to see an old friend; but hurt has arose, and it is pricking my soul. I'm trying to hide my tears from my daughter, but I'm washed into a sea of painful history. Remembering the night I had read the poems of a dead man who loved me, and now to see his best friend doing what I would have loved to have heard Delvin do—the man who loved me, it's piercing my heart. To hear Roylyn, and remembering Delvin, an explosion is going off in my soul.

Boom...boom.

Roylyn makes his way off the stage to a loud applause, and comes my way. He may be blind, but he walks assured of himself. He seems to guide his walking stick as if he's telling it where to go. All I could do is run out the side door into an alley. It might have been the most dangerous ally in the world, but for a moment, I felt I had to be there. I need to let these tears run.

"Mom," my daughter calls out. She's in this ally with me now, and I don't want her out here with me. Mommy *force field* kicks in, as I need to protect her from whatever can happen in a Washington, D.C. alley.

"Mom, I know you and he have some history. Now, I'm not sure I did the right thing...I thought you meeting him would be a good thing. I'm sorry if I overstepped my place."

I kissed her face. "Roberta Delroy Rasheen, that man is a big part of why you are here in this world."

Her face showed shock. I thought about how I had just said what I said, and how it may have sounded.

"My dear, Roberta, please understand me. He is not your father. Who your father is, is something of strange circumstances as I have told you. I have always told you, you are God's child, and you have made life so much easier for me by accepting what I told you. Yet, that man in there, I can say he was close to the situation of who your father might be. He doesn't know, but he was in my life as my friend when you were conceived. That man in there, who I don't know where you know him from, he was a good man who helped to save my life when I was in the Operation Desert Storm war."

"Mom, I met him here while performing. He came up to me and said he thought he knew my voice. You know, you and I sound alike. Anyway, as strange as it is, he knew my voice, and said he thought he might know my mother. I told him your name, and his face almost glowed in a smile so wide and bright, it was like the sun was beaming at night."

I collected my composure, and went back in to see if I could talk to an old friend. Whatever has happened in his life, I was proud of him. In some ways, I feel Roylyn was honoring his old friend. I had to face a mix of new and old history. My daughter went to go lead the blind man to me. He stood in front of me, my daughter scanned both me and him. I nodded to her, and she walked away.

"Hello, Roylyn," I took the blind man's hand. "It's me, Bobbie Pen from back in the army days."

"I would never forget that voice. I hear your voice, and I know it's you, Bobbie Pen," his low, passionate voice sailed high with a long sigh.

"Yes, it's me," I said. "How are you? I heard you out there on stage, and you are so gifted, but please tell me how are you?"

"I'm ok, I'm fine. I can't see, but I can hear and feel," he said as he laid his other hand over mine and touched me softly.

"Roylyn, while listening to you on stage, I can tell you still have that dirty mind. I like the poem you recited though, but I wonder about you. But no matter what…it's really good to see you."

I quickly reflected on saying, *good to see you.*

"It's good to see you too, if you know what I mean," he said, and chuckled.

I told him just how I was feeling, but I did not want to remove that smile on his handsome face. "Roylyn, I'm bit confused. I don't know what I'm supposed to say right now. It has been a long time since that day. I…"

"That day…killed so much in so many ways. I spent a six-year journey learning to walk and care for myself. Learning that I was losing my sight was just another way to see the world that people will never understand until…if and when it happens. I spent years feeling sorry for myself. I spent years letting strangers wash my body, prepare my food, and even feed it to me. I spent years thinking like a wounded man."

"But you look so good, and to hear you out there on that stage, I…"

"I had lost faith in God and stopped talking to Him. Then one day — like all the others before of feeling sorry for myself, I was giving hell to someone, treating them badly. Because I had been so foul to this woman orderly, she dropped me in the shower, and she left me there as the water turned cold because I was being an ass to her. She told me that God helps babies and fools. She added that I was being a fool by choice, and that God had better things to do. She was hard on me for me being hard on myself. She said if I wanted to die in a self-imposed helpless state, I would have to find someone else to watch my demise, and wash my ass. I needed the harshness of her words and the tough love she saw fit to give me that day. I woke the hell up, and pulled myself up out of the funk I was living in. I took my therapy seriously after that. I wanted to write, so I learned brail. I wanted to live like everyone else in this world, so I learned to live again."

"Oh wow, Roylyn," was all I could muster.

"No oh wow, I just had to see…see God still had a plan for me. So here I stand."

"Sounds like a made-for-TV movie, and you should have married that lady for helping you see that you were still a man capable of accomplishing many things."

"I did marry her. My Lynda died six years ago of cancer."

"Damn Roylyn, I'm so sorry. I joke about a movie, and you have lived with so much pain, and then to lose your wife, that's..."

"No, I don't live with pain. I was able to take care of her, and I helped her be strong to the end, as she did for me when I wanted to die. She gave me love, she gave me courage, and she gave me a beautiful daughter. My daughter's name is Delynda, and she is a grown twelve years old. I promised my wife Lynda that I would live on as she had taught me to. So, here I am doing what I always wanted to do."

"You do it well."

"Well, thank you, doctor. Your daughter told me that you do great works too, and that her brother is doing great."

"Yes, he's a fine young man, and as you heard, my daughter is a rare pearl."

"Some time ago, when I heard your daughter's voice, I knew something was different in how she spoke and sounded. It took me a few weeks to place her voice; but then one day, she was humming and reciting while doing a spoken word piece. She has your voice, but she...she has Delvin's hum."

Boom...boom.

I grabbed my head at the temples. I felt dizzy; almost pregnant morning sickness queasy. I woman never forgets that feeling, and at this moment I'm sent back in time to when I realized I was pregnant. Roylyn telling me that he thought my daughter sounded like Delvin's humming ability, took me back to wishing Delvin was her father. It also made me hate the uncertainty. Science could prove one way or another what he had told me, but I knew now for sure. I am soul-certain. Delvin's hum...all these years I never thought to think about it.

"Roylyn, what have you told my daughter?"

"Bobbie, I haven't told her much, other than my best friend and I and you were friends from the war. As far as what I do know...I have thought since I put two and two together from meeting your daughter, that you might have had some struggles. I know what happened in the desert with those guys that night.

Delvin and I knew, but we just never brought it up. At least I didn't."

Roylyn went silent; maybe he was waiting for me to respond, but my mouth was dry, and my throat had closed up.

His head bowed when he spoke. "That experience was for you to do and say what you needed and wanted to do. We just wanted to be there for you to help you process the way you needed."

"You guys knew?"

"Yes, you were bleeding pretty badly that night, and maybe the shock you were in did not make you aware of the visual that showed when we got back into the camp lights. I'm so sorry."

I shrugged my shoulders and looked away. I looked away from a blind man, wishing I could go blind to the thought of that night.

"Delvin's seed though. So..." Roylyn stopped mid-sentence.

"I...I believe he is her...but I have never made myself face that issue. I have always just said she's God's child," I said, hanging my head as if he could see my actions.

"Amen!" Roylyn's deep smooth voice sounded like someone who would narrate the Bible. He reached out and found my shoulder. "As far as you and Delvin, I knew you two had got it on. All of a sudden, you and he were acting so strange, and I know war had its effects on all of us, but the both of you were acting as if you got caught in the basement by your parents. He couldn't look me in the eye, and you avoided the both of us. But it was as it was, and it is what it is. I had my own feelings to deal with."

"Roylyn, what were your feelings?"

"Tell me something...I have to know..." he paused for a long time then asked, "Did you ever get the box of letters?"

"Yes, and I still have all those letters and poems Delvin wrote me."

I could hear pain in my own voice.

"Delvin wrote!" he inhaled all the air that his lungs could hold, and then exhaled. "I wrote those letters. I wrote those poems to you!"

Boom...boom.

The world I knew, blew up. All I could give back to him at the moment was long silence. Days were passing in my head before I could respond. My lung felt on fire, as if I had just run ten miles in the desert heat. I can hardly find enough air to support words that I was trying to find, if I could find any.

"I...I thought...they were...from Delvin."

"No...no. I asked a soldier who helped air lift me out, to make sure you got the box, not knowing if I would ever see you again, and thinking that I was going to die."

Boom...boom.

"But Roylyn, before what happened between me and him, he had been reciting poems to me like the ones in the box. The letters in the box, I thought, addressed the feelings he had for me. He had read me some poems before he died that..."

I had to turn away from Roylyn, even though he can't see me or my reaction. My fingers seem stuck in my hair. *Why am I trying to finger comb it, when I don't do that any other time?* I see my daughter over by the wall. I know my daughter's look. She's not sure if she should smile, or if she has offended me, or if there is something even more troubling going on. I need to attend to her feelings about this. I turned a complete circle to check to see if the walls are real. *Is all of this real?*

I finally compose myself and say, "He wrote good poetry in the style of the letters and poems in the box."

"Bobbie Pen!"

There is sorrow in his voice with this confusing revelation. Roylyn and I were sharing soul-splintering news.

"Delvin, was trying to recite *my* poetry. I was too shy to recite my romantic—I love you poetry. I thought you would avoid me if I came out and told you how I felt about you. My way of flirting with you was to talk with an immature mouth. I didn't have the confidence to tell you how I felt about you, but I could write my feelings; but even then, I couldn't share them with you. Delvin hardly wrote anything, but he was my best friend over there besides you in that sweltering nightmare of a war. I guess in a strange way, I wanted him to feel love just as I did. He shared with me that he had never been in love; he let me know that he had never had sex. I encouraged him to give you some of my poems as if he had written them; so at least for him, he would feel something. We…him and I, had planned to tell you, but then you and he happened. For me, that was another kind of war infringing on me. Those were my feelings."

Boom…boom.

"All those letters and poems…"

"Do you remember this one?

> *The morning windstorm of sand clouds my vision*
> *But you, my dear, are clear*
> *Clear to me that you are the life in my world*
> *That life rests in my heart*
> *So waking*
> *Seeing you*
> *Not seeing you*
> *Brings no fear*
> *The morning haze of blowing hot desert sand clouds my vision*
> *You are a beacon of light, leading me to places I need to be*
> *So blessed to be anywhere near you, my dear*
> *No matter where you are*
> *I am nearer to you than the air we breathe*

My heartbeat slowed. Seconds now felt like years. I felt as if I was sinking into the floor. His eyes can't see, but Roylyn he must have known tears were rolling down my cheeks.

His hand reached and found my slumped chin. He felt my warm tears drip on his hand. He removed some of the moisture with his finger. He kissed my salt of the earth.

"I imagine you are still so beautiful with those jawbreaker cheeks that are getting all wet." His voice soothed. "You know while listening to you and your daughter recite on stage, it was like old times. It's almost as if you and Delvin in a strange way were doing a duet as we used to do.

My heart is racing looking at the man who I had really been in love with. His love, his spirit, had lived in me. I needed emotional bearing, for my love compass has been off course. My mind and body felt numb.

"Roylyn, I need to go tend to my daughter, but could we get together somewhere and talk? I need to share some things with you."

"It's not late, Bobbie, and my condo is just two blocks from here. You and your daughter are welcome to come to my place. I would like for you to meet my daughter. I can send the babysitter home early."

"Is that really okay?"

Please come; and bring your daughter, my daughter will love meeting her. She treats her babysitter as a big sister because she wants one so bad. So, just maybe, since your daughter is going to school out here, she can be a big sister. I guess it could be looked at as she really is, you know, if you think about it."

Roylyn smiles at me and I nod my head, but then I realized I needed to give a verbal answer.

"Yes, but you and I need to talk, because I've been living with my soul mate in my heart since the days of Desert Storm."

"Huh, what?"

"Let's go and share all we have, so we can be closer than the air we breathe. Love may be blind, but it has its own undeniable set of eyes."

Boom...boom

The end